His Study in Scandal

The eyebrows rose higher. "It seems to me, Your Grace, that there are many experiences you haven't had that you deserve to have."

"And you know this from speaking with me one evening?" she replied, sounding doubtful. Doubtful at his words, yes, but also doubtful that someone like him actually existed: a gentleman who wasn't insistent on owning every action himself, but had confidence that things would work out as they were supposed to nonetheless.

He shrugged, still leaning casually against the tree. "I know this because I saw to your pleasure. I also knew you wanted to have fun, and I heard you say to your stepdaughter that you hadn't truly ever had fun."

She considered that, then regarded him. He was so good-looking, it nearly hurt to gaze at him. His dark eyes, his strong nose, and the blades of his cheekbones.

The faint stubble on his cheeks.

And his mouth.

"I am going to kiss you," she warned, and that mouth curled up, inviting.

"I am counting on it," he said.

By Megan Frampton

HIS STUDY *in* SCANDAL

A School for Scoundrels Novel

MEGAN FRAMPTON

AVONBOOKS

An Imprint of HarperCollinsPublishers

HIS STUDY IN SCANDAL. Copyright © 2023 by Megan Frampton. All rights reserved. Printed in the United States of America. No part of this book may be used or reproduced in any manner whatsoever without written permission except in the case of brief quotations embodied in critical articles and reviews. For information, address HarperCollins Publishers, 195 Broadway, New York, NY 10007.

First Avon Books mass market printing: May 2023

Print Edition ISBN: 978-0-06-322422-3
Digital Edition ISBN: 978-0-06-322423-0

Cover design by Amy Halperin
Cover illustration by Victor Gadino
Cover image © imageBROKER/Alamy Stock Photo (background)

Avon, Avon & logo, and Avon Books & logo are registered trademarks of HarperCollins Publishers in the United States of America and other countries.

HarperCollins is a registered trademark of HarperCollins Publishers in the United States of America and other countries.

FIRST EDITION

23 24 25 26 27 BVGM   10 9 8 7 6 5 4 3 2 1

To anyone who has dared.

HIS STUDY
in
SCANDAL

Chapter One

Two years and one day.

Two years and one day more than she would have wanted to mourn her husband, but Society insisted the widow of a duke must spend that long in sad contemplation of her loss.

Every so often, Alexandra wanted to ask Society just how one was supposed to contemplate sadly. She imagined it would involve many hours of sitting in a mountain of black, staring at the seat he used to sit in. Perhaps choking on a few silent sobs when Cook served his favorite dish of boiled ham and potatoes.

She hadn't done any of that. And she loathed boiled ham and potatoes.

Instead, Alexandra had ordered a few black gowns and taken to doing all the things her husband had frowned on her doing while he was alive. Things like tending the garden, reading novels, taking afternoon naps, and having a second biscuit at tea. Talking to their daughter

Harriet about nothing, rather than instructing her in proper deportment. Things that a duchess shouldn't deign to do—according to her late husband—regardless of how the duchess in question felt.

All while waiting until the day she didn't have to wear black and pretend things she didn't feel. Vowing not to waste a minute once she was safely past the time she might scandalize society with her flagrant weed-pulling.

Which was why, two years and one day after her husband had died, she was standing on a small platform in the middle of a fitting room in a London dress shop, about to destroy her mourning clothing.

Preparing to order an entire new wardrobe so she could chaperone her daughter's delayed debut into Society.

"Hand me the scissors, please?" Alexandra said, turning her head to address one of the two seamstresses in the fitting room.

"You're actually going to—" her stepdaughter Edith said in an admiring tone. A tone Alexandra appreciated, since Edith was by far the most adventurous person Alexandra had ever met—so adventurous, in fact, that Edith's father, Alexandra's husband, had always gotten a peculiar expression on his face when her name was mentioned.

Which was probably why Edith spent most of her time traveling, far away from her father's judgment.

"I am," Alexandra said firmly.

They were in Madame Lucille's Fine Millinery, a shop just off of Bond Street that Alexandra had learned about from her late husband. Before he died, of course.

The duke had been adamantly opposed to creating laws that would improve working conditions for seamstresses, saying they would embolden female workers. He had disdainfully cited the establishment because Madame Lucille offered close to a living wage for ten hours of work a day, not far less for far more hours.

Madame Lucille herself had at first welcomed Alexandra and her stepdaughter, Edith, with trepidation, as though anticipating the dowager duchess had arrived to continue the work her husband had begun. That changed to glee as Alexandra explained what she wanted, accompanied by Edith's whoops of encouragement.

The shop was small but immaculately clean, and Madame Lucille had given the two ladies a tour. Alexandra was relieved to see cheery seamstresses in the back work areas, all talking among themselves as they plied their needles.

Madame Lucille had then shown them into the small fitting room, far smaller than in the shops that the duke had insisted Alexandra patronize, then excused herself to locate the bolts of fabric she wanted to make up Alexandra's new post-mourning wardrobe.

The wardrobe she would wear, all the while

hoping Harriet would find a man—eventually—with whom she would fall in love, not make a strategic dynastic pairing. When Harriet spoke about her Season, she talked about meeting new people, and seeing as much of London as she could, and didn't seem to want to get married right away.

Alexandra felt a fizzing awareness of her future, something she hadn't had since before she was married. She'd wear as many colors as possible, drink champagne with insouciance—or *souciance*, if she felt like it—and generally behave as she wished to, not as others wished her to. Perhaps even take a *third* biscuit, if the biscuits were particularly delicious and she was feeling decidedly peckish.

Once her daughter was safely and well taken care of, of course. Until then, she would have to maintain her duchess facade. But clad in colors and fabrics *she* chose.

And she would never allow anyone to make a decision for her. Losing her freedom again, even if she did the unthinkable and fell in love with someone, would be untenable.

Two of the young seamstresses remained in the room, on hand for any assistance if needed. Both of them seemed overwhelmed by having an actual duchess in their midst, even if Alexandra was now just a dowager duchess.

Alexandra took the scissors the shorter of the two workers handed her, then directed her attention to putting her fingers in the appropriate places, pointing the sharp edge of the shears at her neckline, which caused one of the two workers to emit a startled squeak. The neckline was uncomfortably high, and the black bombazine fabric was stiff and unyielding.

Rather like my late husband, Alexandra thought. She nearly shared the quip with Edith, but she didn't want to scandalize the seamstresses.

The metal of the scissors was cool against her heated skin, and she uttered an involuntary gasp before positioning herself awkwardly so she could cut.

The first close of the scissors wasn't the triumphant action Alexandra was hoping for; the fabric of her gown was apparently too determined to withstand the scissors' onslaught.

But then she clamped her jaw and readjusted her grip, and the scissors bit into the unforgiving material, the two sides falling away as Alexandra continued the downward motion.

She was strong enough to overcome the obstacle of something that was stiff and unyielding.

The snap of the scissors and the whispered shush of the fabric were the only sounds in the room.

Until, finally, she reached the bottom, cutting through the ruffled hem and sighing in satisfaction as the two halves of the gown fell apart, revealing her undergarments, a stark white against the dull black of her outer garment. Still holding the scissors in one hand, she straightened, tugging the two sides of the gown apart until they were on her body only because of the sleeves encasing her arms. She turned to hand the scissors back to the worker, then began to slide the sleeves off, biting her lip in anticipation.

No more black. No more mourning.

"Bravo!" Edith cheered. Alexandra looked at her stepdaughter's face and grinned in response. "This calls for a celebration," she added, a mischievous look on her face. "You've got one night before the rest of the family arrives and the Season starts. Let's have some fun."

THEODORE OSBORNE PLUCKED the last sheet of paper on the left of his desk, laid it directly in front of him, scanned it, then picked up his pen and signed his name with a flourish. He picked up the paper and perched it atop the enormous stack on the right, emitting a sigh of satisfaction.

He leaned back in his chair, folding his hands behind his head.

It was done. For today, at least.

And when he married the Duke of Chelmswich's sister, he would have accomplished all his late father wished for him.

The duke had paid a call earlier that day, suggesting an arrangement that would suit both parties. Theo would marry Lady Harriet, and in exchange for the family's impeccable bloodlines, Theo would make several strategic investments into the duke's struggling interests. It was no small thing for a man like Theo, a literal bastard, to marry into a family as well-born as the duke's. It epitomized everything Theo's father wanted.

That the duke could also wield certain legal tactics to Theo's advantage might have been mentioned as well.

It was the kind of coldhearted bargain that only the most aristocratic families engaged in. Theo was willing to forgo the opportunity of marrying for love if it meant he could both improve his business and fulfill his late father's dream.

Osborne and Son had grown, over the course of Theo's stewardship, to include one shipping line, various wholesale industries, a railroad, several London shops, and a pleasure garden.

It was the last item he was thinking of now; he'd purchased it a few years ago, when he'd found himself returning for, well, *pleasure* over the course of a month.

Unlike Vauxhall Gardens, which had been wildly popular in his father's youth, and still offered a variety of familial entertainments, the more discreet Garden of Hedon was for adults who wished to indulge their desires. Anything and everything were permitted, as long as everyone involved agreed.

And Theo often found himself there agreeing wholeheartedly. It was a place where he could forget, for a few hours, that he carried the weight of hundreds of people's livelihoods on his back.

Forget that most of the gentlemen he met during the course of his business were just as likely to look down on him for his low birth as they were to take his money.

Fucking for forgetfulness was his second favorite hobby. His first was his monthly meetings with his friends, four fellow orphans he'd met at the Devenaugh Home for Destitute Boys.

Each of the five had been placed with good families. In his case, he'd been placed with a gentleman who'd never married but who longed for a family of his own. Theo and Mr. Osborne had been as close as any actual father and son, and Mr. Osborne had taught Theo everything he knew about the business.

Theo had stayed close with his fellow orphans through the years, and they'd been his solace when Mr. Osborne had finally succumbed to a nasty cold. The monthly meetings were his only regularly scheduled time away from work.

But since the next meeting wasn't for a few days—he hadn't even bought the book they were to discuss, Charlotte Lennox's *The Female Quixote*—he'd take himself to the Garden, where he hoped to find a like-minded female for some mindless mutual enjoyment.

It would be the last time he would allow himself to go there. As a patron, at least; he was to meet his intended at her debut, and he wouldn't continue his usual activities once he'd met her. His loyalty was something aristocrats likely would scoff at, but Theo intended to be faithful to his wife, regardless of how he came to marry her.

So tonight would be very special.

"Good evening, Mr. Osborne," the guard said as Theo alighted from the hackney.

Theo leaned in and spoke in a low tone. "Remember, no names. We take pride in our discretion."

The guard's eyes widened, and he snapped to attention. "Of course, Mr. Os— That is, Mr. Mysterious Gentleman."

Theo smothered a grin at the guard's attempt at subterfuge, then strolled through the gates, glancing around at the medium-sized crowd already in attendance.

"Theo!" a voice called. So much for keeping his identity secret.

He swung around, seeing his friend Lucy. Lucy owned a millinery, and she rented the space for her business from him. Much later, they'd run into one another at the Garden, spending a few hours together several months ago. They had both agreed it was enjoyable, but that they'd rather stay friends than try it again.

Theo was just as happy, since he didn't want a commitment with anyone. Not even anyone he'd fucked to exhaustion. His business took up enough time as it was; he didn't have time for any kind of relationship, no matter how mutually beneficial it would be.

Which did rather beg the question of what

introducing a wife into his life would look like. But that was the whole point, wasn't it? To marry, and utilize the duke's connections to ensure he could step away from his business interests and live the life of a gentleman of leisure. It would take some doing, but he wasn't scared of hard work.

Tomorrow, he promised himself, he would plan all of it. *Not tonight.*

"How are you?" he said, kissing her cheek.

As always, she was garbed impeccably, a walking advertisement for the excellence of her shop.

"I'm wonderful. I'm dressing a duchess now, if you can believe it. A dowager duchess, to be sure, but a duchess nonetheless."

"Excellent! Am I going to have to raise your rent?" he asked, accompanying his words with a wink.

She poked him in the chest. "No, she hasn't paid her bill yet." She gave him an assessing look. "And you, you're here because you've been working too hard?"

"How did you know that?" he asked.

She rolled her eyes. "Because you're always working too hard." She gave him a gentle push toward the middle of the Garden. "Go have fun. Heaven knows you deserve it."

"Thanks, Lucy."

"And make sure to tell the lady how fortunate she is to get you," she called over her shoulder, waving a goodbye.

"I shouldn't have to tell her," Theo murmured. "I'll have already shown her. Preferably a few times at least."

He surveyed the crowd, most of whom were watching a contortionist twist herself into a pretzel on stage. While the Garden was a place for anonymous couplings, it also hosted a variety of other entertainments, most of which weren't salacious at all.

The guiding ethos of the Garden was that whatever anyone chose to do, it should be fun. Whether that meant sexual exploration or a sprightly game of chess, it didn't matter.

Theo believed strongly that if one worked hard, one should also play hard. The Garden was for the hardworking people of London, people who had a few spare pence to afford the admittance fee. Some of the patrons—the ones from the best families—had expressed surprise that they were elbow to elbow with the merchants they purchased pottery from, or the bankers they did business with. Theo would then strongly suggest those complainers leave the Garden, never to return.

"What are we doing here?" he heard a woman say somewhere behind him.

"We're here," another woman replied, "so that you can know what it feels like to have fun." The second woman spoke firmly.

"I know what it feels like—" the first woman began, then trailed off. "Never mind. You are absolutely right. There's fun, and then there is *fun*. What kind of fun are we talking about? Oh, I see a chess game over there! And look, some people are riding donkeys! I've never ridden a donkey. That seems fun!"

Theo smothered a smile at the woman's excited tone. It was rare, if not entirely unique, for a person to have reached adulthood in the city and still have that ability to find joy in small moments. He envied that, if he were being honest.

"We are not here for you to ride a donkey, for Heaven's sake," the second woman said, sounding aggrieved. "Look, there is a gentleman up ahead. Why don't you ask him what he likes to do here?"

"You mean go up to a stranger and begin talking?" the woman said. From the way she spoke, she might have been suggesting standing on her head while reciting poetry, it was such an outlandish idea.

"Why not?"

Silence as the first woman seemed to process the idea. "Fine. But if I do not have fun, it is your fault." She spoke in a gentle, teasing tone.

"Go," the second woman said. "I'll meet you back here in two hours. I'm going to find my own type of fun."

Theo turned to look at the two women, nearly stumbling into one of them, who was heading directly for him.

This must be the first woman, the one who had never had fun.

She was striking, if not necessarily tradition-ally beautiful; her eyes were wide-set, and dark; not brown, but perhaps a dark green, with strong eyebrows set above. Her nose was strong as well, giving her an almost haughty appearance. Her wide mouth curled up into a smile, and her lips were full and rose-colored and eminently bitable. Her hair was a medium blond, at least in the flickering light, and looked as though it tended to waviness. She had it pulled back into a practical chignon, a few strands falling out from her coiffure.

He would have expected her to be young, but this woman seemed older than he. She also ap-peared to be indefatigably curious, finding de-light in small things.

"Good evening," he said as she opened her mouth to speak. "Are you here for the entertainment?" he said, gesturing vaguely toward the main area of the Garden.

"I don't know what I'm here for," she muttered, but Theo heard her.

He held his arm out for her. "Allow me to show you," he said as she took his arm. "And you can tell me what you want."

For some reason—a reason he couldn't define, even to himself—it was important that he be able to elicit her joy.

Chapter Two

And you can tell me what you want.

Had a gentleman ever asked her that before? Wanted to know what she wanted, not what he wanted her to want?

It felt wonderful. And it was a totally novel experience. All because she was determined to reclaim her life—destroying black clothing, coming to this kind of place, being open to an experience that might be dangerous. Or exciting. Or both.

She'd have to keep that in mind. It would be too easy for her to fall back into her meek ways, but that wasn't who she was. Who she needed to be.

And she was about to make her own decision, not one made for her. It felt glorious.

Alexandra walked with the gentleman on a path that led them further into the enclosed area. There were buildings of varying sizes ringing the center, which seemed to be an elaborate garden with a few high hedges, as though they were part of a maze.

Torches spilled firelight over the path, lighting their way, while she could hear the distant murmur of voices. It felt like the moment before one dipped one's toe into a warm bath—filled with anticipation, knowing that what was to come would envelop one in utter bliss.

Even if she didn't know that for certain. But she guessed it would. After all, this was the cleverly named Garden of Hedon, a name that Edith had had to explain the meaning of, which promptly made Alexandra blush once she understood.

That a forty-year-old dowager duchess was still prone to blushing revealed just how sheltered she'd been heretofore.

At least she was providing amusement for Edith; her stepdaughter had laughed for at least three minutes at Alexandra's blushing.

"So . . . ?" the gentleman prompted.

"So . . . ?" Alexandra repeated blankly.

He put his hand over hers, the one that held his arm, and squeezed her fingers. "Tell me what you want."

She took a deep breath. "I don't know," she replied simply. "I suppose I want to do what I want, which sounds both redundant and also incredibly unhelpful."

He uttered a soft snort of laughter.

"At least you're honest," he replied. "Most people say what they think the other one wants, which is even more unhelpful, because most people don't actually exchange ideas, real ideas, with one another."

"Perhaps we could begin with you telling me what you want," Alexandra rejoined.

He drew her closer, and she felt her breath hitch. "I am here for pleasure," he replied simply. Easily. "This is a pleasure garden, after all."

Was it that straightforward? Say what you want and just—get it?

"Do you want to play chess?" she blurted as they passed a line of tables where people were playing a variety of games.

He didn't reply, instead drawing out a chair at an unoccupied table and seating her at it, then taking the opposite chair.

The board—for the table was painted like a chessboard—was all set up with the pieces in readiness. At least, Alexandra presumed so; she'd never actually played herself, and she didn't have the faintest idea how to begin.

"Chess is an interesting game," he began, moving a small piece on the front ahead two spaces. "It was created in India, I believe, about fifteen hundred years ago." He tilted his head toward her as though confiding a secret. "I only know that because one of my friends is a fount of knowledge, and insists on sharing that knowledge." His tone was fondly indulgent, as though the friend both delighted and annoyed him.

She folded her hands in her lap and regarded him as he spoke.

Goodness. She hadn't gotten a good look at him before, what with the flickering light and all, and now that she did, she didn't understand why he'd been alone.

He was remarkably and vibrantly handsome. His hair was dark, a few indolent curls hanging low on his forehead. His nose was a strong, straight line atop a full, sensual mouth. His eyes were keenly direct, a dark color also, and he had a dimple on his right cheek when he smiled.

Which he was doing now.

Heavens, it felt as though his smile was the warm bath—as though she was dipping her toe in his essence, breathing in his scent through her skin.

"What are you thinking about?" he asked, and she felt herself shiver at the dark intensity of his tone.

"I'm thinking I don't actually know how to play chess," she admitted, startling him into a bark of laughter.

He . . . laughed. He didn't mock her, or ridicule her for admitting her ignorance. He seemed to find it charming.

She was already enjoying herself far more than she had in a long time.

He put the small piece back where it had been, then rose, holding his hand out to her. She took it, allowing him to assist her up.

"Well, is it something you wish to learn? Or is there something else you'd like to discover?"

Alexandra was naïve, but even she couldn't mistake his meaning. Not when he said it in that low, intimate tone. Not when he was gazing directly into her eyes as though he was eager to hear her answer.

And, she found, she absolutely wished to discover things. What it would feel like to have that full mouth pressed against hers. What he might do with his fingers, if given encouragement. How she might lose herself in the warm bath of him, in this place that felt as though it existed in a dream, outside of a world where she was a widowed duchess on the verge of bringing her daughter out into Society.

In a place where she could just be herself, with wants and, yes, *needs* that could be. She had just one night; she should make the best of it. And the wickedest of it. And do everything she had never allowed herself to do before.

With him.

"Should we go somewhere more private?" he asked. "Only if you wish to, however." His tone was gentle. Kind, even. "If you would like to sit back down and learn how to play chess, I am happy to do that as well. This night is for you to have fun. Isn't that what your friend said?"

Alexandra took a deep breath as she weighed her options. Her first option was to take him up on his offer, learn how to play chess, and likely spend some time gazing at his handsome face.

The other option—the one that made her heart race and other parts of her tingle—was to go somewhere quiet with him, to let him show her what a pleasure garden was truly about.

To immerse herself in him.

Though she wasn't really weighing her options, was she? She already knew what she was going to do, had known as soon as Edith had explained where they were going in the hackney cab over. Even though she'd distracted herself with thoughts of chess and donkeys.

"I'd like to go somewhere," she said in a soft, low tone. "Somewhere with you."

His lips drew into a smile so knowing, so wicked, it made her breath catch.

"Excellent," he replied. "And you will be certain to tell me what you want, won't you? Often and with force, if necessary? I want you to experience as much pleasure as you'd expected when you made the choice to come here."

"I didn't actually—" she began, but then stopped herself. What did it matter that Edith had been the one to urge her into it?

It didn't. What mattered was that she was here, Sir Warm Bath was there, and she had the evening to explore before she picked up her responsibilities again.

"Take me somewhere," she said simply.

THEO FELT THE familiar sizzle of anticipation curl inside him as he led her deeper into the Garden. The moments leading up to everything were often the most enjoyable for him; the delicate dance between potential partners, the shared looks and conversation.

He found her enormously appealing, and not just because of her appearance. There was something in how she held herself, as though she was unaware of her own power, but wanting to push herself, to see who she could be.

Perhaps he was reading into her earlier words, but he didn't think so. This was a woman who seemed to be both safe and fearless, who was brave enough to confront what she didn't know.

She was unlike anybody he'd ever spent time with—either in or out of bed. It was intoxicating.

If it ended up that they spent their time together sipping champagne and flirting, perhaps exchanging a few kisses, he would be fine with that. Because it would be what *she'd* decided.

He already knew he wanted to give her what she wanted—he'd asked her to tell him just that. Somehow, he felt as though it was more important that she be given the space to be who she was.

Even though tonight was his last night here as a patron. Perhaps especially because of that.

He prided himself on being an unselfish lover, of ensuring his partner was as, if not more, satiated than he, but this was something else. Something he'd never encountered in himself before. An extension of his always wanting to help, to solve things to everyone's satisfaction.

"Who was the woman you arrived with?" he asked as they made their way along the path.

The path itself wasn't narrowing, but the torch-lights were spaced further apart here, giving the semblance of privacy.

"My stepdaughter," she replied in a fond tone. "She is actually older than I by a few years, and she is also my best friend. I am so fortunate to have met her."

"You are married?" he said, halting on the path. He didn't indulge with married women—it wouldn't be right, not when the whole point was to be free to do what you wanted without obliga-tion. Marriage was very much an obligation.

"No, I am a widow," she said quietly. "He died a few years ago."

"Ah." There was a stillness in her, as though there were things she held inside and wouldn't, or couldn't, say. He decided to let her be the one to broach more of that topic, instead focusing on the one that clearly brought her joy.

"Your stepdaughter—what is it you like about her? That she brought you here?" he added, a hu-morous tone in his voice.

She laughed. "Yes, for one thing. She is—she is fearless. She does what she wants when she wants. She did not get along with her father, my husband. But that didn't seem to bother her. In-stead, she focused on herself. I envy that."

"Which is why you are here with me."

She nodded. "There are . . . things I have to do starting tomorrow. But tonight, Edith encouraged me to come here, to let myself feel the freedom she has. Just for one night."

He chuckled. "Your Edith seems as though she cares for you."

"She does," came the answer. Spoken firmly, and with obvious love. "She dares me to challenge myself, and I admire her so much."

She spoke about her stepdaughter as Theo would about his friends.

"I am here for just one night as well," he said, feeling a tightness in his chest. "There are things I will be doing tomorrow that will not allow me to visit." But he didn't want to think about his future bride, not when this woman was his future. For the next few hours, at least.

"So we are both free for tonight. Only for tonight. Which means we should make the most of it, shouldn't we?" She sounded both hesitant and bold.

"And that freedom means being here with me? Alone?"

"Yes," she said simply.

That eased the feeling in his chest, and he offered her a warm smile.

They stopped in front of one of the small cottages, prettily decorated with greenery in front and painted a bright white. Torchlights stood on either side of the building, casting a welcoming glow. He knew this particular one was empty, because he'd reserved it for his own use earlier.

"We're here," he said.

"Do we just . . . go in?" she asked.

"If that is what you want. There are refreshments inside. It is whatever you wish to do."

"Oh," she said, sounding awed. "I've never—"

"Let me guess," he said as her words trailed off. "You've never done just what you want to do."

"Never."

He gestured to the door. "Then go ahead, my lady, and enter. We will figure out together just what it is you want. For tonight." He needed to make certain she got what she wanted. Make certain she received her joy.

She turned to regard him, her face tilted up so she could look into his eyes.

She was tall, nearly as tall as he, which lent her more of a commanding presence. Her figure was lush, her breasts round and full, her hips also wide. Just the sort of plush softness he wished to sink himself into, to surround himself in and surrender to.

His cock was already stiffening, and he hadn't touched her, save her arm.

He felt an almost primal urge to give her pleasure, to ensure her one night of being herself was the most intoxicating and marvelous night she'd ever had.

Yes, he wanted to fuck her into oblivion, but he also wanted to please her, which was far more complicated than inserting his cock into her pussy. For one thing, it might not even involve that activity; it was whatever *she* wanted.

Though he did hope that activity occurred at some point in the evening. He wasn't *entirely* altruistic.

He already knew this final night would be momentous and unforgettable.

"Thank you," she said, leaning up to kiss the corner of his mouth. He let her lead, let her rest her soft mouth on his for a moment before she withdrew, stepping in front of him to enter the cottage, turning her head to give him a dark look of seduction before walking inside.

He hastened after her, his whole body feeling as though it was burning up with desire.

Already knowing that nothing before or after this could compare with the night he was about to have.

Chapter Three

Alexandra looked around the inside of the cottage, pleased at how welcoming it felt. It was small but immaculately clean, candles set on nearly every available surface. The floor was dark wood, with a few scattered rugs. The eye immediately went to the sofa, set underneath a paned window. It would fit two or three people, if the three were slim and felt comfortable squeezing together. It appeared to be made of dark red velvet, a lush fabric that evoked images of decadent sensuality. There were bottles of unidentified liquid set on either side of the sofa, while a low table held a tray with a bottle and several glasses.

"Did they think a party was on its way here?" Alexandra asked, moving to pick up one of the glasses.

"The Garden prepares for any occasion," he replied. "If a guest wishes to indulge here, we wouldn't want anyone to have to hunt for a glass."

"We?" she said, turning to face him. Realizing

at that same moment that, for God's sake, she didn't even know his name. Nor he hers.

He shrugged. "I might have some ownership here. I like to make certain everyone who pays a fee gets their money's worth."

Her eyebrows drew together. "So is this," she said, gesturing to the space between them, "just you trying to please your customer?" She frowned. "And you said this was your last night. Does that mean you're selling it?"

He shook his head. "No, it's more complicated than that. Let me assure you, I am entirely here for pleasure." He frowned, as though considering what he was about to say. "For your pleasure, in fact. I have this feeling," he said, gesturing to his chest.

She knew what he meant. She had that feeling, too. Frankly, it scared her. But she couldn't allow herself to get scared by it; she had to lean into it. That was the whole point, wasn't it?

He shook his head, as though clearing his thoughts. "I bought into the venture because I enjoy it here so much. But after tonight—" He shrugged, letting his words hang there. "Let's forget all that. For now."

He advanced toward her, predatory, and she couldn't help how her breath caught and her heart raced. This was a confident man, one who knew precisely what he wanted and that he would get it, of that she had no doubt. "As for my pleasing anyone—I am just here to please you."

"Oh," she said, her exclamation coming out with a gasp. "I see."

"You don't," he said, shaking his head slowly, still advancing, until he had slid his hands onto her arms, her bare arms, his palms hot and tender on her skin. "I want to please you. I wasn't certain what I was looking for until I saw you. But now I know. Your pleasure is what I want tonight." He lowered his head to her neck, his lips just grazing her skin, until he reached her ear. "Are you going to give it to me? Or do I have to beg?" He laughed, a dark, low laugh that went straight *there*, where she already pulsed. "I can do that, if it is what you want." He paused. "Please," he said in a husky voice.

She shuddered, her hands coming around to clasp his neck, feeling her pulse beat fast. And then she tilted her head back, meeting his eyes as she took a deep breath. "I am going to. As long as I can do the same for you. It is your final night as well, after all."

And with those words, it was as if she'd set him in motion. He bent and picked her up, hoisting her against his chest as though she didn't weigh a thing, then set her on the sofa sideways, her head leaning against the arm, her legs stretched out to the other end.

Then he got on his knees on the floor in front of her, his hand coming to her face to cup her chin.

She swallowed at the sheer desire she saw in his eyes. Nobody had ever looked at her like that before. Nobody had ever made her so keenly aware of her body before. It felt as though every inch of her was tingling, was waiting to be touched, caressed, petted.

His gaze lowered to her mouth, and then he paused, his glance flicking up to meet hers again. "Tell me," he said.

"Kiss me," she replied, and one corner of his mouth tilted up, that dimple flashing. Then she couldn't think of anything except his mouth on hers, the feel of everything too much and yet not enough.

He was deliberate and gentle, as if he knew she didn't have much experience. Her husband had rarely kissed her, had spent perhaps ten minutes at a time when he'd visited her bedchamber, most of that time spent getting himself ready to enter her.

This felt like he was wooing her, was seducing her with just his mouth, and then with his tongue, which licked at the seam of her lips until she opened on a sigh.

He made a noise low in his throat, and then he was kissing her with far more alacrity, sliding his tongue inside her mouth, licking and sucking as his hand moved to her neck, his fingertips trailing over her neckbones, to her upper chest, playing with the neckline of her gown.

This . . . this was truly happening. She was at a pleasure garden, alone with a stranger, allowing him to kiss her, telling him what she wanted.

What she wanted was to do more.

"Touch me," she said, taking his hand and placing it on her breast. "There, please." The juxtaposition of the polite word combined with what she was actually asking for almost made her laugh.

If she wasn't so intensely involved in this whole kissing business.

Tentatively at first, then more boldly, she tangled her tongue with his, licking as he had, feeling her body tighten in new and unusual and very pleasant ways.

His palm cupped her breast, and he began to move it, grasping its fullness as she felt her nipple harden. Making her long to remove the barrier of fabric that separated his skin from hers.

"Do you like this?" he murmured. "If you need to stop, tell me."

Again, he was giving her the option. The choice. How had she gotten so remarkably fortunate to find a man who would allow her to make her own decisions?

"Don't stop," she said.

She arched her back, thrusting her body up, moving her legs restlessly as though she couldn't get comfortable. And she couldn't. She was on fire. She was focused only on him, and his mouth, and his fingers, and how everything felt alive. She wanted it to continue so she could feel what would happen next, and yet she never wanted this to stop—rather like reading an excellent book she couldn't wait to get to the end of, but didn't want to stop reading, ever.

And then he put his mouth lower, onto her neck, his hand still palming her breast. He kissed her skin, nipping it too, then running his tongue over the same spot.

"Do you want more?" he asked, his words rumbling against her.

"Mmm," she said, still restless. "Yes, please."

He straightened, pulling her up also, then shifted so he could reach behind her, reach the buttons of her gown.

"Oh!" she exclaimed, and his fingers stilled.

"Is this still good?" he asked.

"Still good," she replied.

He undid her buttons, then drew back to face her, sliding the fabric down off her shoulders, her arms, until her gown had fallen to her waist. Her corset followed soon thereafter.

Her chemise was thin, made of the finest linen, and she knew it was likely sheer in the candlelight. His eyes drank her in, and she felt as though she was a flower unfurling under his gaze.

She jerked her chin toward him, raising her eyebrows. "And you?"

His mouth curled into a crooked smile, and his hands went to his cravat, making quick work of removing it, tossing it to the floor beside him. He shrugged his jacket off next, then yanked his shirt from his trousers, pulling it over his head.

Revealing his chest.

Alexandra leaned forward, her hand going involuntarily to his chest, her palm flat against his warm skin. He put his hand over hers, pressing down. "Touch me," he said, echoing her earlier words.

And she did. His body was hard and muscled, with interesting ridges on either side of his abdomen, a line of dark hair running down the middle into his trousers.

She grazed her palm over his nipples, and he made a low, encouraging noise deep in his throat. She grasped his shoulder, squeezing it, feeling the hard strength under her hand, then put her palm onto his side, sliding it down the ridged muscles.

He had put his hand on her leg, and he was sliding the fabric of her gown up, up over her ankles, her shins, the cooler air feeling like its own caress.

"Is this what you wanted?" he asked, his voice husky. Husky with desire, and lust, and passion, Alexandra knew, though she had never heard anyone speak to her with those emotions threading their voice.

"Yes," she replied in a firm tone, making certain he knew she meant it.

"Stand up," he demanded, and she did, then let him remove her gown entirely, folding it carefully on a chair before returning his attention to her.

His eyes blazed as he placed her back on the sofa, now seated as one would sit on a sofa, albeit clad in only her chemise and stockings.

"You'd make an excellent lady's maid," she said nonsensically. Unnerved by what was happening. He grinned, waggling his eyebrows until she laughed in response.

He'd seen she was in unknown waters, and done something to make her feel more comfortable.

Goodness.

He returned to kneeling in front of her, and she frowned in confusion. "What are you . . . ?" she began, but then his hands were on her knees, pushing them wide, and he'd lowered his head to tuck it underneath the hem of her chemise, his breath on her skin.

He kissed each thigh, and she trembled, holding her breath as she waited for whatever he was going to do next.

His hands held her legs wide, open for him, and she blushed to think of what he was seeing— things nobody had ever seen. Even the doctor who'd delivered Harriet had put a draped blanket over her for modesty's sake.

And he kept kissing her skin, sliding his mouth up until he reached the crease of her hip, the chemise ruched up so her lower body was exposed.

"You're so beautiful," he murmured, and she warmed at the compliment—it was sincere. There was nothing he needed to say to get her to continue. The whole point was continuing. Now there was just honesty and emotion and feelings and desire.

Now there was just them in this fairy cottage, away from all responsibility and what it meant to act with propriety. If anybody saw them, even had a hint of what was happening, she would be entirely and permanently ruined. Cast out of Society, relegated to some shadow world where disgraced women were allowed to exist.

Perhaps that was what made it so appealing, so provocative. That one moment could change a person's life forever, for better or for worse.

She forgot everything regarding reputation, what she was to do tomorrow, and nearly forgot her own name when he put his mouth *there* and began to work some sort of magic with his tongue.

THEO LOVED WOMEN. He loved the way they smelled, their soft roundness, how they tried to squelch their cries of passion when they really wanted to scream.

But most of all, he loved how they tasted.

And she—she tasted the best of any woman he'd sampled thus far.

Her musky aroma teased his nose as he licked her, flicking his tongue against her clit, feeling her tremble in response. He let go of her knee to bring his hand to where his tongue was, stroking and caressing as he continued to kiss her.

He heard her frantic breaths, her tiny moans of pleasure, and he smiled against her skin, against her delicious pussy, as he listened to her reactions to figure out what would make her explode in passion.

His fingers—first one, then two—entered her narrow channel, curling up and stroking as he worked her with his mouth. His cock was so hard and so stiff in his trousers that it actually hurt, but it was a delicious agony, one that made him anticipate everything still to come. So to speak.

It felt as though he had never been anywhere but here, under her chemise, one hand on her soft thigh, holding her open for him, the other pressed against her, finding the pressure that made her moans increase.

He didn't know when he'd realized this was an experience different from any of the ones he'd had before. Perhaps as early as when he'd heard her talking to her stepdaughter? Before he'd seen her? When he'd heard the joyful excitement in her voice?

It scared him, if he were being honest. But he also knew it meant something.

"Oh God," she said. He heard how close she was and redoubled his efforts, now sucking on that tiny button, now releasing it to give a slow, steady lick. Then he thrust his tongue inside as she clenched around him.

"Oh God," she said again, and this time her voice was higher, more strained. He smiled against her skin, knew that she was about to climax. He wanted to see her face when she did, but more than that, he wanted to watch her pussy spasm in orgasm, feel how her walls would close in and hold him so he couldn't let go if he wanted to.

He did not want to. He never wanted to.

"Ah, ah, ahhh," she cried, and he stopped thinking, just kept up his lapping of her, not stopping until the last trembling pulse was done.

Then he gave her one last pat and pulled his head back from between her thighs to look up at her.

And the expression on her face was more than enough satisfaction for him.

He'd have been fine if she decided now she was finished with all of this, thank you very much. Her expression was sated, and sensual, and languorous, and redolent with everything they'd done thus far. She looked like a cat who'd lapped up all the cream, and knew she well deserved it. Her eyes were closed, and he allowed himself to drink her in, cataloging the shape of her nose, her fine, strong eyebrows, and her determined chin.

She was so lovely. Brave and careful, bold and cautious. A mystery he wanted to solve.

Only he had just one night.

Then her eyes fluttered open, and widened when she saw him looking at her. Her cheeks began to turn pink in the candlelight, and he reached up to cup her breast. "You are gorgeous," he said, at which she turned even pinker.

"Thank you. Not just for the compliment, but for—" she said, biting her lip when she couldn't seem to find the words. Or was too shy to say them.

"For making you climax? I told you, didn't I?"

"You did," she said on a sigh.

He got up from the floor, wincing a little as his knees felt what he'd been doing for the past half an hour or so, and sat beside her on the couch, immediately drawing her into his chest, adjusting her so her head lay on him.

His cock throbbed, aching for release, and he shifted to ease some of the pressure. He had to be poking her in the back, which might've been awkward if he allowed himself to think about it.

But he didn't. Because if he thought, he might remember this would all be over soon.

She put her hand on his thigh and squeezed, then let out a happy little sigh that made him smile.

"You are quite good at that," she said, her voice low and sultry. "Not that I would know if you are exceptional, since that is the first time—"

"The first time anyone has kissed you like that?" he said. "I assure you, I am one of the best." He was only speaking the truth. He'd been told the same often enough.

"It's a good thing I am only here for one night. I think you might have ruined me for anyone else," she replied simply.

She wriggled in his arms to turn toward him, looking in his eyes. "And what is next?"

He shrugged. "There doesn't have to be anything next, not if you don't want." It might kill him not to climax, but it was more important for her to feel in command.

"Oh, I want," she said, her tone eager. "I figure

if you can do *that*, then the things with which I am familiar will be spectacular. I'd like to feel how it's *supposed* to be done."

"Oh, you would, would you?" he said, smiling at her.

"Mmm-hmm. I'd like to hear you make the same kinds of noises I just did."

He arched a brow. "Give a woman one orgasm and all of a sudden she is demanding the world."

"Not the world. Just *you*," she replied, before leaning in to kiss him.

Just you. The words echoed in his mind, making him think of things he'd never considered before—actually being with someone because he wanted to, not just because of business, or leverage, or any of the other terms that actually meant compromise.

Just you.

Alexandra felt as though she'd not only entered the warm bath, but that she had become it, unable to maintain any kind of distance between who she was and her body. Clearly she had been missing out on a lot during her two decades of marriage; her husband had never done anything close to what her stranger had, and definitely had never elicited an orgasm, as he had.

She felt blissful, but also curious. Wanting to know what else could happen tonight, the one night when she could do what she wanted and with whom she wanted.

"Well then," her stranger was saying, "if you want me, then perhaps we should move to a bed." He gestured to a door. She hadn't noticed before. "It might be awkward, if not impossible," he continued, "for us to fuck as we both wish to."

She gave an involuntary gasp at his crude language—ridiculous, given where he'd just been— and he smirked at her, as if aware of her shock.

"I imagine you've never said that word aloud, have you?" he mused. He jerked his chin toward her. "If we are to continue, I want to hear you say it." Challenging her.

She swallowed. "Say it?" she echoed.

"Yes. If this is your night, your night of fun, and you want to see what else there is, you'll need to be bold enough to ask for what you want."

"Ask—"

"And I will do whatever you say," he said, his voice low and redolent with desire. "But you have to ask." How did he know that was what she needed? To voice her desires?

She took a deep breath, then met his gaze steadily. This was the moment she could prove to herself that she was standing up for herself. Expressing what she wanted, not what anyone else wanted for her.

"Will you—will you fuck me?"

He shivered, and she felt a moment of exultation. She had made this handsome, confident, charismatic man tremble.

"No," he said, "we will fuck each other. Come."

He pushed her off him so she stood on the floor, and he swept her up in his arms again, stalking to the far corner of the room, where he kicked a door open and strode through.

The room was dominated by a massive bed that was almost too big for its space. It was a regal four-poster with lavish bedding, anomalous in this humble space with its simply painted white walls and discreet windows.

He placed her on the bed, then stood at its foot, keeping her gaze as his hands went to the placket of his trousers. Soon he was wearing nothing, and clambering toward her on the bed, reaching for her chemise so he could slide that over her head.

His body was a work of art. Smooth skin stretched over taut muscles, dips and planes she wanted to explore with her hands and her mouth.

He grinned at her, as though delighted, and it was impossible not to return the smile, even though she didn't think this much smiling was customary for this act.

Then again, what did she know? Her late husband thought a few minutes of grunting and pushing was enough sexual congress between a husband and a wife, and clearly he'd been wrong.

Perhaps smiling and feeling happy was the way to do it properly. It was definitely far more enjoyable.

"I think," he said, stroking her body as they lay side by side, "that I can make you come again."

She stared at him. "Again?"

He laughed. "It does happen, Angel. Sometimes even three times."

"For you, too?" she asked. She hated that she was so ignorant, but it wasn't as though she would ever see him again. Not that that made her sad. Even though she was lying to herself when she thought that.

Perhaps she could find a way to do this again—not permanently, as she never wanted another husband—but with someone who would know what to do. Someone who was as set on impermanence as she was.

"No, usually it's just the once." He took her hand and placed it on himself, there where he was rigid and yet velvety smooth all at the same time.

"You have encountered this before, I presume."

She didn't move her hand, just let it sit on his—on his male part, and nodded. "Yes."

"But you've never done anything with it before."

"How can you guess?" she asked.

"It's not a guess," he said, laughter in his tone. "Here, try this," he continued, putting his hand over hers and sliding it up and down. "Mmm, like that, yes."

He gripped her hip, his fingers digging into her as she kept moving her hand up and down. After a minute or two his jaw tightened, and he bit out, "You'll have to stop, I don't want to come like this," and she dropped him immediately, wondering if she'd done something wrong.

He shook his head slowly as if reading her mind.

"That was perfect. I need to know, however, what it feels like inside of you. Do you want that?"

Oh. Oh, in the midst of all this kissing and touching and stroking of various parts, she'd completely forgotten about the one thing she'd done before.

And she couldn't wait.

"Yes, please," she said, and he gave her a wicked smile, that dimple flashing.

"So polite," he said, shifting so he was kneeling between her legs again, holding himself in his hand as he gazed at her.

"Please," she begged, feeling that ache again as she stared at his naked body.

The thought went through her mind—dangerous, naughty, and so unlike her she nearly gasped— that he was fucking *gorgeous*, and she wanted to eat him up with a spoon.

He leaned forward, bracing himself on the bed with one hand, the other still holding himself. She felt him at her entrance, and glanced down, the sight the most incredibly erotic one she'd ever seen.

And then he began to slide in, and her breath hitched as he filled her, pushing in until they were flush against one another, skin to skin.

He stilled for a moment, his eyes closed, and then he kissed her, plunging his tongue into her mouth as he began to move.

The movement became more vigorous, and his hand went between their bodies. His fingers were there, right where he'd had his mouth. She could feel the pressure as he kept moving and pushing. Then he was leaning back, hoisting her legs over his shoulders so she lay wantonly open to him, his penis thrusting in and out, his fingers stroking her in rhythm as she felt herself start to climb that peak again, the one he'd made her summit with his tongue.

He increased his speed, and the bed was jostling beneath them, the wood frame creaking with their movement. She wondered if someone would burst in because of the noise, but she didn't care, she didn't care at all. Then his fingers kept going, and she was holding her breath. His head was bowed over his chest as he fucked her—yes, he was fucking her, and it felt so good, so good to feel and so good to think. Then she summited the hill just as she felt him explode inside her, emitting a harsh groan as his seed spurted.

He collapsed on top of her, sweat slicking his chest, the bed still gently rocking, and she had never felt so satisfied and content in her life.

And it was only for tonight, and she wanted to cry, because she was already missing this, missing the kind of freedom that being the dowager Duchess of Chelmswich could never have.

Unless she took it. Found it and held it close. This was just a taste of what could be, if she was brave enough to do it.

Chapter Four

Theo's hands shook as he did up the buttons on her gown. Her hair hung down, fallen from her chignon, likely when they were on the bed.

He'd never experienced anything like that before, and he wasn't certain he liked it.

That is, he loved it, but he didn't know if he *liked* it—liked feeling as if he was in thrall to someone else, as if he could just close his eyes and drift into a world where it was just the two of them.

He'd never wanted to spend more time with one of his partners before, not the way he wanted to spend time with her. It wasn't in his nature to be introspective, and yet here he was, wondering what was going on inside his own head.

Why? Why *her*?

He couldn't answer that.

Except it had something to do with her being so open, so trusting, while also so ready to enjoy everything offered to her—the comfort of the cottage, his kisses, the possibility of a game of chess, for Christ's sake.

"That's done, then," he said, his voice rough. She turned around as she lifted her hair off her back, twisting it into some semblance of a respectable hair style.

Her face was flushed, her eyes sparkled, and he didn't think he'd ever seen anything more beautiful in his entire life.

"Can I get you something to drink before we leave?" he asked, picking up the bottle of champagne.

She glanced toward the door, a frown wrinkling her eyebrows, then she turned back to him, giving him a nod and a smile. "That would be lovely, thank you."

"So polite," he murmured, seeing her blush at his reference to when she was begging him to enter her.

He poured two glasses of the sparkling liquid, then set the bottle down. He had put on his trousers, but remained shirtless, since his heated skin wouldn't tolerate fabric at the moment. Not when he could be bare with her, even if it was just his chest.

"To tonight," he said, tapping his glass against hers.

"To tonight," she repeated, then took a sip, her eyes widening in delight as the champagne touched her tongue.

"It's excellent quality," he said, unable to resist boasting. "It's imported from France, of course, and comes from a small vineyard."

"It does taste good," she said. "Not that I know anything about—" she began in a self-deprecating tone.

"Stop," he said, putting his hand on her arm. "You know you like the taste, don't you?" He shrugged. "That's all you have to know." He brought his glass to his lips to take another sip.

It felt important to reassure her. About the champagne, about how she'd made him feel in bed.

She drank as well, a contemplative expression on her face. "Just like I know I like how you taste me, even if I have never experienced it before."

He nearly choked on his champagne, she startled him so much with her frankness. If less than one entire night of play could unlock this in her, imagine what—

He couldn't and wouldn't allow himself to imagine it. One night. That was all he ever expected, all he ever wanted.

Even though he wanted. Just . . . wanted.

"Exactly," he said when he was able to speak again. He finished his drink, then set it down on the table and glanced around for his shirt.

It was likely past time to leave the cottage. The Garden closed promptly at two in the morning, and it had to be past one o'clock now. How long had they been there?

It seemed as though she'd had the same thought, since she finished her drink also, then sat on the sofa to put on her slippers.

"Come, let me walk you to meet Edith," he said when she'd finished.

She rose from the sofa, smoothing her skirts. "Thank you."

"And will you tell her you had fun?" he couldn't resist asking.

"The most fun," she said, giving him a look that made him want to do it all over again.

Instead, he opened the door for her, holding her arm as she stepped off the stairs back onto the path. He spotted one of the Garden's workers in the shadows and tilted his head toward the cottage, indicating that there was cleaning to do.

They walked together in silence, a companionable silence that Theo nonetheless wanted to disturb: *Who are you? What is your name? What are you doing in London?*

ALEXANDRA'S PACE QUICKENED as they walked toward where she was to meet Edith. She had no idea of the time, no idea if it had been two hours or two days since Edith had sent her off to have fun.

But she had had fun, and she had Edith to thank for it. Not to mention the mysterious gentleman.

"Alexandra!" Edith called as they came into view.

"Alex," he murmured behind her. "Your name is Alexandra."

He'd called her Angel before. She liked that.

"I'll leave you here, now that I know you'll be taken care of. It was my distinct pleasure, Alexandra," he said, then melted away into the shadows before Alexandra could reply. Or ask his name.

Which was just as well.

Edith had changed from a few hours ago; her hair was done differently, and she wore black lace gloves that Alexandra knew she hadn't had on before.

"Did you have fun?" Edith asked, her eyes sparkling with curiosity.

Alexandra took a deep breath. "I did. But we should be going," she said, feeling suddenly desperate to leave. Not because she wasn't having fun anymore, but because she was. The prospect of never having it again, of never feeling the way he'd made her feel, hurt so much it was nearly palpable.

She needed to go home and readjust herself, back to being the dowager duchess who was going to serenely and sedately chaperone her daughter through the rigors of a London season.

Not be the woman who demanded her own pleasure, who said things no modest woman would say.

The woman she wanted to be, honestly. Though she'd have to pretend a bit longer to be the previous iteration of herself. Just until the Season was over.

"Of course," Edith replied.

One of the many things she loved about her stepdaughter was Edith's acceptance of whatever Alexandra wanted. Not that she wouldn't challenge her stepmother, if she felt it was warranted; but she could sense what Alexandra needed, sometimes almost before Alexandra herself did.

It had been the only bright spot in her marriage, at least until Harriet was born. Without Edith, Alexandra didn't know how she would have survived.

She walked swiftly to the exit, an unaccountable feeling of sadness washing over her. Wanting to cry, even though she'd just had the most incredible evening of her life.

But no. Tonight was for her pleasure. He'd said that, he'd *meant* that, and she wasn't going to let pesky feelings of loss and emptiness get in the way of that.

"Did you have fun?" she asked Edith.

Edith gave a vigorous nod of her head. "Absolutely—I don't want to shock you, so I won't describe it, but it was perfect. Just the sort of thing I needed before having to deal with William and Florence." William, Alexandra's stepson and Edith's brother, and Florence, his wife. Edith wrinkled her nose as she spoke, making her feelings absolutely clear.

Alexandra looped her arm through her stepdaughter's, nudging her shoulder as she did so. "Don't you dare ruin tonight by mentioning what is ahead of us."

"That's true," Edith replied. "There will be time enough to think about them in the weeks to come."

And time enough to think on this evening of bliss. Alexandra already hugged the memory close.

"Sɪʀ?"

From his secretary's tone, it sounded as though he'd been calling Theo's name for some time.

"Yes, apologies, Taylor."

It was the morning after his visit to the Garden, and he'd spent a restless few hours in his bed, his mind replaying everything that had happened. Every touch, every sigh.

He didn't usually think about his trysts once they were over—there was always another one to look forward to. What was the point, he surmised, of being young, handsome, and wealthy if one wasn't going to indulge one's cravings?

And his partners always benefited.

But for the first time, he wished there was more. He wished he knew more about her than just her name—Alexandra—and that she was a widow. He'd been tempted to follow her, but that felt unseemly, as though he was overstepping. Both of them had made it clear the evening was a unique one, not to be repeated.

But he wanted to repeat it. More than that, even more frightening than that, he wanted to know more about her—what she liked, why she was in

London, if she enjoyed reading the same sorts of books he did.

How she was able to maintain an open, hopeful mien when it was painfully clear that in at least one aspect of her life, she'd been underwhelmed. Not even satisfied at all, he'd guess.

"The Duke of Chelmswich has sent over the papers for your review. He sent a note."

The Duke of Chelmswich. The man who'd been clear on the benefits Theo could expect if he wed the duke's sister: favorable trade terms with the government, expedited agreements, and the patronage of the duke himself.

Yesterday, it had seemed as though it was a good idea. Something to lift Theo even further from his birth, something that his adoptive father would have bragged about to all his friends.

But today? Today that idea seemed unpleasant and beneath him, and besides, his father was dead. The only person left to impress was himself, and he wasn't impressed at all with the Theo of yesterday's decision.

"What does the duke's note say?"

Taylor frowned at his employer. "Are you certain you wish me to read it, sir? It was marked 'private.'"

"Taylor, you have been with me for . . . five years now?" Theo asked. "You know all of my business, and I see no point in hiding anything from you now."

Taylor gave a discreet cough in agreement, then

unfolded the note. "He writes, 'My sister will be making her debut at the Leighs' ball in a week's time. I expect you to attend, as you will be able to meet her there.'" Taylor paused, his eyebrows raised in what Theo might call disdain for a more expressive man. "'Meanwhile, this paperwork details the various scenarios that would benefit our mutual alliance.'"

Taylor raised his head and met Theo's gaze. "That is all, sir."

"Thank you," Theo said. "You may go." He waved his hand, and Taylor nodded, then left the room.

If Theo was less pragmatic, he might think his mysterious lady of the previous evening had appeared just in time to show him the course he was considering was the wrong one.

But Theo was pragmatic, which was why he'd agreed—tacitly, but it seemed the duke took it to be agreed upon in truth—to the arrangement.

It wouldn't be possible for a woman to be as perfect for him as she seemed, would it? Surely it was just him regretting what he was about to do, wishing for a happier future?

But then, her wondrous expression as she sat at the chess table, as she touched his bare chest, as she drank the champagne, told him otherwise.

It would be possible.

It was just that he didn't know who she was, how to find her, and if she'd even consider him if they did meet again.

"YOUR GRACE."

Alexandra drew a deep breath before pasting a faint smile on her face—not too broad, since it wouldn't do to appear overenthusiastic, nor too dour so as to seem unwelcoming. Her stepson William rose from behind his desk as she entered his study, already filled with his belongings as though he'd been there for months.

He had arrived that morning with his wife Florence and Alexandra's daughter, Harriet. There had been a flurry of unpacking, with a variety of frantic servants rushing to and fro while Florence barked out orders from the foyer like a general overseeing her troops.

Alexandra had peeked out from her bedroom at one point, only to retreat quickly when she'd heard Florence insisting the library be repurposed as a secondary sitting room.

"Your Grace," he replied, inclining his head.

The two of them were close in age, with Alexandra only a year or so older than her stepson.

She had tried to forge a relationship with him when she'd married his father, but he was too much like her husband—rigid, correct, and dismissive—and they had endured one another for the duration of her marriage. Very different from how it had been with William's older sister, Edith.

It had been a relief when her husband's death meant she was relegated to the dower house. Florence had immediately changed everything on the estate, and it felt as though Alexandra had never lived there.

Most dowager duchesses would have had some authority in the home they'd lived in for decades. But Alexandra's husband, when he'd been alive, had made his views of his second wife absolutely clear, and as a result, neither Alexandra's stepson nor her stepson's wife had any respect for her. She was more than happy to leave, even though she knew the staff, at least, regretted her departure.

But now they were all under one roof again, this time for the purpose of marrying Harriet off. Her stepson had promised a reasonable dowry for Harriet when she married. Something Alexandra hadn't been certain of, since he and Florence were tight-fisted with their money.

At least they shared a fondness for Alexandra's daughter—Harriet was polite enough for William and Florence to approve of, and she had an open and genuine enthusiasm for many things. It would be hard to dislike her.

Though Alexandra wouldn't put it past Florence to try, if the circumstances were different.

"Thank you for meeting with me before all this begins," William said, waving his hand in the air. "I understand it might be difficult for you to undertake, what with your recent loss."

William seemed to be of the opinion two years wasn't a long enough time to mourn a husband one didn't particularly like, and Alexandra was not going to try to persuade him otherwise.

He probably liked boiled ham and potatoes also.

"I want Harriet to have a lovely debut," she replied. Keeping her tone noncommittal.

"We want her to have a *successful* debut," William said, sounding as though he was correcting her. "And to that end, I have made a list of potential husbands for her." He picked up a piece of paper from his desk. "I do not have to tell you that Harriet's marriage is most important to the family."

"Surely not as important as it is to Harriet," Alexandra said, trying not to sound panicked. She did not want Harriet to have to go through what she had—marriage to someone who didn't love her, someone who wanted her just because of how marriage to her would reflect on him.

"And her husband should provide something the Chelmswich name is in need of." He looked up at Alexandra, his eyes narrowed. "We have more than enough respectability. Enough land. Enough heritage. What we don't have enough of is money."

Alexandra gave him a confused look. "I wasn't aware of that."

William's expression turned uncomfortable. "Yes, well, there have been some unfortunate setbacks recently."

Ah. In William's vernacular, that meant he had made some bad investments, and wanted to sell Harriet off to foot his bill.

"I've already contacted a few gentlemen to discuss an arrangement," he said.

"You mean a marriage." Her chest tightened, and she wanted to scream—*No, no, no, you are not going to make Harriet do what I did.*

"Yes." He spoke as though it was a simple thing, as though trading one's sister—even a half sister—was as easy to do as purchasing a hat, or taking a carriage ride. "The person I believe will suit the best is a Mr. Osborne. He inherited his adopted father's business some years ago, and has increased the holdings substantially, and is still only twenty-eight, eight years older than Harriet, which will give him the wisdom to guide her. He comes from a low background, and will be grateful for the prestige of our name."

"You've already discussed this with Mr. Osborne?" Alexandra couldn't help the furious tone of her voice, which immediately raised William's hackles.

"As the head of the family, I do not have to explain myself, Your Grace, but yes, I have. If this or another equally lucrative marriage does not occur, I would have no choice but to withdraw the funds for Harriet's dowry."

Extortion. He was going to force Harriet into whatever marriage he wished because of his own bad management. Instead of the joyful experience Alexandra hoped for her daughter, the one she herself had never gotten, Harriet would have to be sold off to the highest bidder, as Alexandra had been. Not able to make her own choice, or have the opportunity to fall in love.

But she couldn't say anything to William or he would become even more fixed on the idea.

Nor could she tell her daughter; she'd promised Harriet a wonderful debut, one where she could meet people from Society and perhaps settle on one of them for her husband. She'd urged Harriet to take her time, to find someone she truly liked.

Now she had to stand by that while also ensuring the person Harriet truly liked was also wealthy enough to suit William. If not specifically Mr. Osborne of the wealth and low birth.

But she would not stand by, would she? She would do everything in her power to ensure her daughter didn't have to barter her hand in marriage to soothe William's pocketbook.

She hadn't shredded her widow's weeds just to watch, helpless and passive, as William did to Alexandra's daughter what Alexandra's parents had done to her. She would not. She could not.

"I see," she said, digging her nails into her palms. "And if Harriet and this Mr. Osborne decide they do not suit? And Harriet doesn't find another husband straightaway?"

William gave her a cold look. "Harriet is appealing enough. Let us hope it does not come to that." His mouth compressed into a thin line before he spoke again. "But if it does, it will be your responsibility, as Harriet's mother, to ensure she marries someone of sufficient wealth."

He rose, indicating the conversation was over. Not that it was much of a conversation; it was

William informing her of what would happen, and the consequences if it didn't.

"Thank you," Alexandra replied, rising as well. "I will you see you at dinner."

"Indeed."

She turned and walked out, her pace increasing as she came closer to her bedroom. She would have to find a way out, or hope that Harriet fell madly in love with Mr. Osborne at first sight.

She would not let what happened to her happen to her daughter. No matter what she had to do.

SIX DAYS LATER, and Alexandra hadn't had time to think about anything except what was directly in front of her, which both irritated and relieved her. Because if she had had time to think about things, she might have thought about that night. How bold and fearless she'd felt.

The expression on his face when he'd spent into her. How his skin felt pressed against hers.

What it felt like to come against his tongue.

About the next morning.

William's ultimatum.

Her own future.

Instead, the days were filled with visits to Madame Lucille's for finishing touches to both Harriet's and Alexandra's new wardrobes. Harriet had discarded her black clothing with nearly as much alacrity as her mother, and now it was time to reap the fruits of their labor—meaning the hours they'd each spent up on the dressing podium as seamstresses pinned hems, adjusted waistlines, and added a variety of trim and furbelows.

It was the evening of Harriet's debut. Time to focus on her daughter's future, and then when that was solved, her own. Not as soon as tomorrow, but in a few weeks, if all went well. If Harriet and this Mr. Osborne suited one another.

"How do I look?"

Harriet's tone veered between supreme confidence and extreme trepidation. Similar to her mother's, Alexandra thought wryly.

Alexandra patted her daughter on the arm. "You look lovely," she said, not for the first time. Or for the hundredth.

"Mama, you're certain?"

"I am, dearest. You are perfect."

They were all in Harriet's bedroom, Alexandra seated on her daughter's bed as Harriet posed in front of the mirror, Edith and Harriet's maid, MacLean, hovering nearby. Harriet wore white, as debutantes were supposed to, though Madame Lucille had added a few pink satin roses at the bottom of the gown, which matched Harriet's flushed cheeks. Harriet took after Alexandra in appearance, though her hair was lighter, and her eyes were blue like her father's, not green.

She *did* look perfect, Alexandra thought fondly.

"Is my hair all right? I could ask MacLean to change the style."

Alexandra shook her head as she met the aforementioned MacLean's gaze in the glass.

Harriet's lady's maid was a model of patience, but even she was beginning to sigh as Harriet continued fussing.

"You are perfect," Edith said, sounding impatient. "As your mother said."

Harriet wasn't making her debut at her own ball—neither William nor Florence had wanted the bother of hosting a party, not to mention the expense—so they would all be going to the Viscount Leigh's home. The viscount had a daughter in her second season, so this party would be for both of them.

"Your Grace! Harriet!" William called from below. He sounded impatient. He sounded like his father.

Thirty minutes later, they were inside the Leighs' home.

Harriet was chatting with Lady Cassandra Leigh, both of them giggling and darting glances at the various guests.

The ballroom was spectacular—wide, with polished marble floors and a high ceiling from which hung several chandeliers. The viscount, a widower, had enlisted his sister to act as hostess, and she had outdone herself in decorating the room. Glorious bouquets of flowers studded every table, while an inordinate number of servants circulated among the guests, distributing champagne and bite-sized treats.

A trio of musicians played a delicate accompaniment to the chatter, the music a pleasant underpinning to the party.

Like Harriet, the party was perfect.

Madame Lucille had worked hard on Alexandra's gown as well, a rich purple color with black velvet trim. Black velvet bows adorned her sleeves, while the neckline was lower than she usually wore. Her maid had pulled her hair back into intricate curls, winding a black velvet ribbon through them. Amethyst earrings swung against her neck, and she wore white gloves with amethyst bracelets. She felt beautiful, but more than that, she felt comfortable in what she was wearing.

"Why do we have to go to all this bother if Harriet's future is already decided?" Edith asked in a low tone as William introduced Harriet to a few of his fellow peers—Mr. Osborne, he'd informed them with a hint of displeasure, was occupied with business until later.

Alexandra had told her stepdaughter everything, needing a sympathetic ear if not a solution to the problem.

Edith had railed against William's high-handedness, but there wasn't anything she could do. The two siblings already had a fraught relationship, even more tension-filled than Alexandra and William's, and William would not take kindly to his sister's interference.

In fact, Florence had suggested more than a few times that Edith might want to go back to "that traveling nonsense," as she did whenever her sister-in-law expressed an opinion.

Edith had staunchly refused because she would

not leave Alexandra and Harriet to "those narrow-minded pedants," as she liked to refer to her brother and his wife.

Small wonder they didn't get along, given their respective opinions of one another.

"We have to go through with this not just because I want her to have a choice," Alexandra began.

"Even though William has made it clear she doesn't," Edith interrupted.

"But also because she has been looking forward to this since your father died," she finished. "We spent hours talking about it—who she'd meet, where she'd go, what she'd wear. Just because your brother is—" She hesitated.

"An unmitigated ass," Edith finished.

Alexandra heard the frustration in her step-daughter's tone. One that echoed the fierce angry burn in Alexandra's own chest.

The fact remained that William, as the head of the family, held all the decisions. At least for now. He doled out Alexandra's allowance, paid for her and Harriet's new wardrobe, and funded living in town for these months.

If he withdrew his support, Alexandra and Harriet would be back at the dower house with only Alexandra's meager inheritance from her parents to live on. Harriet wouldn't have a dowry, and without a dowry, she would have much less of a chance to marry. The only suitors she would likely attract would be gentlemen who wanted to exploit the cachet of marrying a duke's daughter, and those were precisely the type of suitors Alexandra wanted Harriet to be able to avoid.

Edith had enough money to live on her own, but just barely, and when given the choice, preferred not to have any home, but to travel instead. She had offered to help if Harriet didn't want to make a match William approved of, but Alexandra wouldn't allow her stepdaughter to curtail her own life. Edith had managed to get out from under her father's—and by extension, William's—thumb, and Alexandra didn't want her to have to go under it again.

No, this was something Alexandra alone would have to solve. There were worse things than not having enough money to purchase whatever one wanted—Alexandra had had that, and she'd been miserable. Well-clothed, but miserable.

She knew Harriet would prefer to make her own choice, even if that choice meant she didn't have a dowry. Not that she could tell her daughter that, at least not until after she met Mr. Osborne. Not until she'd exercised all other options.

"Do you suppose he is handsome?" Harriet asked, having returned.

Alexandra couldn't pretend not to know whom she meant—William had discussed how Mr. Osborne had decided he wanted a wife, at long last, and that the duke had met with him on other business. He hadn't told his sister that he was bartering her in exchange for Mr. Osborne's investment money, but he had told her that Mr. Osborne was eager to meet her. There had been no mention of the other names William claimed to have on his list.

"I do not know," Alexandra replied lightly. It was on the tip of her tongue to remind Harriet that appearance wasn't the only thing that made a person likeable—her late husband had been attractive enough, but he was still the Original Pedant. Grim, judgmental, and rigid, forcing his views on anyone who had less power than he.

Which was everyone.

But only William had met the gentleman thus far, and she didn't want to dissuade her daughter from the match just because her chest tightened and her heart hurt at the unfairness of it all.

"Now, remember," a voice said, piercing Alexandra's musings, "you are Mr. Osborne's superior in everything, but you should not reveal it. That is the mark of good breeding."

Florence, William's wife and the new Duchess of Chelmswich, spoke as if her listeners were far too addled to understand anything themselves.

She was the daughter of a good family that could trace its antecedents to the Crusades—which to Alexandra just meant Florence's ancestors had gone to war to prove a point, a stubborn, contentious point that only men with too much leisure time would think of—but it had been a coup for her to marry William, who would one day be a duke.

She spent more time than the duke himself thinking of their family's importance, which meant she was constantly reminding everyone of what a ducal family should, and should not, do.

Just one of the many reasons she and Edith loathed one another.

"Yes, Your Grace," Harriet replied, not even baring her teeth as Alexandra would if addressed in that condescending way. Though she did shoot a quick glance toward her mother.

Oh. Alexandra actually *was* baring her teeth, she discovered. Baring her teeth for her daughter by proxy, which wasn't helpful, given the sway Florence had over her husband, and the sway her husband had over all the rest of them. Perhaps that was why Harriet was looking at her. Reminding her that William and Florence had control.

How she wished her daughter hadn't learned that lesson already. Though it seemed she had, and Alexandra could only be proud of Harriet for observing the inequity. It would make it far easier should Alexandra have to present Harriet's options to her.

"He should be here soon. He told William that business—" and here Florence's nose seemed to recoil from the stench of commerce "—would delay him, but not for long."

"If you'll excuse me," Alexandra said, feeling suddenly stifled, "I need to speak to—" and she made a vague gesture, not that anyone was paying attention to her.

She walked off, inhaling deeply. The first time since they'd arrived that she had been able to do anything for herself. She didn't have an idea of where to go, just that she didn't want to be with them for a moment longer, or she would scream.

"Good evening," a low voice said, and she started.

It was him.

Chapter Five

Her breath caught. "Oh. Good evening."

She glanced back to where her family stood. None of them was looking at her, thank goodness. Because she could feel her cheeks turning pink.

"I realize we haven't been introduced," he said dryly, "but can I persuade you to step out onto the terrace with me for a moment?"

The terrace. It would be cooler there, and perhaps she could regain her composure. Though she doubted it.

"Please?" he added.

Please. He'd said that that night, when he'd said all he wanted was her pleasure. "Yes," she agreed.

He held his arm out for her, and she took it, enjoying the fact that he was so tall—taller than she, and she was usually taller than most of the men she spoke with. Both her late husband and William seemed to resent her height, since it meant she topped both of them by a few inches.

"I haven't been able to stop—" he began.

"Ssh," she admonished. "Wait until we're outside."

"Of course," he replied.

It shouldn't be so remarkable, a man following her instructions, but it absolutely was. She had little experience in the men in her life actually listening to her, and yet here he was.

Here he was.

Until she saw him just this minute, she hadn't realized how much she'd wanted to see him again. She'd smothered that wish, along with all her other desires, because Harriet's situation demanded it.

But dear Lord, she'd wanted to see him again.

He wore evening clothes, as the other gentlemen here did, but his fit flawlessly, highlighting the impressive physique she knew was underneath.

His hair was tamer than it had been the other evening, and she found herself missing those delicious curls.

They slipped onto the terrace; there weren't very many people there, since the ball had begun just a half hour or so earlier. Later, when the guests were tired of dancing or just wanted a moment to get away from the noise and the cacophony, it would be more popular.

But for now, for all intents and purposes, they were alone. At least in her imagination.

"I haven't been able to stop thinking about you," he said, taking her hands in his.

She looked down at them, at their clasped hands, wishing neither one of them was wearing gloves. She glanced back up, meeting his gaze in the shadowed darkness. And then she withdrew one of her hands and reached up to pull a curl down, back onto his forehead where it belonged.

"There," she said in satisfaction. "I like it better this way."

"Then that is how I shall keep it," he replied, his lips quirking at one corner.

His expression grew serious. "I am grateful to have found you this evening. There is something I am supposed to do, something I have nearly promised, but I don't think I can. Especially now." He took a breath. "I've spent every evening since thinking about you. And now you're here, just at the last minute. If this was a work of fiction, I would think it far too convenient."

"What do you mean?" Alexandra asked, puzzled. "You have to do something but you don't want to because of me?" How was that even possible? It had been just one night, and she had surmised that for him, it had been one night out of many. For her, of course, it was different.

He took a deep breath, looking away from her, into the night, but it was clear he wasn't focusing on anything. "I am supposed to marry a woman who will bring me respectability, and I will bring her money." He returned to looking at her, and the intensity of his gaze made her knees wobble. "It's an age-old barter that I agreed to." He gave a crooked smile. "Until less than a week ago, I would have been fine with the arrangement. But I cannot stop thinking about you, and it would not be fair to enter into a marriage with anybody when all I want is—"

"Stop," she replied, putting her gloved fingers on his mouth. "You can't. I just—I just got my freedom. I can't promise—"

"I know you can't," he said, taking her wrist in his hand as he drew her fingers away from his mouth. "I would not ask that of you. It is a bit early to ask that of anyone." Again that crooked smile. "But I want to see you again. And I won't woo one woman while desiring another. It wouldn't be right."

"Oh," she said in a soft voice. It wouldn't be right. A man of honor, then.

"Will you? Will you meet me at the Garden tonight?" he asked in an urgent tone.

She gazed at him for a moment, then shook her head. Regretting the decision as soon as she'd made it, but knowing it was the only decision that she could make, given Harriet's situation. "I cannot. My obligations start in earnest this evening, and I cannot add something like you into my life."

His eyebrows rose. "Something like me?"

She waved her hand in the air, conscious that even now, the air between them felt like it was sizzling. Vibrant with passion.

But it was only desire. She didn't know anything

about him, except that he was likely younger than she, and quite adept in certain unmentionable skills. That he seemed to care how she felt and thought about things.

It certainly wasn't a basis for any kind of ongoing connection.

"Something like an affair, if you want to put it bluntly," she said.

"Ah," he said, drawing back a step. "I understand." He swept into a low bow. "Thank you for your time. Can I escort you . . . ?"

"You shouldn't," she interrupted. "I don't want anyone to see me with you." She felt her cheeks heat as she realized how insulting that might sound. "That is—"

"I understand," he bit out, then bowed again. "Good night."

"Good night," she replied.

He stepped past her and strode back inside, leaving Alexandra alone.

THEO GROUND HIS teeth together as he returned to the ballroom, grabbing a glass from a passing server and downing it in one swallow. Perhaps it was champagne, or white wine, or flour soup, he had no idea.

He'd never been refused before.

Then again, he'd never asked one of his sexual partners for anything more than the one night. Lucy had become a friend, but other than that, he didn't see any of them beyond nodding when they'd returned to the Garden.

But even though she'd said no, he couldn't go through with what had seemed so reasonable a week ago: marry the Duke of Chelmswich's sister, with the understanding that the duke would use his personal political power to ensure Theo's businesses didn't encounter any unexpected snags. That his ships could come and go through the ports easily, and if there were future opportunities, that Theo would be one of the first to hear of them.

It felt sordid, trading his money for respectability and leverage.

Even though it was something the aristocracy did all the time, which is why he'd contemplated the idea when the duke proposed it. And he had to admit, he'd been flattered, and had thought about what Mr. Osborne would say if he knew his son had married a duke's daughter.

But he couldn't go through with it.

It would be tricky to extricate himself from it, however. He hadn't promised to follow through explicitly, but the arrangement was one they had discussed at length in Theo's offices. And clearly one the duke thought settled.

Settled only an hour before he'd gone to the Garden.

"What are you so glum about?"

Theo jerked his head up to see Simeon Jones

and Bram Townsend, two of the Bastard Five, as he liked to call himself and his group of friends. Bram's wife, Lady Wilhelmina, was in the corner chatting with a few old men, likely members of the astronomical society she belonged to.

Simeon was garbed in his usual eye-catching way, wearing a waistcoat that could only look good on someone as handsome as Simeon was. An artist, Simeon delighted in pushing the envelope of what was respectable behavior, and frequently caused scandalous talk, talk that would ruin a less prepossessing man.

Bram was a solicitor, and had recently married an aristocrat, so he'd had to appear at these types of functions more than he had before. He was hoping to be appointed to a judgeship—a possibility Theo had discussed with the Duke of Chelmswich as part of their negotiations—and was therefore attempting to be friendly to people who might put in a good word for him.

"I'm not glum about anything," Theo replied smoothly, clearing his expression of anything remotely glum.

Simeon and Benedict both shot him skeptical looks.

"Fine. Yes. I'm irked, but nothing worth discussing here."

"Mr. Osborne," he heard a voice say, and he turned to see the Duke of Chelmswich striding toward him.

"Good evening, Your Grace," Theo replied. "May I intro—"

"No time for that," the duke replied, making Theo realize—not for the first time—how terribly rude having a title allowed one to be. If he were to behave the same way, he'd be rightly shunned. But because the duke was a duke, he could get away with it.

And this incredibly rude gentleman was supposed to be his brother-in-law.

Theo regretted even more giving the duke the encouragement he was now taking as confirmation that Theo would go through with marrying the duke's sister. He could not go through with it. Not when he'd thought so much about Alexandra, about that night.

"Excuse me," Theo said to his friends, both of whom were staring at the duke in shock.

But he'd have to figure out how to tell the duke he'd decided against it.

And that, he knew, might end up costing him more than money. Both his personal and professional reputations would be at stake if the duke took his refusal badly. Not to mention the harm done to his potential intended—people would gossip that there was something about Lady Harriet that made him change his mind about the marriage.

He had no idea if the duke had spoken of their conversation, but he had to assume so. Especially if the duke owed money, being able to confide that Mr. Osborne and his vast wealth were soon to join the family would make creditors breathe a little easier.

Dear God, what a mess.

"Where have you been?" Florence exclaimed as Alexandra returned. She'd stayed a few minutes after him on the terrace, hoping the cool night air would do something about her heightened color.

Not that anybody besides Edith would notice— William and Florence were too engrossed in themselves, and Harriet was too excited for her debut, as she should be.

"I've just—"

"Here he is," William said, striding up with another person in tow behind him.

Alexandra exhaled, relieved she wouldn't have to find a polite way to say how little she wished to spend time with either Florence or William, which was why she had disappeared so abruptly.

"Allow me to introduce you, Mr. Osborne, to my sister, Lady Harriet." William didn't wait for the two to exchange words before turning to Florence. The gentleman was still hidden from Alexandra's view, since Florence's feathered headdress obscured the man's face. "This is my wife, the Duchess of Chelmswich," he said, "and this," he continued, inclining his head toward Alexandra, "is the dowager duchess." He spoke in a decidedly less enthusiastic tone when speaking Alexandra's name.

Alexandra held her hand out, waiting for him to turn to her. He bowed over Harriet's hand, then took Florence's for a moment, and Alexandra felt a prickle of something she didn't understand begin to flow through her skin.

It was her turn, and he reached her, taking her gloved fingers in his, bowing low. "Good evening, Your Grace." Then he raised his head, and Alexandra's eyes widened as she saw who it was.

"Ahh," she began, and his gaze flickered, recognition flooding his eyes. She inhaled, trying to keep herself from fainting.

Dowager duchesses of a certain age did not faint. Not even when the man who'd licked her *there*, who'd brought her to pleasure not once but twice, stood in front of her in excellent evening wear, those dark, enticing curls still resting on his forehead.

The dimple decidedly not in evidence.

"The pleasure is mine," he said in a stilted tone of voice, and then she was convinced she actually *would* faint, because last time they'd met, he'd insisted that the pleasure be *hers*. He had found it for her, brought her to it, but now it was gone. He was here, here of all places, here to woo her daughter, and he was the worst possible person for reasons she could never divulge.

THEO WAS ACCUSTOMED to hiding his emotions. He'd been scoffed at and derided for his birth most of his life, and even after Mr. Osborne took him in, he'd been subjected to comments and sidelong glances and the like.

Even now, now when he had more money than most men he met, he'd see the look in their eyes, and do his best to ignore it.

Until it was time to best them at business, or steal a lady they'd been courting, or anything that would prove he was actually better than all of them, despite his birth.

So it wasn't impossible for him to keep his composure when meeting her, even though he was horrified. What was the likelihood that the woman he'd tasted and kissed and touched a week before was the mother of the woman he was supposed to marry?

The woman he did not want to marry in the first place, now that he'd thought about it, and now really could not possibly marry, given the circumstances. This was far worse than anything he'd read in fiction.

She, however, was not as adept as he at hiding her feelings. And he knew, from what he had intuited from her stepson, that her situation was not entirely comfortable.

The duke hadn't come out and said anything of the sort, but he had intimated during their initial meeting that his stepmother had taken advantage of his father, and that was the reason this marriage was needed—to prop up the family's fortunes after she had used her influence on the duke, having him make several bad investments in a row.

"May I ask the dowager duchess for a dance?" he said, addressing his question to her, but also to the duke.

He could already tell the duke was filled with his own consequence, what with being a duke and all, so this invitation might make the duke think that Theo was endeavoring to curry favor with Lady Harriet's mother to get her acceptance for the suit.

Rather than speak to her without fear of eavesdroppers.

"I am—" she began hesitantly, a bright flush coloring her otherwise pale face.

"You would be delighted," the duke interrupted. "Just the sort of proper behavior one expects from a gentleman," he said, his tone holding a hint of surprise.

That Theo wasn't crawling about on the floor snatching crumbs from untidy eaters? That he wasn't stamped with some sort of marking indicating his illegitimacy?

Good thing he wasn't allowing himself to show his true emotions, he thought wryly.

And it was fairly rich that the gentleman who'd rudely pulled him away from his friends was now complimenting him on his behavior.

"Ah, yes," she said, swallowing.

"And then you may dance with Lady Harriet," the duke announced.

Theo held his hand out to her, and she took it,

allowing him to place her into the correct dancing position.

She was as lovely as he'd recalled. And he'd recalled many times since that evening, usually when he was alone at night in his bed with his cock in his fist.

Though he thought about her during the day as well—far more troubling to his state of mind.

Her eyes were a vibrant, verdant green. On their night together, he hadn't taken note of their unusual color, he'd been so transfixed by . . . other things.

Which were lushly displayed in a sumptuous purple gown, black trim a subtle reminder of her widowed status.

And then he remembered what Lucy had said. "Did Madame Lucille create this?" he asked.

She blinked. "I did not think the first thing we would speak about was my gown," she said in a determinedly pleasant tone, "but yes." She lifted her chin. "My late husband attempted to thwart Madame Lucille's business, so I thought it would only be right to patronize her shop."

Theo felt himself grimace. "Did you expect me to begin our conversation with an acknowledgment of what we are to one another?"

"What we are to one another is nothing," she said, low and urgent. "We have to forget any of it happened."

He tightened his grip on her waist in an unconscious response. "I can't forget," he replied simply. "I said it before, and now it is even more true."

He was so angry he could barely speak. Not at her, of course; but at the injustice of all of it. The mean-spirited humor of the gods, or whatever fates were playing around with his life, to create this situation.

Her lips thinned, and she glanced away. "I wish you would." She returned to meet his gaze. "I won't say it was a mistake, but I will say that it . . . complicates things."

He gave a dry chuckle. "You could say that."

"I could say a lot of things," she shot back, and then he couldn't decide if he wanted to applaud her or kiss her senseless.

Probably both.

Which wasn't helping the current situation at all.

"Meet me at the Garden of Hedon tonight, after the ball," he urged. "We can discuss what is to be done about all of this."

"Besides me taking up residence in an isolated castle and threatening any visitors who try to visit?" She shook her head. "No, that wouldn't work. I would have to see Harriet at some point. Oh!" she said, her voice brightening to a sharp tone. "What if I announce I will see no gentlemen for the rest of my life, and then I would never have to see *you*."

"You say that as if that's a good thing," he said through a clenched jaw.

"Well, isn't it?" She lifted her fingers from his

shoulder and waved them vaguely. "You're going to marry my daughter, and I will have to bear it, and we can never tell anyone, and—"

"Meet me at the Garden," he interrupted. "We can discuss it calmly, like adults, rather than coming up with harebrained schemes."

Her eyes narrowed. "I *am* an adult, Mr. Osborne. In case you haven't noticed, I am twelve years older than you, as well as being the mother of the woman you intend to marry."

I intend no such thing.

But he couldn't continue to argue with her. He could see the duke and Lady Harriet both watching them with avid curiosity, and he hoped they wouldn't ask just what they were talking about. If things got any more heated between them, it would be obvious, and the problem between them would expand to include everyone involved.

And he could not allow that to happen. Not for himself—he didn't care, and he had enough money to withstand any scandal—but for her. He knew what a damaged reputation could do to a woman, even a dowager duchess.

There was a reason she'd come to the Garden anonymously, and he was determined to protect that.

He just hoped she'd meet him later. To ensure she was properly protected, of course. Not because he wanted to see her again.

Even though he did.

"THANK YOU, MR. Osborne," Alexandra said as he returned her to where William, Florence, and Harriet were standing. Edith had wisely taken herself off somewhere, likely to avoid her family.

Not for the first time, she wondered what Edith and William's mother had been like—neither of them spoke about her much, and the late duke never had. Alexandra suspected that she had been like Edith, perhaps even more unhappy in her marriage than Alexandra had been. Whenever she'd tried to ask Edith anything, her stepdaughter had changed the subject.

Alexandra wished she could run to where Edith was currently hiding, but she would not desert her daughter, no matter what.

And this was definitely a *what*. As in, What had she been thinking? What was he going to do? What was Harriet thinking about all of this? And more than a few *why*'s as well. Why did it have to be him, of all people? Why did her traitorous heart have to leap when she saw him? Why couldn't she just forget all of it, behave as though it was nothing, a mere moment in the course of her life?

Like a man would, she thought. Her late husband had kept a few mistresses during the course of their marriage, and he had seemed to manage going from their beds to hers without any twinge of conscience.

Though Mr. Osborne had looked nearly as

emotional as she had, even if he had tried to disguise it behind his calm mien. So perhaps it *did* mean something to him, more than just one night of pleasure.

Which might make it even worse, though she didn't think it could be any worse.

Holy hell, what was she going to do?

Worse yet, what was *he* going to do?

"Your Grace?" William said, sounding impatient. Likely not the first time he'd tried to get her attention, then.

"Pardon?" she replied, pasting a smile on her face.

"Mr. Osborne has asked Harriet to dance."

"Ah," she replied. She didn't know why William was fussing, since he'd already declared the two would dance.

"It is a waltz," he continued, "and Harriet wished to make certain that was acceptable with you." He sounded annoyed, likely because Alexandra appeared to have a tiny bit of control.

"Oh. Yes, of course," she replied, meeting her daughter's gaze.

Harriet looked dazed, likely from looking at the beauty of Mr. Osborne.

"May I?" he said, holding his arm out to Harriet.

She colored, and took it, and he led her onto the dance floor, Alexandra watching as they stepped into the pattern for the waltz.

"They already make a lovely couple," Florence simpered.

"They do. And he could do no better than Harriet,

that is certain. It is a great honor we are bestowing on him," the duke said in a pompous voice.

A great honor that you will make him pay richly for, Alexandra thought. If he even agreed to it—and if he did, what then?

How horrific would it be to keep that secret the rest of her life? To gaze at him knowing what he looked like naked, that he'd put his mouth on her and listened as she'd told him bits and pieces of her life. As he'd ensured her pleasure.

But if Harriet ended up falling in love with him—Alexandra would just have to figure out how she would tolerate it all. She would not break her daughter's heart because her mother spent one impetuous night with a stranger.

"We'll have to invite everybody to the wedding," Florence continued. "Which will mean a lot of expense."

"He can well afford it," William said in a curt tone. As though he was resentful Mr. Osborne had succeeded financially where he had failed. As though William hadn't squandered what he'd been given.

"Is there any thought of what might happen if they don't suit?" Alexandra asked, even though she'd asked William before, and he'd been dismissive. Her voice sounded strained, and she hoped that William's and Florence's usual self-absorption would keep them from noticing the difference.

"That won't happen," William said confidently.

"Harriet needs to marry a gentleman who can afford her," William replied.

You mean afford you. How had he mismanaged everything so badly? Within just two years? The ducal estate was rich in land, and Alexandra's late husband had always relied on his land stewards to balance the accounts and improve the holdings.

She recalled that William had blustered about having to sack some people right after his father died. She hadn't paid much attention because he had made it absolutely clear that her knowledge of what his father had done was not wanted. And Florence had been occupied in moving Alexandra as quickly as she could to the dower house, so Alexandra herself had been busy packing. Gleefully, if she had to admit it; it was a relief not to have to manage the household.

How bad was it? How much financial damage had William done already?

If her stepson wasn't able to sell his half sister in his devil's bargain, that would mean Alexandra's own livelihood was in jeopardy. He wouldn't extend any kind of grace to his stepmother, not if her daughter didn't do as he required.

"Harriet is fortunate that Mr. Osborne is so good-looking," Florence said, sounding envious.

Alexandra darted a quick glance at William, whose expression had tightened.

"It is a shame about his birth, of course," Florence continued. She sounded genuinely mournful.

"What about his birth?" Alexandra asked. William had mentioned his "low background," but hadn't offered specifics.

"He's—well, his parents were not married," Florence said in a whisper. As if it was a secret only she knew. "He grew up in an orphanage. The man he called his father, Mr. Osborne, wasn't his father at all."

"That's enough," William said. Florence paled, no doubt because of his harsh tone.

Alexandra rarely felt sympathy for her step-daughter-in-law—the woman was too narrow-minded and judgmental, just like her husband—but she did flinch at how derisive William could sound.

He usually sent his wrath anywhere but his immediate family, but even they tried his sorely tested patience at times.

"And there are no other possibilities for Harriet's hand?" Alexandra asked, trying to keep her tone light. As if it was a meaningless question she asked out of idle curiosity, and not something that would determine her future actions.

"Nobody nearly as rich," William replied, keeping his voice low. "A person with his antecedents will pay handsomely for the privilege of being associated with our name. People with good breeding would be far more reluctant to enter into that kind of agreement. I would prefer to have the matter settled as soon as possible."

Alexandra absorbed that as her eyes sought them out. They were easy to find; he was one of the tallest men on the dance floor, and Harriet's golden hair caught the light, making it seem as if it was lit from the inside.

They moved together fluidly, and Alexandra felt her chest tighten as she watched. What if they did suit? What would she do then? If he wanted to go through with it, and Harriet agreed?

From the expression on Harriet's face, it looked as though she was half in love with him already.

Though she had met so few gentlemen, it wasn't surprising she would be so taken by one of the handsomest men she had met. And her expression could be because she was finally here, in London, after waiting impatiently for the mourning period to be over.

Perhaps the same could be said of Alexandra? That she'd been waiting so long for something joyful, something just for her, that it felt more meaningful?

If she went and did the same sorts of things she'd done with him with somebody else, would it render that night less important in her mind?

The thought was both appealing and repellent.

But there was another reason to return to the Garden of Hedon tonight—to see how she felt when she was back there, where she'd experienced the most pleasure she'd ever felt in her entire life.

Perhaps she would feel nothing. Perhaps it was just that one night, an anomaly in an otherwise circumspect life.

Maybe more terrifying, perhaps she was a hedonist all along, and hadn't realized it.

Most terrifying of all was that she was somewhere in the middle, intrigued and seduced by a particular man. A man who was on course to marry her daughter.

She'd know in a few hours.

"He's very handsome," Harriet began when she'd returned from her dance.

Alexandra couldn't pretend not to know who Harriet was speaking of.

"He is," she said, in as neutral a tone as she could manage.

"Although he—" Harriet said, then hesitated.

"He what, dearest?" Alexandra replied. She glanced around to see that William and his wife were in conversation. "We won't be overheard."

"He is so solemn," Harriet said. "I know he is only eight years older than I, but he behaves as though he is *your* age." Her tone made it seem as though Alexandra was withered, with one foot in the grave already.

Alexandra tried not to laugh at how horrified her daughter sounded. "He is likely quite cognizant that most people here might look down on him for his birth," she said in response. Even though she absolutely should not be encouraging Harriet to give him a second chance, but her spirit of fairness didn't let her stay quiet. "He likely overcompensates by maintaining a serious mien."

"That's it," Harriet said in a triumphant tone. "He's the type of person who'd use the word *mien*, like you do. I don't know if I can tolerate someone who is engrossed with business and elegant language and behaving properly all the time." She got a faraway look in her eyes. "We've spent so long in the country just sitting. I want to *do* things, and have *fun*."

Mr. Osborne definitely knows how to have fun, Alexandra thought, before she could stop herself.

But she did not want Harriet to experience his version of fun.

Her daughter was right; from what she knew and had experienced of Mr. Osborne, he had sophisticated tastes and was focused on his business interests. William had made that clear. He wouldn't be interested in guiding a girl just out of mourning around town, having ices, going to the circus, and observing various acts of entertainment.

He was the type who would want to be the entertainment, to want to entertain himself. As he had with her at the Garden.

"Whom else have you met?" Alexandra asked.

Harriet shrugged. "So many gentlemen, most of them quite pleasant. But no matter what William says, I want to take my time before deciding on anything." Her chin lifted stubbornly. "I don't see the point of hauling us up here and spending all this money on gowns when all that is going to happen is that I get married in a few months. I want to have fun first."

That's my girl, Alexandra thought proudly. Aloud, she said, "I am certain your brother will be amenable to you making whatever choice you wish, dearest," even though she was not certain of that at all. "We can speak with Florence, and she will ensure he listens to reason." Which was more possible, since Florence was easily swayed, and she and William collaborated on most decisions. Anything she could do to forestall the perhaps inevitable moment when she would stand up for her daughter as no one had ever stood up for her.

"Thank you, Mama," Harriet said.

Chapter Six

Theo stood just inside the gates, in the shadows, waiting.

He'd been here for at least an hour, pacing under the large tree just to the left of the entrance.

One of the guards had attempted to engage him in conversation, but had quickly realized that was fruitless, as Theo replied in monosyllables, if at all.

She had to come. Didn't she?

It was a confounded mess, he had to admit.

When the Duke of Chelmswich had approached him, he'd thought the match a good idea—if the lady was pleasant, and intelligent, and attracted him. The duke's half sister, Lady Harriet, was all of those things, but he couldn't even imagine her as his wife.

In fact, even though the thought terrified him, the only woman he could see as his wife was *her*. His Angel.

And he knew he was the last person she would

want to marry—that anyone would *allow* her to marry.

If she didn't appear tonight, he'd have to find some way to get to her. To let her know he had no intention of marrying her daughter.

Would she find it reassuring? Disappointing? Would she understand why it would be abhorrent for him to marry her daughter?

Did she feel the same way he did about their night?

A carriage drew up just as he was pondering that, wondering if it was just something she'd done that she had no intention of doing again. If it scratched an itch that no longer needed tending.

Or worse, something she enjoyed while she was doing it, but then went home with regrets, regrets that grew until they overwhelmed her.

Theo never indulged in regrets—he'd done a few things he wished he hadn't, but he didn't deny their importance in his life, nor wish he hadn't done them.

He learned from each and every one of his experiences.

For example, he'd learned how she sounded when she came—her gasps, her sighs, her quickened breaths.

He'd learned what she tasted like.

The softness of her body, and how she kissed.

That he couldn't stop thinking about her.

"Mr. Osborne."

He jerked himself out of his thoughts, his heart beating faster when he saw her.

"You came," he said, stupidly, since she was standing here. She knew that already.

"I did."

She wore a dark cloak over her evening gown, glints of the luxurious purple fabric peeking out from the dark folds. The hood was pulled over her hair, and her face was partly in shadow.

The moonlight caught the sparkle of the jewels hanging from her ears, and the pale skin that gleamed despite her attempts to disguise herself.

"We need to speak somewhere privately," she said in a low tone, while he stood there, drinking her in.

"Of course," he said, annoyed at himself for being so transfixed.

Theo Osborne was never transfixed.

He was suave, capable, and adept at any situation he found himself in.

He was not flummoxed or struck dumb.

And yet he'd been both in the past minute.

He took her arm, folding it through his, and began to lead her on the path to one of the quiet rooms reserved for more salacious activity than conversation.

"Not—not there, please," she said.

"Not where?"

"Where we were—before," she replied, her voice low and firm. "I don't want to go back there."

"I am taking you somewhere else," he said. He

had considered taking her there to see what might happen a second time. Tempt her with the memory of what they'd done, and how it had felt. But he couldn't be that underhanded.

He'd gotten over the initial shock of seeing who she was. His mind had leapt into planning—figuring out what he could do to extricate all of them from this situation.

It wasn't just the two of them who would be affected. Lady Harriet would suffer unless Theo managed to navigate his refusal to marry her properly.

But for now, he just had to talk to her. The dowager Duchess of Chelmswich.

Alexandra.

Angel.

He took her to another part of the Garden, the one normally used just by the staff. He had an office in one of the buildings, a room that was primarily for him to meet with vendors and clients who required the utmost confidentiality.

"Mr. Os— Sir, we hadn't expected to see you tonight," one of the Garden's managers said, looking surprised. She stood in front of one of the three buildings comprising the managerial and staff area.

Mr. Osborne tucked the dowager duchess closer into his side, then addressed the manager. "Please make certain we are not disturbed, Miss Howatch."

She nodded to indicate her understanding,

moving swiftly away from where he now took the dowager duchess.

He opened the door of the building containing his office, stepping aside to let her walk in first.

He followed, quickly lighting the lamps that hung on either side of the entrance.

"We won't be disturbed," he said.

"I was there when you issued that order," she replied, her tone amused.

At least she was capable of finding humor in something. Perhaps things weren't as dire as he'd imagined.

He unlocked the door to his office, then busied himself with lighting lamps and candles in here.

It was a cozy, comfortable space, more fitted for a meeting room than a place for actual work.

The majority of his work was done in his other office, the one in the Osborne and Son building in a different neighborhood.

Here, he met with diplomats, politicians, entertainers, and other high-profile men and women who wished to indulge their desires at the Garden without the concern for their reputation.

And with a dowager duchess who was curious and passionate, uncertain of what she wanted, but willing to explore to discover it.

"Please sit," he said, indicating one of the chairs.

Like everything Theo surrounded himself with, the chair was well-made and comfortable, expensive without being opulent, cushioned in a dark green fabric and heavy oak.

She sat, folding the hood of her cloak back.

Her hair gleamed in the lamplight. She sat straight-backed, as he presumed any duchess worth her ducal salt would, entirely proper and correct, a neutral expression on her face.

Her eyes, however, were wide and wary.

He wanted to assure her he wouldn't hurt her, that he'd do whatever it was she wanted—only he couldn't promise that, could he?

Because if she wanted him to marry her daughter, he'd have to refuse. Because he would not marry one woman when desiring another. That wouldn't be honorable, and he might be a bastard, but he always did the honorable thing.

He took the chair opposite, folding his hands in his lap.

"Well?" he said, bracing himself for whatever it was she wished to say. "We have an interesting conundrum, don't we?"

ALEXANDRA COULDN'T HELP the sharp burst of laughter that emerged from her at his words. "You could say that," she said, when she'd settled herself. "We have an impossible situation," she said, correcting him.

He sat across from her, his hands lying in his lap, his expression, she imagined, deliberately bland. Or perhaps not—perhaps his downplaying what had happened, what *might* happen, was because he was frequently strung up by things he had done here.

What other women had he played with that he then encountered in society? Yes, he had wanted to continue the liaison, but perhaps he asked that of all of his playmates.

The thought was lowering. Because she could imagine the number of women that might encompass was an awful lot, given his expertise in the whole "interesting conundrum."

He folded his arms over his chest. "I want to tell you, I have no intention of marrying Lady Harriet."

She digested his words, her thoughts racing frantically in her head.

"Why not?" she asked eventually.

His eyes widened, and he spread his hands out in an explanatory gesture. "I already told you before. Because of what happened between us, naturally."

"Even though William—the duke, my stepson— insists you will marry her? How will you wriggle out of that?" she challenged.

"Do you *want* me to marry your daughter?" he asked. His voice had a sharp edge to it.

"God, no," she said in a vehement tone. "But I don't know how you will get out of it."

He arched a brow, and gave her a knowing look. "I am very good at navigating personal relationships," he said, and she felt herself heat from the inside out.

"You don't know William," she replied when she'd settled herself. Her voice was bitter. "He wields power, and he likes to wield it."

"Has he threatened you?" Mr. Osborne asked, and from the way his body shifted, it looked as though he was on the verge of leaping up and doing something if the answer was in the affirmative.

It wasn't his business, and she felt uncomfortable trusting him with any information he didn't already know—information like William's saying he would sell Harriet to the highest bidder, or that Alexandra's own livelihood would be in jeopardy. Moreover, she didn't like his immediate leap to her defense, as though she wasn't capable of taking care of herself.

Not that she was necessarily entirely capable, to be honest. But she hadn't explored all the ways she could figure this out without asking for help from the man she—she fucked one evening. And she would figure it out, no matter what she had to do.

"What happened between us," she said instead, "is an unfortunate incident."

"An unfortunate incident," he echoed, and his tone was menacing—not toward her, but toward her choice of words.

Rather like how his choice of saying *interesting conundrum* had affected her.

"And I appreciate that you say you won't marry my daughter, given everything, but I also know how things work in Society. Word gets out that a certain lady is supposed to become betrothed, and if she doesn't, Society wonders what is wrong with her."

"There is nothing wrong with your daughter. I am not saying that." He scraped his hand through his hair in obvious frustration.

"Thank you," Alexandra said tightly. "I am well aware of that."

"I didn't mean—" he began, then leapt up out of his chair and began to pace. "The point is," he said, walking swiftly around the room, his hands still raking through his hair, "that I am normally adept at navigating things to my advantage."

"And?" Alexandra asked, confused.

"And I can't stop thinking about you." He shook his head. "You're in my thoughts, and no matter how much I remind myself I need to focus on other things, I cannot."

He stopped in front of her chair and dropped to his knees in front of her. "And I have not been the same since that night."

She stared at him, stunned. This was far more than what he had said earlier on the terrace.

He gave a snort of laughter at her expression. "Yes, well, it surprised me nearly as much." She didn't think that was a compliment.

"What are you saying?"

He shook his head, clearly frustrated. "I have no idea. All I can say now is that I have no intention of marrying your daughter, but I understand the potential for problems, if your son—"

"Stepson," Alexandra interrupted.

"Stepson is set on this match."

"So what do we do in the meantime?" she asked.

He shrugged. It was not the response she wanted. The best thing for her peace of mind—and Harriet's future—would be for him to suddenly recall urgent business in Tanzania, and take himself there immediately, not to return until Harriet had chosen a groom.

But that wouldn't be fair to him, asking him to do anything of the sort. And it would mean that William would become more desperate, and perhaps find someone who was even worse of a suitor than Mr. Osborne, whose only bad attribute was that he had pleasured his potential bride's mother a day before meeting said potential bride. Other than that, he was ideal. Definitely the best option for—for anyone.

Focus, Alexandra.

"In the meantime," he said, still kneeling at her feet, "what does your daughter think of all this? Of me?"

She chuckled. "Well, she said you behaved much older than you are. Apparently you don't seem as though you would be fun."

His eyebrows rose. "Not fun, hmm? Once she gets to—"

Alexandra held up a hand. "Please don't finish that sentence, whatever you do."

He flushed, and he looked almost—almost—abashed. "I certainly didn't mean it that way. My apologies."

"Apology accepted," Alexandra replied, wishing

she wasn't feeling so many emotions—anger, resentment, protectiveness, and yes, passion.

Because seeing him again made her want to do everything they'd done the other evening, only more so.

Before, it had been an exhilarating adventure; now it was just dangerous.

She rose, and he leapt to his feet as well.

"I should be going home." She glanced at the clock that sat on the table next to his chair. "It is nearly four o'clock."

"Let me see you home," he urged, and she warmed at his protective tone, while also feeling angered by it.

Too many conflicting emotions, to be sure.

"I will be fine. I told the coachman to wait for me outside. He is to be trusted, and he will ensure my safety."

He nodded, his lips pressed together as though he wished to argue, but decided—wisely, she would say—against it.

"I will see you soon, Your Grace," he said.

She grimaced. "Yes, likely you will. Goodbye, Mr. Osborne."

And she strode out, trying not to look back, trying not to imagine what could happen if she stayed just a bit longer.

Wishing the situation—the interesting conundrum—wasn't so quite interesting.

Chapter Seven

*Y*our mind is elsewhere, Theo," Simeon said, flicking Theo on the back of the head.

It was the evening of the monthly book club, and Theo, Simeon, Benedict Quintrell, Bram, and Fenton—just Fenton, though his last name was Ash—were in the Orphans' Club in their private room.

The five had met when very young, all orphans, all eventually sent to live with people who wanted children but didn't have their own.

They had maintained their close connection since, and Theo was grateful to have the other four as his family, especially since Mr. Osborne had died.

"I didn't read the book," Theo replied shortly. He hadn't even *bought* the book.

The room was comfortably appointed, with plush sofas, a few chairs, and a pleasant fire crackling in the grate. Food was laid out on a side table, mostly cheese and bread.

Bram, who'd just gotten married, the first one of their group to do so, arched a dark eyebrow. "Working too much?" he asked. He tsked. "It's not like you to miss a deadline," he remarked.

Simeon snorted as he stepped to the table and plucked an apple from a bowl. "Likely Theo's been *playing* too much at his club." He bit into the apple, keeping his gaze on Theo's face.

They all knew about the Garden of Hedon, though only Simeon had ever gone there, his appetites even more voracious than Theo's.

"As a matter of fact," Theo said in a haughty voice, "I haven't been there since—" and then he stopped, because for some reason, he didn't want to tell them about her. About the night itself, and its potentially devastating consequences.

"Since . . . ?" Benedict prompted.

Benedict was the most meticulous one among them, working in government doing some sort of mysterious thing, or things, that none of them understood and that he didn't bother to explain.

"I imagine it's a woman," Fenton said, making everyone turn to stare at him.

Fenton was their resident genius, having parlayed his considerable maths knowledge and keen insight into market gains, and his overall worth was close to Theo's now.

It was just a matter of chance the Duke of Chelmswich hadn't approached Fenton to marry Lady Harriet. As a consequence, none of this would be happening.

Then again, Fenton would likely wander off in the middle of the proposal, so his marriage to the duke's sister wouldn't be happening in any case.

"Is it?" Simeon asked, now working his way around the apple's core.

Theo shrugged. "Perhaps." He rose and poured himself a drink from the sideboard. Something dark, smelling strongly of alcohol. It didn't matter what it was, to be honest. He didn't usually drink, unless it was champagne, but if he gave up going to the Garden—and he hadn't any desire to go, not since having her there—he would need to replace his sin with something else.

Drinking seemed like a good idea.

He took a sip, then scowled at the glass, his nose wrinkling. Resisting the urge to cough.

Never mind. Bad idea.

"Oh dear," Simeon said in a knowing tone of voice, the kind that made Theo want to box his nose or make him wear ill-fitting clothing—either would hurt Simeon just as much. "Theo is drinking. It must be a woman. A very special woman."

Theo snorted. "*All* of your women are very special. Which begs the question, if they are all special, doesn't that make them all the same?"

Simeon shook his head slowly. "Don't try to wriggle out of this by changing the subject."

"And Theo is right," Fenton said. "If everyone is special, then no one is special. The Theo Paradox."

Theo made an elegant bow. "I've always told you I was brilliant. Fenton just confirmed it."

"Who is she?" Simeon persisted.

"I can't tell you," Theo said flatly.

"You mean to say you could, but you won't," Fenton said, ever the pedant.

"Correct. I won't."

Simeon clapped Theo on the back. "Excellent news. Perhaps you are finally going to settle down."

Theo looked at his friend with suspicion. "You're only saying that because it would mean that there would be less competition."

Of the five of them—four, now that Bram was ridiculously head over heels in love with his new bride—Theo and Simeon were the most rakish, with each topping the other in their respective scandalous conduct.

Simeon sniffed. "As if you are an equal opponent to me."

"Can you two stop brangling for a moment?" Benedict sounded exasperated, which was a common occurrence for him—he was the de facto oldest brother of the group, the one who was able to talk reason to all of them, and was the first to point out their less than admirable attributes.

If he wasn't so intelligent, honorable, and loyal, he would be damned irritating.

"It's clear, from how he's behaving, that Theo is in some sort of trouble. As his friends, it is up to us to help solve it."

"Since he won't be able to do it himself," Fenton observed, in such a mild tone Theo couldn't take offense.

Theo sighed, knowing he'd have to tell them, his closest friends, his family, the trouble he was in. Though he wouldn't tell them he hadn't wanted to go to the Garden since, and that his nights had been haunted by images of her in that small room, lit only by flickering candlelight.

How her gasps had become moans, and how she'd come against his tongue.

"The thing is," he began, and told them the situation, omitting specific names, though it wouldn't be difficult to figure out.

It was good to tell them, he thought afterward. Even if the solutions they offered ranged from ineffective to ridiculous.

It wasn't as though he could keep away from Lady Harriet forever, for example; the duke would want to know why Theo had changed his mind, and what that meant for their future business dealings.

And it also wasn't as though he could do what Fenton suggested and pursue the dowager duchess. For Fenton, the best solution was the simplest, but it didn't take anyone's personal feelings into account.

And he wouldn't allow himself to be found in a scandalous situation, one that would ensure the duke rescinded his offer. It wasn't worth bartering his own future happiness to salvage this particular moment in his life. Because while an aristocrat might bluster his way through any sort of awkwardness, a bastard with uncertain parentage would never be allowed to. And what if he wanted to marry at some point in the future?

But for now, he'd avoid Lady Harriet and her mother. At least temporarily. Even though he ached for the latter.

It was for the best.

"Your Grace?"

Mrs. Davis, the housekeeper, stood at Alexandra's door, an anxious expression on her face.

Not unusual, since most of the staff had worn anxious expressions since William and Florence had arrived. Nothing was done the way they wanted it, and Alexandra had lost count of the times she'd heard Florence complain about the staff. Whether it was that her gowns weren't ironed quickly enough, or the duck was room temperature, or the fire in her bedroom wasn't blazing when she awoke, there was always something for the current Duchess of Chelmswich to gripe about.

Alexandra tried to overcompensate by asking for very little from any of them, but since she'd been raised not knowing how to do anything, that proved difficult as well.

Perhaps instead of going to the Garden of Hedon, she mused, she should have taken herself for a night of debauchery where she'd learn how to clean shoes, or polish silver, or fold her own linen. Something practical, not the bliss she'd experienced—and had been missing ever since.

"Yes, Mrs. Davis?" she replied.

"The duke wants to see you in his office straight-away," the housekeeper replied. Her hands twisted in her apron.

"Of course."

Alexandra took a moment to glance at herself in the mirror, then bustled downstairs, wondering what William could possibly have to say to her.

For the most part, the two factions—she and Edith on one side, William and Florence on the other—managed to keep themselves separated. Harriet moved between the two easily, but that was likely because neither William nor Florence realized Harriet had her own opinions about things.

They'd been in town for two weeks already, Harriet had garnered a wide array of potential suitors, and Alexandra had been relieved to observe that Mr. Osborne was not currently one of them. He had not appeared at many of the events since the night of Harriet's debut, and when he had, he hadn't danced with anyone, and had left shortly thereafter.

She wished that that reality didn't also mean she missed him. But she did, even though she knew that was ridiculous—to miss someone you'd had one night with, and now shared a very awkward situation with. She couldn't lie to herself, however, and she wished she could spend time with him, even if the time wasn't intimate.

But meanwhile, she was at the threshold to

William's study, and she needed to enter and see what new complaint he would lodge.

"Come in," he said, as she tapped on the door.

He rose, gesturing for her to sit. An almost genial expression on his face.

What did he want? He had to want something, if he was being pleasant.

She settled herself in the chair he'd indicated, and he took the seat opposite.

The room was filled with intimidatingly large furniture made of dark wood. It was deliberately designed to diminish the confidence of anyone who entered who wasn't William. Or her late husband, who'd occupied the room prior to his death.

She loathed this room. Usually, she felt helpless when she entered—knowing something was going to be told to her, and she'd be forced to do it.

But ever since that night—when she'd discovered some of her own wants, needs, and yes, desires, she'd felt more like she was in control of her own destiny. Now that her husband was gone, she had only to ensure Harriet was taken care of, and then she could do what she wanted.

Except that what she most wanted would be forever forbidden.

Enough of that, Alexandra, she reminded herself.

"Thank you, Alexandra, for coming to see me."

You sent the housekeeper to fetch me. I could not refuse.

"Of course," she replied.

William crossed his legs and placed his folded

hands atop one knee. "It seems we have a bit of a problem."

Her eyebrows rose. "We do?"

He nodded. "Yes. Mr. Osborne is not paying the proper attentions to Harriet. I've tried to arrange an appointment with him, to discuss the matter, but he has been too busy—he claims—to meet with me."

She felt her pulse fluttering. He had said he would not marry Harriet, and he was sticking to his word.

"Since he will not meet with me, I want you to speak with him. To discuss his intentions regarding Harriet, and remind him that the House of Lords can—and will—examine his business interests."

"Is he engaging in anything nefarious?" she asked.

He shrugged. "Does it matter? If I ask for an investigation it will be done." William smiled, though it was a smile with no warmth. "I do not presume it will come to that, but I wanted to let you know, in case he proves reluctant." He leaned forward to meet her gaze. "He and I spoke about it prior to Harriet's debut, and I believed it to be settled, but perhaps he does not. But it needs to be, for many reasons."

"Surely we need not depend on Mr. Osborne for Harriet's hand?" Alexandra asked. Her stomach felt as though it had knotted up. "There are other gentlemen who have been calling, and bringing flowers, and asking her to dance."

William shrugged. "None of them have the funds Mr. Osborne does. He also owns businesses that could directly benefit the estate, and I wish to leverage those to my—that is, the estate's—advantage." He folded his arms over his chest in a decidedly militant posture. "Florence has made inquiries—discreet inquiries, of course—and confirmed that Harriet's other suitors are either not serious about courting her, or are hoping she will bring a substantial dowry." His mouth thinned. "Mr. Osborne is unlikely to ask for a dowry, and if he does, we will just—" and he made a vague gesture in the air.

You will give him money you will then manage to get back as soon as the two are wed.

She'd always known he was unpleasant—his treatment of her while his father was alive was just barely polite—but she hadn't known the depths of his duplicity.

He would be a grotesque caricature of evil even if he was a fictional character in a melodrama.

Unfortunately, this was all too real, and it would affect her and her daughter's lives.

"I will speak with him," she said, knowing she had no other choice.

"Yes, you will," William replied smugly.

Chapter Eight

"Mr. Osborne?"

Theo turned at the sound of her voice, wishing his heart didn't want to leap out of his chest. He'd come to the ball that evening to try to clear his head, since nothing else had worked. He needed to do something to get over this intense feeling of want, to put it all in the past. As he had with so many of his prior sexual encounters.

It had been two weeks since they'd last spoken, and it felt like so much more time than that. He hadn't returned to the Garden, he had tried to immerse himself in work, and still he found himself thinking about her at odd moments—wondering if she had gone back there, with a fierce burn at the thought, then thinking whether she would prefer the newest champagne brought in on one of his ships. Hoping she was able to find some fun, even in the midst of her daughter's Season.

"Your Grace," he said stiffly, sweeping into a low bow.

Over her shoulder he saw the duke watching them avidly, while the duke's wife was trying to disguise her curiosity.

Lady Harriet, he noted, was on the dance floor with some young lord or another.

Her cheeks were flushed, and she looked happy. That was some comfort, at least.

"May I speak with you?" Alexandra said in a low tone. "Privately?"

His thoughts immediately went *there*, and he felt his whole body react, only to realize moments later that that was most certainly not what she meant.

"Yes, of course. It would be my pleasure," he said, and he didn't miss how she bit her lip at his last word.

He knew she felt the same—or nearly the same—attraction he did. He also knew how awkward that would be, lusting after the gentleman one's daughter was intended to marry.

It would certainly make family gatherings very uncomfortable.

The thought almost made him laugh aloud. Almost.

"Come with me," he said, holding his arm out for her. "I know where we can go."

She took it, and he led her through the crowd, attracting a few curious glances, but nobody stopped them.

He found a door at one end of the ballroom and flung it open, waiting as she slipped inside, then went after her, shutting the door behind them.

He'd been to events at this family's house before, and had stolen a half hour in this very room with a remarkably flexible woman who appreciated a good desk, and there was one at the other end.

"What can I help with?" he asked, trying not to think of all the ways he'd like to help.

She drew a deep breath, then met his gaze.

Her eyes were so lovely. Dark green, like emerald in shadow.

"My stepson, the duke—"

"I know who he is," he said, imbuing a hint of humor in his tone. "He's the one who offered your daughter up as though she was an evening jacket instead of a human being." He gave her a pointed look. "Though I imagine one could try the evening jacket on before purchase."

"Or know beforehand it won't suit you," she added, then turned bright red. "Never mind, I didn't say that."

He smothered a laugh. "Marriages might work out better if the respective parties were able to try one another on for size, so to speak." He took pity on her, and steered the conversation back on course. "So, you were saying, your stepson, the duke—"

"Yes," she said, glancing away from him, "it seems he is concerned that you are avoiding my daughter."

"I *am* avoiding your daughter," Theo replied. "Clearly the only possible solution, given—" and he made a vague gesture in the air between them.

"Yes, well," she said, taking a deep breath, "William wanted me to speak with you. To remind you that he and his fellow lords in the House of Lords have the ability, he says, to make your life more difficult than it is."

Theo's eyes widened. "He actually said that?"

She met his eyes. "Not in so many words." She considered that. "No, actually he did say it in so many words. That the House of Lords would 'examine your business interests.'"

Theo resisted the urge to put his hands on her shoulders. To try to comfort her as he muddled through what she was saying. "I understand this is difficult for you—"

"That is putting it mildly," she said in a dry tone.

"But if he follows through, he could indeed make my business interests more problematic. I don't wish to upset you, however, so I'll just have to make adjust—"

"Wait a minute," she interrupted. Her color had returned to its normal shade. "What if—what if I were to tell him you needed more persuading?" She snorted. "I could tell him that you are not convinced Harriet will make a good wife, and it will be up to me to talk you into it." She lowered her head, and took his hand in hers. Squeezing it as she spoke. "The most important thing is that Harriet not fall in love with you, and there is no doubt you are handsome and charming."

He wanted to preen at her praise, but knew that would be inappropriate, given the circumstances.

"So even if you were to offer no encouragement, if the two of you spent time together, it might end up that she would fall in love with you. We must keep you separated." Her tone was urgent. "So if—"

"So if you and I were to spend time together," he reasoned out, "then your stepson would believe that his plans were moving forward, and he wouldn't tamper with my business. At least not yet."

"No, and perhaps in that time, Harriet will have found someone suitable to fall in love with."

They both stopped speaking, just staring at one another as their thoughts whirled. At least, Theo assumed her thoughts were whirling as much as his were. It wasn't a very clever plan, but he couldn't think of anything better.

And it would mean he could spend time with her.

Which might be very dangerous. Because she was handsome and charming as well, and he could easily see himself falling in love with her. The second to last woman he should ever consider marrying.

But he would deal with that later on.

Now he had a charade to fulfill.

"Is it a bargain?" she asked, holding her hand out.

He nodded. "It is."

She exhaled in relief. "Thank you."

"ALEXANDRA," EDITH SAID, bustling into Alexandra's bedroom, "Mr. Osborne is here, only Harriet is out with Florence. He's asked to see you."

It was a few days after they'd agreed to their bargain, and Alexandra had been on tenterhooks waiting for him to implement it. She'd told William she'd spoken to Mr. Osborne, so William had been glaring daggers at her as each day ended and Mr. Osborne hadn't come to call.

She wished she could go beard him in his own den, but that would be completely inappropriate, even though they'd done worse together.

"Oh, thank goodness," she said, leaping to her feet.

Edith gave her a curious look. "You're that eager to see him? I thought you didn't want him to marry Harriet, at least not until Harriet decided if she liked him."

"It's not—it's a bit more complicated than that," Alexandra said, feeling her stomach start to knot. She didn't want to lie to Edith, especially since her stepdaughter was very good at ferreting out secrets.

"You'll tell me when he is gone," Edith said. It was not a question.

Alexandra smoothed her skirts and descended the staircase, giving Mrs. Davis an inquiring look.

"I've put him in the small salon," the housekeeper said. "Will you want tea?"

"No, thank you," Alexandra replied.

She went down the hall, turned the knob, and stepped inside.

He was standing in front of the fireplace, turning to look at her as she entered.

If only—she caught herself thinking, then firmly shoved that thought away.

"Good afternoon, Mr. Osborne," she said, keeping her tone even.

"Good afternoon, Your Grace," he replied, equally polite.

She sat, gesturing for him to do the same. "I suppose, given our connection, that we need not be so formal. At least not when we are alone," she said. She took a deep breath. "You can call me Alexandra."

"Theo," he said, an easy smile on his mouth. It was hard to remember that she wasn't supposed to find him intriguing, wasn't supposed to recall their night together, when she saw him. Especially when they were alone.

"Well, Theo, I have to say I am disappointed," Alexandra said, feeling a tight knot in her chest. "You were to spend time with me, and you have not come to call or made any indication of your intentions."

His eyebrows rose. "And you—you were just as able as I to send a note, or pay a visit?"

Alexandra's eyes widened in surprise. "You know I cannot. I am a woman."

"I had noticed," he replied in a wry tone. "Otherwise we might not be in this situation." He made an apologetic gesture. "I am sorry. I shouldn't have said that. I had some business that interfered in my schedule. I had intended to come before this."

Had he found time to visit the Garden of Hedon? She didn't want to know, but the thought tickled at the edge of her consciousness—had he already repeated the experience of a few weeks ago with someone else?

"Thank you," she replied in a quiet tone. "I appreciate that this circumstance is not uppermost in your mind, that you have other things occupying your time."

He held up a hand. "Let me interrupt to say that this is the most important thing in my life right now. I cannot have you or your daughter suffering because of me."

"And we cannot allow William to make you suffer," she replied.

His lips curled into a feral smile. "He won't. I have been making certain adjustments to my business to ensure he can't do his worst." His smile turned warmer. "Perhaps he can do some damage, but not irrevocably so."

"That is good," Alexandra said, relieved.

"Though that doesn't actually help you," he pointed out. "How about we go out for a carriage ride?"

"Now?" Alexandra said in surprise.

He shrugged. "Why not? Unless you have other plans."

She shook her head, an amused look on her face. "Not unless you consider sitting in my bedroom staring out the window having other plans."

He gave her a wide, open grin that made her heart

flip. "Excellent. I promise to be more entertaining than the view outside. Are you ready now?"

She glanced down at what she was wearing—a simple day dress, one that her husband had never liked because it didn't have enough ornamentation on it. "I just need a hat and my gloves," she said, rising.

"I'll wait for you," he promised as she made her way to the door.

Alexandra rushed upstairs, feeling an inexplicable sense of warmth.

Though it was explicable, wasn't it? It was him. Which was absolutely dangerous.

She barely knew him. Why did his presence make her feel so—so good?

Because, a knowing voice said in her head, *he gave you something you've never had in your entire life—the feeling of being desired. Of being worthy of giving and receiving pleasure.*

Her husband had wanted her, yes, but he had wanted her for how her appearance reflected on him. He hadn't wanted who she was or what she could be, beyond "duchess" and "mother."

Until she'd seen Theo that first night in the ballroom, she hadn't even known his name—but they had known one another intimately, the most intimate way two people could.

And now she was beginning to discover that inside his beautiful facade was an equally kind and caring person.

Why else would he agree not to court Harriet?

She could well imagine someone else, someone like her late husband or William, ignoring all the uncomfortable awkwardness that would arise in the same circumstances.

Though she couldn't see either one of those men at a place called the Garden of Hedon, but she also didn't want to imagine it too much.

"Where are you off to?" Edith said, walking down the hall with a book in her hand.

"Mr. Osborne—" *Theo* "—is taking me driving."

Edith's eyebrows arched in a far too understanding way. "Ah, so—"

"Stop right there," Alexandra said, pushing open the door to her room. "I'll explain later, I promise. Right now I need to find a hat and gloves."

"I'll help you. You don't need to call your maid for just this," Edith said, following her in. "I'll pick out your hat if you want to find gloves."

Typical, Alexandra thought with a hidden smile, that Edith wanted to decide on Alexandra's choice of headwear. She liked making her own decisions, which was just one of the myriad reasons she loathed residing with William and his wife.

What would it be like to be Edith? she thought as she rummaged through her drawer for gloves. For one thing, she wouldn't feel shame or embarrassment about having gone to a place like the Garden, for example—it was clear that Edith had been there before, and that she had found the pleasure she sought.

Alexandra strongly suspected Edith hadn't spent her time there playing chess.

"This one, I think," Edith said, withdrawing a hat from one of the hatboxes on the wardrobe shelf.

The hat was the most opulent one Alexandra owned—made of blue velvet, it had alternating silk flowers in a variety of shades festooning the brim, wide satin ribbons tying it on.

"Of course you would choose that one," Alexandra said fondly, taking the hat from Edith. She moved to the mirror and put it on, adjusting the hat so it fit snugly while still allowing her to see beyond its sides.

"You look lovely," Edith said. She winked at her stepmother. "Mind you behave with Harriet's purported intended," she added, her tone indicating she suspected what kind of relationship Alexandra and Theo had.

Was it that obvious? Or was Edith that observant?

She couldn't think about that, especially when she was about to go driving with him, supposedly to convince him to marry her daughter.

THEO HELPED HER up onto the seat of his curricle, then stepped around to leap up beside her.

The day was warm, but not unbearably so, and the few clouds from the morning had disappeared, leaving a blue, open sky, rare for London.

If he wasn't trying to escape the impossible mess he'd made of his life, he might almost enjoy himself.

Though that wasn't fair; he *would* enjoy the day, simply because she was here with him in his carriage, and they could speak undisturbed.

Now that she'd presented her bargain, and he'd agreed, it felt as though there was an easing of the tension between them.

"Where do you wish to go?" he asked, flicking the reins on his horses' backs.

"I don't have a preference," she said. "Just somewhere not here."

"Of course," he said, urging the horses into a fast trot.

They rode in silence for a few minutes, and while it wasn't an entirely comfortable silence, at least it didn't feel fraught.

Progress, Theo thought wryly.

"Have you thought of what to do?" she asked suddenly.

He glanced toward her for a moment. Her face was turned toward his, and she was biting her lip in what he now recognized as an instinctual habit, born out of anxiety, or nervousness, or a combination thereof.

"What was your marriage like?" he asked instead.

She gave him a pointed look. "You are not answering the question."

"Neither are you," he retorted, at which she laughed, her expression surprised, as though she'd startled herself by laughing.

"I haven't thought of anything yet," he admitted.

"We can stall your stepson for a little while, but eventually he is going to realize that this marriage will not happen."

"Are you so certain of that?" she asked, her voice soft. It would have been difficult for an ordinary person to hear her over the sound of the wheels, but he was so attuned to her, so determined to pay attention to her, that it felt as though he'd never miss a word she said.

"Absolutely." He leaned closer to her, an unconscious reaction to how he knew she must feel. "I won't do anything to hurt you, Alexandra." He quirked a smile toward her. "I believe I promised you pleasure the first night we met."

She gave a sharp inhale, her fingers tightening around his. "Thank you," she said, still in that soft voice. His heart clenched at her words.

He'd never felt this kind of empathy before. Not for someone who wasn't one of the Bastard Five.

"It's just us here alone, Alexandra." He swallowed against the lump in his throat. "Angel."

"Oh," she said on a sigh. "Oh."

They had driven through several busy streets, and were now on a quieter road, one that flanked one of the many small parks dotting London. He slowed the horses, then turned to look at her. Their hands were still entwined.

He jerked his head to the side, indicating the park. "Would you like to walk for a bit?"

"Yes, please," she said, leaning past him to look at the greenery. "That would be lovely."

He dismounted, then assisted her from the carriage. "You there," he said, calling to a group of boys across the street. One left his friends and scurried toward them.

"What d'ya want?" he asked. He was likely about twelve years old, with bright blue eyes and brown hair that was stuffed under a grubby cap.

"Hold my team," Theo said, pulling a coin from his pocket. "And there will be more when we return."

The boy's eyes widened at the sight of the coin, and he touched his fingers to his cap. "Indeed, my lord."

"I'm not a lord," Theo murmured, though it didn't matter, not to this boy. The only thing that mattered was that Theo had money in his pocket and could pay for anything he wanted.

Which was the whole point, wasn't it? He had enough money to overcome the duke's anathema to his parentage. He should be able to buy his way out of this predicament, only it wasn't that simple.

And it wouldn't get him what he wanted, which was her.

Was it just infatuation? After all, he barely knew her. Just that she was shyly adventurous, was loyal, and wanted her freedom.

That's what she'd said. *I just got my freedom.* And that was why she had been at the Garden that night—her stepdaughter had encouraged her to see what freedom would be like, he recalled.

He couldn't try to tie her down, not now, not

when it was so important. For one thing, she wouldn't allow it; for another, he couldn't do that to her. Even if she let him.

"Where are we going?" she asked in an interested tone.

He jolted himself back to now. He was here with her now.

"I'm not sure," he replied. "I suppose it's where we want to go."

"Ah," she said, almost slyly, "so we're back to that."

"Back to—" he began.

They stood a few feet away from a small pond, with ducks swimming around while small children and their nursemaids tossed bread.

"Back to choice, and freedom, and doing what you wish."

"You can have choice, you know," he said.

She turned to face him, one eyebrow raised. "Choice means a very different thing when you are a forty-year-old woman, Mr. Osborne." She glanced away, biting her lip. "You asked about my marriage. My late husband chose everything for me—how I dressed, where I went, who I saw. I couldn't do anything about it because he was my husband. Edith and I became friends, which helped, and then Harriet arrived—" her face softened "—and she made everything much better." She met his gaze. "But now my stepson is determined to force Harriet into something the same way I was."

Theo wanted to expostulate that he was nothing

like Alexandra's late husband, but that wasn't the point. "So in addition to figuring out how I will successfully avoid getting married to your daughter, we'll have to figure out how you can have the choice and freedom you deserve." His tone made it sound as though the tasks were entirely reasonable.

She stared at him for a few moments. Then she began to giggle, her eyes crinkling at the corners as she covered her mouth. "It's impossible," she said in between chuckles. "If we had written this as a French farce, it couldn't be more ridiculous."

"At least it's not *boring*," Theo pointed out.

Which made her laugh harder, and he joined in, catching the attention of a few of the small children and their caregivers.

"It's most definitely not boring," she agreed, when their laughter subsided.

Chapter Nine

Alexandra never expected to have so much fun contemplating the impossible situation—the *interesting conundrum*—she'd gotten herself into. Her stomach hurt from laughing, and he was wiping his eyes with his handkerchief. She'd had more fun in the last few minutes than she'd ever had with her late husband.

If she thought about it for too long, and with her old Alexandra mindset—accepting everyone else's premise, following along with what she was supposed to do—she would have been on the brink of despair.

But things weren't that dire. And she refused to be that Alexandra any longer. She was the Alexandra who shredded mourning clothes, who went to a pleasure garden and had *pleasure*, goddamn it.

The one who would face anything if it meant her daughter would be happy.

He'd said he wouldn't marry Harriet, and she

believed him. What's more, he was as powerful, albeit in a very different way, as her stepson. If she hadn't met him how she had and when she did, William would have had a lot more leverage over everyone's future.

So perhaps it was a *good* thing she'd gone to the Garden of Hedon where he pleasured her not once, but twice.

It was a far better way to approach it, after all. Edith would approve, and Alexandra had vowed to herself to be more like her stepdaughter, hadn't she?

Well. She would. She would find joy, and fun, and all the things she'd been lacking before.

It was in that spirit she said the next words. "Would you mind—that is, is it possible that we could see if this," she said, gesturing to the space between them, "is just an anomaly? I mean, if it turns out it was all just that night, then we don't have a problem."

He advanced a step toward her, and her breath caught.

"Do you mean to say," he began, his voice low and resonant, "that you would like me to kiss you?"

"No," she replied softly, a smile lifting one corner of her mouth. "I would like to kiss *you*."

He blinked, and then his lips quirked into his own wry smile. "Then I accept, Your Grace."

They both glanced around then, realizing that standing near a duck pond with a half-dozen children and their nursemaids was not the ideal spot for a round of exploratory kissing.

Without discussion, they began to walk together to a copse of trees about fifty yards away.

She took his arm as they walked, liking how their shoulders nearly touched. His stride was long, like hers, and it was a treat to walk with a gentleman who wasn't increasing his pace to keep up with her, or forcing her to go at his.

They walked past the first line of trees, into another small grassy area. Alexandra peeked back, and depending on where they situated themselves, they would be impossible to spot.

"This is the place," she said, sounding more breathless than she would have imagined.

He extended his arm in a mockingly gallant gesture, and she grinned at how playful he seemed. Almost as if all of this was fun for him, which Alexandra guessed it likely was.

That was the spirit she wanted—the spirit of a confident, handsome man who knew what he wanted and was superb at giving others what they wanted at the same time. Or nearly the same time, she thought as she recalled their evening together.

She took hold of his shoulders and pushed him back against one of the trees, then regarded him for a moment. He waited, nearly as still as the tree against which he leaned. Just looking at her, as though he was content to let her take the lead.

"That's never happened," she murmured.

His eyebrows rose in question. "What hasn't?"

She gestured toward him. "This. A man waiting for me to do something without demanding he take the lead or saying that I am taking too long or something else that indicates he is the male."

The eyebrows rose higher. "It seems to me, Your Grace, that there are many experiences you haven't had that you deserve to have."

"And you know this from speaking with me one evening?" she replied, sounding doubtful. Doubtful at his words, yes, but also doubtful that someone like him actually existed: a gentleman who wasn't insistent on owning every action himself, but had confidence that things would work out as they were supposed to nonetheless.

He shrugged, still leaning casually against the tree. "I know this because I saw to your pleasure. I also knew you wanted to have fun, and I heard you say to your stepdaughter that you hadn't truly ever had fun."

She considered that, then regarded him. He was so good-looking, it nearly hurt to gaze at him. His dark eyes, his strong nose, and the blades of his cheekbones.

The faint stubble on his cheeks.

And his mouth.

"I am going to kiss you," she warned, and that mouth curled up, inviting.

"I am counting on it," he said.

She put her hands on his waist and leaned forward, tilting her head slightly. Placing her lips gently on his, tightening her grip on his waist.

Still, he didn't move. He just let her do what she wished.

She kissed him, swiping her tongue over his bottom lip before licking at the seam of his mouth, an invitation for him to open to her.

Which he did.

His arms, which had been hanging by his sides, drew up, his hands coming to settle at her waist, to pull her in close to his body.

She breathed in his clean, warm scent, faintly woody, though that might have been the tree they were leaning against, she thought with a trace of amusement.

His body was rigid, as though he was holding himself back. *For me*, she thought. She swept her tongue inside his mouth, licking and sucking there, the sensuous languor already stealing over her, even though they were upright and merely kissing.

But there was no *merely* to what they were doing.

This was an intense kiss, which Alexandra knew, even though her kiss repertoire was quite limited.

Their tongues sparred, tangling with one another in a sexual contest, though they'd both win.

She reached up to cup his jaw, to hold him at just the right angle for the onslaught, to push against him so their bodies were completely touching.

His erection pressed against her there, and she was once again grateful that they were nearly of a height—doing this with someone much shorter or much taller would require a certain amount of acrobatics, and she wasn't confident in her ability to find the right spot.

But she was confident now.

That was due as much as to her own self as to him—she'd decided, right after her husband died, to embark on a second life, once her mourning period was over.

She would be confident, fearless, and take what she wanted, as long as it didn't harm anybody else.

That, of course, was the thorniest issue at the moment.

But this was to see if it was just a fluke—a moment in time that wouldn't mean as much at another time.

Unfortunately, she thought ruefully as she considered how she might get him undressed and in the correct position for more exploration, she did not think it was a fluke.

She wanted him. She wanted him to want her, and judging by his reaction, he did.

She wanted never to stop kissing him, and also to feel him kissing her everywhere else. To explore other positions that might bring pleasure. Perhaps to introduce him to some new types of pleasure, not that she had the faintest idea what those might be.

Just that she wanted to do it.

She wanted to do all of it. With him. And only him.

He kept kissing her, his hands now wrapped around her waist to meet at the small of her back. His legs spread wide so she could nestle herself in, feel his hardness pressed against where he'd licked her before. Where he'd buried his cock and fucked her, hard, making her forget who she was and what she was doing.

This was most definitely not an anomaly.

THEO WAS LOSING his mind. There was no other explanation for how he felt, how just a kiss—a mere kiss—could inflame him to such a height.

He'd kissed plenty of women before, from slow, lingering kisses to ones that flirted with an edge of violence, with teeth and tongue and naughty nips.

But he had never fallen so deep and immediately into passion as now, when he was standing outside in a London park, for God's sake, his back against a tree that was cutting into him, her guiding what was happening between them.

He wanted to give her that control before they began, but now he wanted her to take it, to see what else she might do to him. With him. For him.

Their breathing was the only thing he could hear. Her tongue in his mouth, urgent and insistent, her soft, warm body pressed against his.

His arms were banded around her, his fingers splayed on her back, his cock pressed against her, right where he wanted it to be, if they were wearing far fewer items of clothing.

That is to say, if they were wearing nothing at all.

But while Theo had done his share—more than his share, actually—of adventurous sexual activity, he'd never engaged in outdoor copulation where there was a chance they would be discovered.

It wouldn't be right to force anyone else to partake in his particular sexual appetite, so he'd never found it appealing to risk exposure.

But he had to admit that right now he was sorely tempted.

He reached down to cup the soft roundness of her bottom, squeezing the flesh through her skirts. She made a surprised noise low in her throat, and then she chuckled, leaning further against him, one of her hands still on his face, the other pressing flat against his chest. Exploring with her fingers.

Then she broke the kiss to rub her cheek against his, making a low noise of pleasure.

"I promise I did shave this morning," he said. He spoke in a husky growl.

"Mmm," she murmured. She kissed his jaw, then moved to his ear, taking the lobe in her teeth and biting gently. Sending shivers down his entire body.

"This—this isn't an anomaly, Your Grace," he said, a hint of laughter in his voice.

"Unfortunately it is not," she agreed. She

shifted, making his cock press against her a little more closely.

"You like that, hmm?" he asked.

"I do," she said. "I like all of it. Not an anomaly."

He wished she didn't sound regretful, though he understood it—they were in a difficult situation, to put it mildly, and he still hadn't thought of a way out of it. Though he was even more convinced that he needed to put a stop to the notion before anybody but the two of them got hurt.

"What are we going to do?" she continued. Still leaning against him. Him still holding the soft roundness of her arse.

"I suppose," Theo said thoughtfully, "we continue doing this until we have gotten it out of our systems."

ALEXANDRA TILTED HER head back so she could look in his eyes.

Goodness, he had beautiful eyes. They were brown, a deep, rich, velvet brown that looked like freshly made coffee or a strong stallion's coat.

Though that could be just him—he'd woken her up, like the best cup of coffee and, well, she didn't need to explain the *strong stallion* imagery to herself, did she?

She giggled at the thought.

"Do you find that amusing?" he asked, sounding surprised.

His hand was still on her bottom. She wished he

would do something with his hand—like stroke her there, or perhaps yank her closer to him.

"No, not at all—I was just admiring your eyes."

"Admiring my eyes," he repeated, sounding confused.

"Yes. And—and other things," she continued, pressing her mouth to his throat. She felt his pulse under her lips. "I like that you are taller than I am. It's a rarity. I like how you kiss me," she said, hearing her voice get lower and softer. "I like how it feels when our bodies are touching."

She emphasized the last sentence with another shift of her legs so his penis was hitting the spot that ached for him.

"Do you want me to fuck you against this tree, Alexandra?" he said, his voice ragged.

She gasped, both at the shock of hearing him say the crude words and also how she felt a rush of want—yes, she wanted him to fuck her against this tree.

But they couldn't. Not so close to other people, and not in the daytime.

Though at night it would be nearly as foolish.

"It wouldn't be right," she replied.

"But you want it," he urged. "We can't, I know that, but just tell me you want it."

She swallowed. "I want it." A hesitation. Then she continued, "I want you to fuck me against this tree."

And his mouth was on hers again, and he was kissing her as though this was the last kiss in the world ever, and they were the last two people in the world ever. It felt as though he was pouring his soul into the kiss, into her, and she was melting.

Or no, not melting; that would imply submission, and she was finished with submitting.

Instead, it was a passionate dance between them, one where both of them knew their steps and encouraged the other to do their best.

Dear Lord, he most definitely was doing his best.

His hands were ranging all over her, from her bottom to her back to her arms, and then his fingers were cradling her jaw, holding her still as his tongue dueled and clashed with hers.

Someone was moaning, and she realized it was her—a low, keening sound that was as close to a growl as she had ever gotten.

Then it was over. They had broken apart and were staring into one another's eyes, gasping, him still holding her face, her with her fingers splayed on his chest as she rubbed up against him like a wanton.

Because she was a wanton, she decided. And there was nothing wrong with that, not if the two people were like-minded in their attraction for one another.

And if there were no other imped—

At which she groaned, but not in an *Oh my God, I am in so much pleasure I might die* kind of way; more an *Oh my God, this is the man my rigid stepson has decided will marry my daughter, and*

I can't seem to keep my mind and hands off of him kind of way.

"We'll find a solution," he said, correctly gauging her thoughts.

She exhaled, then compressed her mouth into a tight line, edging back from where she was pressed against him. "I have no idea how," she said.

"Perhaps your daughter will meet and want to marry someone even more suitable than I?" he said, sounding hopeful.

"More suitable than you." She rolled her eyes as she spoke. "Someone more handsome, more wealthy, more in need of the respectability the Chelmswich name bestows, so much that you'd eschew a dowry and instead pay for the privilege of marrying into the family?" She huffed out a breath. "Please."

"Well, when you put it that way, it does sound impossible."

"We should go back," she said, suddenly weary.

"We will figure it out somehow," he promised. "Or we will keep doing this until we are sick to death of it. Like when you eat too much chocolate pudding and then realize you never want to see another bowl of chocolate pudding in your life."

She had to laugh. "You're not chocolate pudding, Mr. Osborne."

"Theo, remember," he said. "I think our recent interactions allow for a certain amount of familiarity?" He gave her a crooked smile, one that was as abashed as it was charming.

"Of course," she agreed with a chuckle as she slid out of his grasp.

He pushed himself off the tree, straightening his jacket where her eager hands had disheveled it.

"Am I . . . ?" she asked, making a gesture to indicate her appearance.

"You're beautiful," he replied. "Though you've got a bit of redness on your cheek from—" and he pointed to the stubble on his face.

"That will ease," she said.

Though she wasn't sure anything else would—could she imagine a time when she wasn't hungry for him? Wanting his touch all over her body? His sexual attentions directed at her?

"You're thinking again," he observed.

"It's rather difficult not to, what with the brain I have inside my head," she shot back. Then was immediately astonished at her own candor.

He grinned at her, not taking offense, and she breathed a sigh of relief.

He wasn't her late husband. He wasn't William.

He was Theo, Mr. Osborne.

Her lover, she presumed.

Until he wasn't.

"WHEN WILL I see you again?" Theo asked on the drive home. He made it sound urgent, as though they hadn't just done all sorts of things against that tree in the park.

Alexandra glanced over at him. "You mean see me, or see me?"

His expression was one of confusion. "What is the difference?"

"Well," she began, ticking the points off on her gloved fingers, "if you see me at a ball, you might ask me to dance, and there would be people all around and William glaring at both of us, demanding we fulfill our respective duties. Perhaps, if we're very fortunate, you can take me for a stroll on the terrace."

"And the other bit of seeing?" he said, his tone warmer.

"The other bit of seeing is where I meet you somewhere—at the Garden of Hedon, for example—and we see one another in a different light."

"I understand now," he replied. "You might say I *see* the difference." He waggled his eyebrows at her as he spoke.

She laughed and swatted him on the arm.

"Can I say both?" he continued. "I do like dancing with you, and the bonus of having the duke glare at us is just a fillip on the delight of the evening."

She shook her head. "You take pleasure in things I do not, I have to say."

"How do you know?" he challenged. "The only

fun you've had recently is with me. Who's to say there aren't more pleasures out there you haven't explored?"

She regarded him thoughtfully. "I suppose you might be right—"

"I usually am," he interrupted.

"I'll speak with Edith about it. Lord knows she is going to want to grill me about today."

"Are we agreed—" he began in a nearly hesitant tone "—that we won't do anything with anybody else we expect to do with one another? Not that I would bind you, but—"

"No, I hadn't even thought of that," she said firmly. "While I appreciate your asking and not demanding—" something most, if not all, gentlemen would not do "—I have no desire for anybody else," she said simply.

"I see," he replied in a soft voice. "Another thing I am able to see, thanks to you."

"Maybe *I* can teach *you* a few things." She spoke in a deliberately light tone. He seemed so sincere, so earnest, that it imbued whatever they were talking about with a resonance that made her feel uncomfortable. As though she was embarking on things she didn't understand.

Which was certainly true, she had to admit to herself. She didn't know how to have fun, she hadn't yet explored all her own pleasure, and she definitely did not understand the fluttery feelings she had when she was around him.

"I will be glad to be at your knee," he replied. "Learning."

The images that came to her mind were graphic and carnal and altogether exciting.

"So you'll meet me?" he said urgently.

"Yes," she replied. "Yes."

Chapter Ten

Theo watched her ascend the stairs to her stepson's town house, noting the lovely sway of her hips, and how elegantly she held herself. It seemed she might not relish all the duties being a duchess held, but she certainly deported herself as if she was a queen.

His queen. For the moment, at least.

And then—then, he didn't want to think about it. Because he knew that she fully intended for there to be an end to all of this, and he was already beginning to suspect he never wanted that. Even though every other time before, he'd been the one to end things.

Unless it was mutual, like how it was with Lucy.

He was deep in thought the rest of the ride. His mind—usually razor-sharp when it came to business—was absolutely befuddled when it came to solving the situation he found himself in.

They found themselves in. Because if it was

just him, and he discovered he and Lady Harriet didn't suit, he'd just—walk away.

But that would leave both Alexandra and Harriet in difficulty, and even besides the whole *I'd like to continue having sex with her* aspect, he did not want anyone to suffer because of something he'd done.

And then there was the whole *I'd like to continue having sex with her* aspect.

He couldn't wait. This time, they knew one another. At least, more about one another.

He knew how she smelled. How she tasted. How she kissed.

She knew he wanted her, though he doubted she knew just how much.

He wasn't certain even he knew how much— just that it was more than he'd ever wanted a woman before.

He didn't want to just know the sounds she made when she came. Or how her skin felt under his fingers.

He wanted to know what made her laugh. What brought her pleasure, and not just the salacious kind. What books she liked to read, if any.

Though if she didn't care to read books at all, he might find himself less interested in her.

But that was something to discover, wasn't it? Perhaps she'd admit she only read pamphlets on skin care, or something like that, and he'd find it easier to walk away, when it was time to do so.

When it was time to do so.

Because there would be a time. She'd made that clear.

What if—what if he didn't ever want to walk away?

Time enough for that, as well, he thought ruefully. Right now he had to solve the prickly problem of being intended to marry the daughter of the only woman he wanted to fuck.

He turned onto the street where he lived, starting as he saw an ornate coach, emblazoned with a recognizable crest, two coachmen standing smartly at attention.

In front of his house.

As he watched, the duke descended from the carriage, glancing around in obvious disdain.

Theo's home was large, but not nearly as enormous as the duke's town house. Likewise, it was in a reasonably fashionable street, but it wasn't Mayfair.

Theo employed servants sufficient for a single gentleman living alone, but not the vast number he imagined were employed by the duke.

However, he thought wryly, if the duke wasn't so determined to impress everyone with his magnificence, perhaps he'd have more cash at his disposal, and he wouldn't have to barter his sister in exchange for some of Theo's merchant money.

Theo slowed the carriage, tossing the reins to one of his coachmen, then alighted to the pavement where the duke was waiting.

"Your Grace," he said, bowing.

Just at that moment, another set of feet descended from the carriage, and Theo was astonished to see Benedict alight.

He gave his friend a puzzled frown, but Benedict just jerked his chin toward the duke as if to say, *Just wait, it'll be explained.*

"May I invite you in?" Theo said, gesturing to the door.

His butler, Greeves, already stood there, ready to take hats and walking sticks and whatever else a gentleman might need when venturing out of doors.

Mr. Greeves was missing an arm, but he had adjusted to his disability and was a remarkably good butler. At least, in Theo's admittedly small buttling experience.

The man had worked at one of the Osborne factories, which was where his accident had occurred. Theo's father had attempted to give Mr. Greeves money enough to live on for the rest of his life. Mr. Greeves was too proud, and refused to take charity—but he would take a position, if there was one to be found that would suit his limited abilities.

"Tea in the library, Greeves, unless you gentlemen want something stronger?"

Both men shook their heads, and Greeves headed off to the kitchens.

"If you'll follow me?" Theo began to walk down the hall to the library, where he conducted meetings. His office was too small to be comfortable for more than just him and his secretary.

"We've been waiting for fifteen minutes," the duke said, sounding peevish.

"If I had known—" Theo began.

"And you haven't replied to my notes." The duke stopped in the middle of the hallway, forcing Theo to stop also and turn back.

"As you know yourself, Your Grace, business does not wait." Theo tried to keep his tone pleasant, when really he wanted to tell the duke just what he thought of his arrogant ways. "And the dowager duchess spoke to me, so I am aware of your concerns."

But if Benedict was here, then likely the duke had come on his own sort of business. Theo didn't want to make his friend's work more difficult because the duke was an ass.

"Just here." Theo walked to the door, holding it open for the duke and Benedict to enter. He followed, shutting the door behind.

"Please, have a seat." He indicated the chairs and sofa, all of which were comfortably arranged around a low table.

He took the chair with its back toward his desk—he didn't want to assert his dominance here by sitting behind his desk, as though the duke was a supplicant for his time and attention, but he also wanted to subtly remind the duke that Theo was the owner here.

Benedict gave him a quick, knowing smile, and sat on one end of the sofa, while the duke settled himself in the chair to Theo's left.

"How may I help you?" Theo asked.

Greeves stepped inside, making his way toward them, deftly placing the tea tray on the table as the duke glared.

"Is there anything else, sir?" Greeves asked when everything was properly placed.

"No, thank you," Theo said. "You were saying?" he continued, speaking to the duke when everyone was holding a cup of tea made as they wished it.

"With the imminent union of our families," the duke began, "the House of Lords, on my impetus, wishes to work with Mr. Quintrell's department," he said, nodding toward Benedict, "to streamline certain redundancies to make everyone's businesses more efficient."

Theo regarded the duke for a few moments, reflecting that people who seldom engaged in business themselves often used language that was deliberately obfuscatory in order to disguise the fact that they had no idea what they were talking about.

No idea why *that* thought came to mind, he thought dryly.

"Making business more efficient is every businessman's goal," he said in a mild tone.

Benedict shot him a sharp look. Apparently not mild enough.

"We're hoping to offer certain benefits if business owners will guarantee a living wage for workers," Benedict said. "The government wishes to make it possible for families to work and live reasonably well while profits go up."

"You've just described an impossible dream," Theo remarked.

"Not impossible," Benedict said, speaking rapidly. "We can do it. We just need everyone—" and then he glanced toward the duke "—to participate."

"Ah," Theo said. He felt the vise tighten.

"The first demonstration of which will be our partnership," the duke pronounced. "When you are married to my sister—"

"*If* I am married to your sister," Theo corrected him. "Lady Harriet and I have made no formal agreement. I barely know her."

"That's because you've stayed away from anywhere she might be!" the duke said, his face turning red.

"Business," Theo reminded him. Benedict gave him a warning look, and he continued in a more conciliatory tone. "I agree with everything you are saying. Of course I want happy workers," he said, even though he doubted the duke had ever thought about his workers' happiness.

"But you will need to present a united front on this endeavor," Benedict said. "If one business owner undercuts wages, everyone will follow so as to increase profits. You have to stand firm, at least until we can make certain the new regulations and improvements will affect profitability."

Benedict likely knew as little as the duke about

the day-to-day running of a business, but at least *he* didn't sound like a pompous ass when he spoke.

"Which means," the duke said in a triumphant tone, "we will have to keep company together more often. You will come to the country with us, and you can take a well-needed break from your business concerns. Mr. Quintrell is unable to join us," he continued in a sour tone, "but rest assured I will be working with him on this matter. I will need to be at my country home to consult my documents, and you will join us there."

It was not a request. Theo looked to Benedict, who gave him a *You have to do this, friend, I'm sorry* look, and Theo suppressed a grimace.

A neat way to get him to appear to be courting Lady Harriet, Theo saw. And if he refused? Benedict would likely not be able to implement his plans, not to mention the workers that would lose out on higher wages. And the other business owners who would be livid that one person's refusal meant they would lose out on possible boons from the House of Lords.

Very neat indeed.

ALEXANDRA WAS ASCENDING the staircase to her room when Edith popped out of her bedroom, her face lighting up when she saw her stepmother. "You're back!" she exclaimed, rushing forward.

"I am," Alexandra replied, walking to the door of her room.

Florence had taken Alexandra's previous room, since she was now the duchess, and given Alexandra a smaller room on the same floor.

But she didn't mind—her new room had a window seat, with windows looking down onto the street below.

It was decorated in muted tones of grays and pinks with a few notes of navy, a tranquil space that felt far more comfortable than the duchess's bedroom ever had.

Though that could be because Alexandra herself was far more comfortable as a dowager duchess than the actual duchess. Some women might have chafed at having to cede control of the household; not Alexandra. She had taken leadership, as it was her responsibility, and she had enjoyed working with the staff. But she did not miss always having to respond, at any time, to any question.

Edith trailed after her as Alexandra removed her hat and gloves, tossing them on one of the small bureaus that were set against the wall.

"Would you like me to ring for tea?" Alexandra asked, as Edith sat down on one of the chairs facing the fireplace.

There wasn't a fire going—it was warm enough without it—but it was still a comfortable place to sit.

"No, I need you to tell me what happened with Mr. Osborne."

Alexandra felt herself flush. "Why would you think anything happened with Mr. Osborne?

William asked me to speak with Mr. Osborne about Harriet, since he is so set on the match. William, that is, not Mr. Osborne."

Edith flapped her hand in dismissal. "Yes, that is what I knew you would say, but that is not true. I saw how he looked at you, Alex."

"How did he look at me?" Alexandra said, unable to resist asking the question.

She had never been the focus of one person's desire. At least, desire not also tinged with the craving for acclaim at having secured a beautiful woman as one's bride. Mr. Osborne—Theo—clearly desired her, but he also *listened* to her, as though her brain might be nearly as attractive as her appearance.

"Like he was in the desert and you were a tall glass of water," Edith said. Grinning.

Alexandra rolled her eyes. "I think you are seeing things."

Edith gave her a narrow look. "I am an *expert* on such things, you mean to say." She raised an eyebrow. "So what are you going to do about it?"

There wasn't any point in continuing to argue with Edith, not when her stepdaughter was so firmly convinced she was right. Since she *was* right.

Edith had been insightful from the first time the two of them had met; she'd waited until the two of them were alone, and then she'd detailed all the ways Alexandra was unhappy. And vowed to help, if she could.

Alexandra had loved her stepdaughter from that moment on.

She flopped down in the chair beside Edith. "I don't know," she admitted. "I don't know anything, it seems."

"You know you find him attractive," Edith said. "Wait a minute," she continued, sounding even more excited, "did you meet him at the Garden?" The last word she practically squeaked.

Alexandra squeezed her eyes shut as she gave a tiny nod.

"Oh my Lord!" Edith exclaimed. "No wonder you're so tied up in knots! I thought it was because William and Florence are so damaging to one's ability to have fun, but no, it's because—it's because you did things with the gentleman who is going to marry your daughter!" Her words were a delighted shriek.

Alexandra smothered her face in her hands.

"Oh my," Edith said. "That is a situation." Her tone was admiring.

Alexandra peeked between her fingers at her stepdaughter as she said, sarcastically, "You think so?"

"He's not going to marry her," Edith continued firmly.

Alexandra raised her head. "I know that, but how do you?"

Edith rolled her eyes. "Because he's clearly besotted with you."

Alexandra was shaking her head before Edith had even finished. "It's not that simple." She frowned as she folded her arms over her chest.

"He's over ten years younger than me. Even without all of—" and she gestured, indicating William's attempt at matchmaking "—it's not going to work. I don't *want* it to work. I want to do what we talked about—be free to make my own choices."

"You *could* choose him, you know," Edith said in a dry tone. "It doesn't have to be either or. You could choose him, and you could also choose other things you want to do. Not everyone is like my father." She spoke the last sentence bitterly, and Alexandra's heart hurt for her.

Bad enough to have lost her mother at a young age; to be left with a parent who didn't understand her, and what's more, didn't particularly care for her, had to be terrible. Small wonder Edith took ownership of herself and her interests. Nobody else would.

"But most gentlemen are like my late husband," Alexandra remarked.

Edith considered it for a moment, then nodded. "True. But I don't think Mr. Osborne is. And you, you have the choice you've always wanted. Why not choose to have fun? With him?"

Put that way—as Edith usually did—it seemed so simple. Even simpler than when she and Theo had spoken about it in the park. Perhaps she should utilize Edith's analysis anytime she was going to do something risqué.

But the point remained: Why not?

Why not enjoy this while it lasted, knowing it

would inevitably end, and she could move on to the next bit of fun?

Though somehow she thought that wouldn't be that easy—the moving on part.

Something in her liked how he looked at her, as Edith said, as though she was a tall glass of water and he was dying of thirst. As though she had something to say to him he would find important, not just something to hear while he was waiting to display her or touch her or treat her as an object, not a person.

But that didn't answer the very real problem facing her. "So how do you suggest I extricate Harriet from William's terrible bargain?"

Edith raised a brow. "Your capable business-man doesn't have a suggestion?"

"He's not my—no, he doesn't," Alexandra replied. "Short of him crying off, which would besmirch Harriet's reputation, which neither of us wants him to do."

Edith was opening her mouth to reply when the door was flung open, revealing a clearly distressed Harriet.

"Have you heard?" she said, her voice raised in dismay. "William is making us go to the country. Right in the middle of my Season!"

She strode into Alexandra's bedroom, fury emanating from every fiber of her being. "I've just had my debut—delayed for two years while we sat in that very same country and wore black, mind you—and now he wants to take us back there. It's not fair!" She plopped down on Alexandra's bed, huffing out a breath.

"Why would he do that?" Alexandra asked, genuinely bewildered.

Harriet gave her mother a pointed glare. "Because he thinks that is how Mr. Osborne will propose."

"Mr. Osborne has been invited?" Edith asked.

Alexandra held her breath.

"Yes," Harriet said grumpily.

"And you don't want that?" Edith said in a probing tone of voice.

Harriet threw her hands up in exasperation. "No! He is handsome, yes, but he and I will not suit. He is far too—" she said, wrinkling her nose "—old and serious. Besides, I don't want to marry for at least five years," she continued. "What is the point of having a Season when you just get married at the end of it?"

"That *is* the point of the Season, usually," Alexandra replied in a mild tone. Though inside she was sending up silent thanks that her daughter knew precisely what she wanted. And that it was not Mr. Osborne.

Harriet folded her arms over her chest. "Not for me. I do not want that. I don't want—pardon me, Mama—to have to marry someone who'll just ignore me, except when I have children."

Harriet's words rang out, fierce and strident, and Alexandra exhaled in relief. Relief and concern, of course, because William could make all of their lives very difficult, if he wished to.

But for now, at least she didn't have to worry that Harriet's heart would be broken if she didn't marry Mr. Osborne.

"Huzzah!" Edith cheered as Alexandra went to Harriet and gave her a warm hug.

"We'll figure it out," she said, her words a promise. Not just to her daughter, but to herself. "We'll figure it out." She tightened her grip on her daughter. "Whatever we need to do, whatever you need to do, will be done. No matter what it is."

Harriet nodded against her shoulder. "Thank you," she said, and her tone was relieved.

All of this meant she most definitely would go to the Garden that evening. She and Theo would need to discuss how to behave around one another in the country.

As well as finish what they'd started on that tree.

Chapter Eleven

ou really can't attend?" Theo said, hearing the note of desperation in his voice.

Benedict shook his head. "Not with negotiations at this critical time, no."

The duke had departed a half hour earlier, clearly triumphant at having finessed Theo into position.

As soon as they'd heard the carriage pull away, Theo had gone to the sideboard and poured a healthy draught of whisky for himself and another for Benedict, handing it to his friend before taking a swallow.

He sputtered, realizing he still didn't like the taste of liquor all that much.

"It won't be that bad, will it?" Benedict asked.

Theo regarded Benedict over the rim of his glass. "You *do* recall my predicament?"

Benedict winced. "Yes, of course. I wish I could come, but—"

"I know. Business," Theo said in a tone mocking his own earlier use of the word.

"Business." Benedict put his hand on Theo's shoulder. "But the duke made it clear that without this, he would not continue to work on the project. It's vital to so many people, Theo, and I wouldn't ask if it wasn't—"

"Pardon me, sir." The men glanced to where Theo's butler was standing at the doorway. "Mr. Ash is here."

"Just Fenton," Fenton said, sounding irritated as he pushed past the butler. "And you needn't announce me anyway. It's not as though Theo won't see me."

"Try me," Theo said, getting up to greet his friend. He clapped Fenton on the back. "What are you doing here?"

"Looking for an escape," Fenton replied, sounding as beleaguered as Theo had ever heard him. "My sister's invited all of her husband's family to stay in London with us as she buys everything she deems appropriate for the baby."

Fenton's sister wasn't actually his sister at all; like the rest of them, Fenton was an orphan. But he'd been adopted into the Ash family at age twelve, and his sister was his elder by two years. He and Eliza—Mrs. Robens now—had grown close over the years, and he opened his London home to her when she was in town from Somerset.

"An escape, hmm?" Benedict said, casting Theo a significant glance.

"You think . . . ?" Theo began, not certain if Fenton's presence would improve things. Their friend was the most erratic and eccentric of them, and there was a strong possibility Fenton might make things worse somehow.

On the other hand, Theo didn't have much of a choice.

"Come to the country with me," he said, going to pour a glass of whisky for Fenton, who took it automatically before glancing down at it and frowning, then putting it down, untouched, on the table. Fenton didn't like alcohol much either.

"Why?"

Fenton sat on the sofa beside Benedict, stretching his arm across the top as he regarded Theo with a curious gaze.

"Theo doesn't want to be alone with the Duke of Chelmswich and his family," Benedict answered.

"Because the duke has decided I will be marrying his sister, even though I never committed to it." If he could take it back, take back that meeting of only a few weeks ago, where he agreed to meet the duke's sister and mentioned he was thinking of settling down—he would have done anything to make that possible.

But then he wouldn't have taken himself to the Garden that evening in a last hurrah, and he wouldn't have met her.

So perhaps he'd have taken the meeting regardless. He just wouldn't have allowed the duke to persist in his schemes.

Dear Lord, but he hoped she would meet him at the Garden this evening. Not only could they strategize what to do—not that either one of them had the faintest idea—but he could touch her, as he'd been aching to do since they stopped kissing earlier that day.

"I'll come," Fenton said, sounding relieved. "The country?" He frowned. "There won't be hordes of delighted women there?" He spoke as though *hordes of delighted women* was roughly analogous to *demons with fiery vats of tar.*

Theo shook his head solemnly. "I expect not."

He couldn't even tempt himself with the tantalizing thought that *she* might be a delighted woman—if they were able to be alone together so he could delight her thoroughly. He was in enough trouble as it was.

Even though seeing her, speaking with her, was the only thing making him not dread this visit entirely.

Well, that and the glee he'd feel when Fenton inevitably did or said something that demonstrated that the duke was most definitely not the smartest gentleman in the area.

Perhaps Fenton would do something so outlandish the duke would decide that allying his family with someone with friends like that would be a grave mistake.

Perhaps a bright spot to having such an erratic friend?

"Excellent," he said. "We'll leave tomorrow. We can take my carriage."

"Good," Fenton said in an absent-minded tone, as though he'd already forgotten what he'd agreed to. "I told Simeon he could use mine anyway."

"Where is Simeon go—?" Theo began, then shook his head. "Never mind." One erratic friend at a time. "Be here at eleven o'clock tomorrow."

Fenton nodded, walking out of the room without another word.

Theo glanced over at Benedict, and the two of them burst into laughter.

At least he wouldn't be *bored*. What with trying to solve his impossible situation, finding time to delight the dowager duchess, and ensuring Fenton wasn't too flummoxing, he'd be very busy.

THERE WAS NO possibility Alexandra would be able to function at a Society party this evening. Her mind was too full of . . . of everything, from Harriet's future, to her own, to what could possibly be done, to how he made her feel.

William and Florence had accepted her excuse without question, and she'd been relieved to be on her own just for a little while.

She stood at the entrance to the Garden, wearing an evening gown that was much plainer than most of her others. A dark cloak covered her from head to toe, and she had the hood drawn down over her face so there was even less chance she would be recognized.

He hadn't arrived, and the thought crossed her mind that perhaps he wouldn't come—what if he assumed she wasn't coming because both of them were expected to go to the country the next day?

That would be a disappointment. But one she could tolerate, because she wasn't a silly girl who lived and died for a man's attentions. She was far too old and, yes, self-confident to react like that.

But she hoped he did come.

While initially she had thought him only to be something to play with, to explore, now she was curious about who he was—his personality, his likes and dislikes, how he came to be who he was despite his humble origins.

That was perhaps more dangerous to her peace of mind than merely desiring his body.

Even though desiring his body *did* take up a fair amount of her thoughts at the moment. Perhaps, if she was to draw a chart of it all, Harriet's future would be forty percent, her own fifteen, what could be done ten percent, her own future another ten, and his body about twenty-five percent.

Did that all add up? Not that it mattered. Her thoughts were a whirl of possibilities and dead ends, of ultimate sacrifices and greater goods and all sorts of things that she would not have expected a woman her age to need to think about.

Women her age, she'd been led to expect, were primarily focused on the prospect of grandchildren and embroidery. If one was able to plan very well, there might be the addition of some light novel reading.

Nowhere in the guide to being a widow did it mention suddenly having lustful thoughts that not only obscured all thoughts of embroidery but obliterated them.

She was still hoping for grandchildren, however. Just not fathered by him.

The thought of it made her feel sick to her stomach.

But she knew it would not come to that. He was adamant against it, but even if he weren't, she would do whatever she had to, even steal away with Harriet in the middle of the night to forge some sort of life elsewhere. And Harriet herself was obviously against it, though in William's eyes, two women's opinions didn't matter as much as his own.

It was the last thought that gave her strength. Her late husband hadn't valued her opinion, and neither did his son. She could only trust herself. Others—no matter what they promised—could change their minds at any time. Other men, that is.

For a moment, she felt a sizzle of impotent rage course through her. Because if not for men, she could live her life as she pleased. Her husband had provided for her well enough, though her stepson controlled the funds; without his interference, she could do as she wished.

Her late husband had also been far too controlling, but he was gone now, so he could no longer tell her how to dress, who to speak with, and what volume her voice should be.

Why was she trusted enough to bear a child and nurture that child to adulthood, but not trusted enough to manage money? What made her stepson so much more capable than she?

She strongly suspected it was that he had a penis, and that was it.

"Argh," she said, feeling as though she was about to burst from it all. Grateful, at least, that she knew she would never marry again. Never allow herself to be controlled by anyone ever again.

"Are you all right?"

She turned at the sound of his voice. This man, at least, wasn't in control of any part of her. Whatever she did or did not do with him was her choice.

Which somehow made it even more appealing.

"I am fine," she said, swallowing down her anger. "Just frustrated."

He held his arm out for her, and she took it, allowing herself to lean against him for a moment.

"You've spoken to William?" she asked.

He gave a sharp exhale, making his spoken reply redundant. "I have. He is making it even more difficult, tying this potential . . . partnership," he said at last, as though reluctant to say *marriage*, "to procedures and laws that will benefit my workers, and workers in general."

"William really must be desperate if he has suddenly turned democratic," Alexandra remarked dryly.

He snorted in reply.

They walked further into the Garden, and at first Alexandra thought he was taking her to the place he'd brought her the first time. But he walked past that building to another one tucked further into the trees.

This building was fashioned after a Greek temple, with distinct marble columns in front, flanking a doorway with a curve at the top. If it had been anywhere else, it would have been a folly, a creation built purely for visual delight.

But here it was visually pleasing as well as serviceable, she presumed.

"You're not taking me to any kind of orgy, are you?" she said, her mind suddenly catching on what she recalled from her bare smattering of Greek history.

He laughed as they walked up the stone steps. "No, hardly. This place is not as often used as the others. I thought you might prefer it to be a bit quieter."

"Thank you," she said as he opened the door, waiting as she entered. "You're correct." Not only had he been able to sense what she was feeling, he actually did something about it.

Remarkable.

Unlike a regular house, the entire building was contained within this one room, with a sumptuous bathtub at one end and a discreetly draped bed at the other.

In between there were well-upholstered chairs and sofas placed around a long, low table that held an assortment of fruits and beverages— Alexandra presumed wine, though she wasn't certain.

"Have a seat," he said, going to the table. "Do you want something to drink?"

She nodded, and he poured her a glass.

"You're not having any?" she asked, as he handed her the drink and sat down without getting anything for himself. He didn't sit next to her, but opposite, meaning, she thought, that she'd have to be the one to get up if she wished for them to be closer.

Was she reading too much into that? Perhaps. But everything felt fraught and dangerous and exciting, and her mind was already racing, so it was seizing on anything it could find.

"I haven't developed a taste for alcohol," he said, shrugging. "But I wouldn't want that to limit your choice."

He was just speaking about whether or not to have wine, but it resonated with her so much more than that.

"Thank you," she said, tipping her glass to him before she took a sip. It was red wine, tasting faintly of dust and much more strongly like grapes. "It's good," she added, placing it down on the table.

He leaned forward to pick up the glass. "Mind if I smell it? I like the aroma. I just don't like the taste."

"Of course," she replied.

He raised the glass to his nose, closing his eyes and inhaling. A low moan escaped from his throat as he held the glass up, transfixing Alexandra with the image.

A gentleman taking a pure, simple delight in something. Rather like their evening together, to be honest, though this was less salacious.

But no less enticing.

"You're staring," he said after a few moments. His mouth quirked at the corners, and his tone was warm.

"You are something to look at, that is for certain," she replied, wishing it didn't feel so brave to be honest.

He inclined his head. "Thank you. I will say the same for you." His eyes traveled over her, his intense gaze making it feel almost as though he was touching her.

She shivered.

"Are you cold?" he asked, springing up.

"No," she replied, meeting his eyes. "I am fine."

"Can I do anything for you?" he asked, still on his feet.

She regarded him for a moment, thinking of all the things he could do for her—but she only wanted one thing.

"Yes," she said at last. "I want you to talk to me."

Chapter Twelve

𝒯heo had not been expecting that.

And yet, somehow, her request was even more precious than asking for other, more physical, things.

Talking required sharing. Trust. Communication.

Not just the exchange of pleasure, or mutual enjoyment.

He walked toward her, taking a seat in the chair next to hers. Frowning as he hitched it closer, close enough for the skirts of her gown to touch his trousers, but not close enough to feel intimate.

He glanced around the room, looking for inspiration.

"Do you want to take a bath while we converse?" he asked suddenly, making her start.

"A . . . bath?" she repeated.

He nodded toward the bathtub in the corner. It was larger than the average bathtub, deliberately so, and had been fitted with the latest in plumbing technology.

Not that he'd talk to her about *that*.

"A companionable bath offers a lot in the way of warm . . . companionship," he said, feeling ridiculous for his words.

He sounded as though he had no idea what he was talking about, when—when he had no idea what he was talking about.

He just wanted to be warm and naked with her.

She gave him a winsomely crooked smile. "Why not?" she said. Her brow furrowed. "But you'll have to help me undress and then dress again."

"Of course," he said, rising. He held his hand out to her, and she took it, laughing a little as she stood. "I did before, if you remember."

"I do," she said. "I don't quite understand what is going on," she murmured in a lower tone, but loud enough for him to hear.

"I don't either," he admitted, "but I am enjoying it."

"Me too," she said, shooting him a smile.

She turned, gesturing to her back.

He put his hands to her buttons, his fingers undoing them one by one.

"Do all duchesses have quite so many buttons?" he asked after a few moments.

Her shoulders shook with laughter. "I have no idea. I've only ever had experience with the one duchess." She twisted her head to look at him. "Do I have an excess of buttons, in your experience?"

He leaned forward to press a kiss to the nape of

her neck, smiling as she shivered. "I don't remember anybody else when I am with you," he said.

"You are quite the charmer," she replied.

His fingers stilled. "I'm not being charming." He spoke sharply. "I'm not saying anything I don't mean." He lowered his voice, putting his mouth to her ear. "Besides, I've already had you. I don't need to persuade you into anything. Nor would I. You should be free to make your own decisions. Always." He paused. "But I do hope you decide to do it again."

She took a deep breath, then exhaled on a sigh.

His hands went back to work on the buttons, and then he was finally finished. He placed his palms on the flat of her back, though there were still layers of fabric between them. He pushed the gown to either side of her body. She began to draw the sleeves down, then stepped out of the gown, leaving her in her underthings.

She wore a corset over her chemise, and he hesitated over the laces for a moment before she nodded in assent.

"Nobody has—" she began, her voice sounding choked. "Nobody has been quite so honest with me before. At least," she amended, "not honest and complimentary," she added, sounding rueful.

Theo's chest burned with a sudden, fierce anger, that anybody would disrespect her. He had only known her for a short time, and yet he knew that she was kind, and caring, and sensitive.

"It's fine," she added hastily.

He must have reacted strongly enough that she was rushing to soothe him. Soothe him, when she was the one who had been insulted.

The last lace was undone, and then the corset was off as well. She turned around then, biting her lip.

The candlelight limned her body under the chemise, and he made a valiant attempt to keep his attention above her neck, even though every part of him—especially his cock—wanted him to look his fill.

"Are you going to get in with me?" she asked. Sounding hesitant, but also as though she was eager.

"If you like," he replied.

"I do like," she said, and the desire in her voice was palpable.

He held his arms out from his sides. "Do you wish to undress me then?"

She inhaled, a sharp gasp of surprise. "You would . . . ?" she began.

"I'd like it very much," he said. "Undress me, Angel."

ALEXANDRA DIDN'T FEEL anything she would have supposed she'd feel when standing nearly naked in front of a gentleman who was not her husband.

Actually, her late husband had never seen her like this either. When he'd come to her bed, she'd already been in it, wearing night rails that he just shoved up while he did what he came there for.

Her body was that of a forty-year-old woman; her belly was soft and rounded, from having Harriet and, in the past two years, having three biscuits at tea. She would have thought, then, that she would feel shame, or awkwardness, or embarrassment.

She felt none of those things.

Instead, she felt confident, and desirable, and natural.

That last one was the most surprising.

It felt right to be here with him, nearly un-clothed. Even though she wasn't thinking about doing anything salacious with him.

At least, not that much.

She put her hands on his shoulders, him standing still for her ministrations. It made her feel powerful, that he was allowing her to undress him.

Of course she knew he could take care of it himself—it wasn't as though gentlemen's cloth-ing was as difficult to maneuver as ladies'—but she wanted to do something of an equal exchange for him.

"I like you touching me," he said, his voice low and rumbly. She slid his jacket off his arms, then took it and laid it over the back of one of the chairs.

"I like touching you," she replied, meeting his gaze.

Her fingers undid his cravat, and then there was his bare throat. Strong, and delicious-looking.

She leaned forward to nuzzle him there, pleased again that they were nearly of a height.

She felt him swallow, and she chuckled against his skin. "I've barely started," she murmured.

"And I don't want you to ever stop," he said.

His hands were by his sides, still not touching her, as though he was waiting for her permission. Perhaps he was.

"You can touch me, you know," she said.

"Is that what you want?" he asked.

She drew back and put her fingers to the buttons of his shirt.

"Maybe not just yet," she said.

He arched a brow. "Making me wait is an exquisite torture," he said.

"Is it?" she asked, her tone innocent.

"You know it is, minx," he replied.

"And here I thought you thought I was an angel." She moved in closer to yank his shirt from his trousers, then slid her palms flat against his belly.

His lips curled into a slow, sensual smile. "Both can be true."

She knew that now. She owned that now.

She slid her hands up, her fingernails raking against his skin as he held his breath. She heard him inhale sharply as her fingernails brushed against his nipples.

"Too much?" she said, drawing back a step.

"No," he said, his voice ragged. "No. Keep going."

She tugged on the shirt, drawing it over his head, then laid it on top of his jacket.

He stood in his trousers and boots, and she frowned down at the latter.

"I suppose you should sit so I can take those off," she said.

He claimed the nearest chair, and she knelt in front of him. A reversal of their first time together, when he'd knelt in front of her. He held his feet out toward her, a grin on his face. "I like how you look at my feet," he said. "Though I like how I look at your feet better. Especially when I'm—"

She wrenched one boot off hard enough to make him lose his balance, and he wobbled on the chair before catching himself. He laughed, and she realized that for a moment she'd been waiting for him to yell at her, to tell her she was doing it all wrong.

Like her late husband used to.

But he wasn't the late duke. She had no tether to him beyond mutual desire, and she could leave if she wanted to. She wasn't obliged to do anything she didn't want to.

It was exhilarating.

The second boot joined its mate, and then she gestured for him to stand, rising herself as she did so.

She couldn't help but notice his trousers tented in the front—still, he made no move to touch her, or do anything that might take her power away.

He noticed her looking, and he grinned in response. "That's all you, Angel."

Her fingers went to the placket of his trousers. They trembled, and he put his hands on top of hers, stilling them. "We don't have to continue if you don't want to," he said, his voice low and solemn.

"I want to," she replied, and he drew his hands away. She immediately undid the buttons, tugging to bring the trousers down to the ground.

"Well," she breathed.

He stood in his smallclothes and stockings, his penis proudly erect, his eyes on her face.

She licked her lips, and he groaned. "Minx," he said.

She placed her palm on his chest again—so warm, so solid, so muscular—and drew it slowly down, keeping her gaze locked with his. "Do we need to call for water?" she asked.

He shook his head. "The Garden has the newest plumbing. We only need to turn the knob."

"Oh," she replied, surprised.

"Shall I?" he said, jerking his head toward the bathtub in the corner.

"Yes, please," she said.

Soon she heard the sound of running water and saw the steam rising from the tub.

"That looks heavenly," she said.

"It does," he replied, but he wasn't looking at the water, like she was, but at her.

She felt a shy smile spread across her face, and then she was pulling her chemise off, now only wearing her stockings. She shot him a quick glance, then leaned over to roll the stockings down, baring herself to him.

"Holy hell," he growled, and she grinned to herself.

Once her stockings were off, she put one toe into the water. Of course it was the perfect temperature—she wouldn't have expected anything less.

"Ahh," she sighed as she got in. She leaned against the back of the tub, the cool marble a welcome contrast to the heat of the water.

"Come in," she said, looking at him.

He shucked his smallclothes and stockings in a moment, then got in behind her, easing her so her back lay against his front.

The tub was enormous, clearly meant for at least two, if not more, people.

He wrapped one arm around her, his hand on her bicep, the other lying on the edge.

"What do you want to talk about?" he asked, his voice low.

IF ANYONE HAD asked Theo to list his favorite things to do, it would not be bathe with another person with no expectation of sex.

In fact, anonymous fucking—like he'd had the first night he met her—would have been top of the list, followed closely by the monthly book discussions with the Bastard Five.

Followed, likely, by other iterations of fucking and possibly completed with eating lemon ice on an exceedingly hot day.

And the last only because Mr. Osborne had

taken him, when Theo had first been adopted, out for ices during the height of summer, when most reasonable people who could afford to had left London.

But not Mr. Osborne, who understood how important it was to stay on top of his business concerns, regardless of the temperature.

Bathing with another human would not have crossed his mind.

And yet here he was, submerged in water, her pressed against his chest, his cock aching while he steadfastly tried to ignore it. Her gorgeous full breasts half in, half out of the water, one of her long legs stretched out, the other bent at the knee.

"The bath was a good idea," she said, not answering his question.

Not that he recalled precisely what his question was—she was too naked, and he was too heated, both from his desire and the bathwater, to remember.

Something about talking. She wanted to talk.

"Do you like lemon ice?" he asked.

She twisted her head to look at him, a surprised expression on her face. Then she shrugged and turned back around.

"I do," she said. "Not as much as chocolate, but lemon is particularly refreshing when it is hot."

He squeezed her arm. "Yes, exactly my opinion," he said, feeling a pure enthusiasm he hadn't experienced for years. Even the monthly book club was occasionally punctuated by discomfort, such as when one of the Five was arguing with another over something ridiculous.

"Do you like to play games?" she asked. Sounding as though she was truly asking, not using a double entendre.

"Are we back to discussing chess?" he said, pressing a kiss to her warm shoulder.

She laughed, leaning her head back against him. Her hair tickled his nose. "No. Though someday perhaps you will teach me how to play."

As though there was a future they might share.

"I like charades, and twenty questions," she continued, "though I haven't played either of those very often." She paused, and when she spoke again, her voice was fondly reminiscent. "Harriet always liked games, but my husband thought that games were for children."

"And Harriet was . . . ?" Theo said, not holding back the scorn in his tone.

"He was not the most rational person," she said.

He snorted. "It seems his son takes after him."

She twisted to look at him again. "Why did you even consider what William proposed?"

He kept his eyes on hers, sorting out his thoughts. "I suppose it is because my father, my adopted father, that is, always wanted me to be more than what I had been born as. He wished for me to enter Society as someone who belonged there, not someone who had bought his way in."

She opened her mouth, but he kept speaking. "But I know that no matter what, anyone who meets me will know just how I got into their world. And," he continued, the realization hitting him hard, "I don't care. I don't want to be in that world."

"*My* world," she said softly.

He pulled her tighter into him. "Not your world. You're just as unwilling a participant as I, only you were born into it. I would very much want to be in your world," he said, emphasizing the *your*.

She swallowed as she kept her gaze locked with his. "I wish I could be in my own world too," she said, and at that moment, he would have done anything to make that happen.

But it wasn't possible. Not just because he didn't have the power to extricate her, but also because he knew she would want only herself to be the cause of her liberation.

Instead, he asked, "What would your world look like?"

She turned back around, her voice thoughtful. "I'd like to be in a world where we are each responsible for ourselves. Where we make our own decisions, and suffer our own mistakes."

The thought crossed his mind that she had suffered a huge mistake already—marrying the late duke—but he also recognized that that hadn't been her mistake, but one someone else made for her.

"I'd like it to be acceptable for people to not have to spend time with people they don't care for."

"Like your stepson."

She let out a sharp laugh. "Yes. And Florence, his wife." She shook her head. "It isn't proper to admit you don't like members of your family, but I have to say, I do not."

"I don't like members of your family either," he replied, a wry tone in his voice.

She laughed, tilting her head back so he could see the lovely column of her throat.

"This is wonderful," she said, when she'd stopped laughing. She gestured in the air toward the two of them. "This, just—being. Without obligation."

He increased his grip on her arm. "I will never oblige you to anything," he said, his voice a low promise. "You deserve nothing less."

Chapter Thirteen

"I'll take the dowager duchess in my carriage."

William's words were not a request.

"Florence, Harriet, and Edith can ride in the other carriage."

Alexandra suppressed a grimace before turning to where one of the footmen stood waiting to help her into the carriage.

It wasn't one of the carriages her late husband had owned; nearly as soon as William had inherited, he had commissioned a new vehicle suitable to his own needs.

His needs, meaning, it appeared, to display his importance as prominently as possible. Whereas the earlier iteration of the carriage was comfortable, upholstered in velvet and with the ducal crest on the outside, William's carriage was upholstered with exceedingly rare and quite delicate silk, the result of which was to have the occupants sliding around on its slippery surface like they had skates on their backsides and they were sitting on ice.

Alexandra tugged her cloak under her, hoping she could anchor herself better for the journey. William followed, sitting on the seat opposite her.

Just as the door was about to close, Edith popped in, her expression full of mischief. "I've decided to ride with you two," she said, swinging herself in beside Alexandra.

William began to sputter, but the door swung shut, and they felt the lurch as the coachman and footmen got into their places.

"I wished to have a word with Alexandra," William ground out.

It was almost worth feeling like a wooden ball sliding across a highly polished floor to be able to see William's annoyance.

Almost.

"Go ahead and speak with her," Edith said in a sprightly tone. "I've got a book to occupy my time." She withdrew a book from her pocket, giving Alexandra a quick wink before opening the book and ostentatiously beginning to read.

"Well," William said, shooting his sister another narrowed look, "Mr. Osborne and I are working with the government—" he puffed himself up before continuing "—and he seems more amenable to the agreement we made."

"He does?" Alexandra said, speaking before she'd realized it.

Edith's eyes met hers, and her stepdaughter made a dismissive gesture, as though William had no idea what he was talking about.

"He knows it is in his best interest. But now," William said, his features hardening into a sour expression, "Harriet does not wish for the match."

"Oh?" Alexandra spoke in an innocent tone, as though she wasn't perfectly aware of her daughter's feelings.

"Oh," William echoed. "It will be up to you to persuade her otherwise."

"You mean to say," Alexandra began, "that it was my job to persuade Mr. Osborne to court my daughter, and now that he seems to be doing so, it is now my job to persuade my daughter to want to accept him?" She couldn't keep the disdain from her voice.

William didn't seem to register her fury. "Yes," he said, giving her a tight smile. "Very good."

"She's not a dog," Edith murmured, and Alexandra nudged her stepdaughter's shoulder.

"What did you say?" William asked, glaring at his sister. "You are welcome as my guest, Edith, but mind you stay out of things."

Edith lifted her hands in a gesture of surrender. Unfortunately, that meant she was no longer clutching the seat to steady herself and she pitched forward, falling onto the opposite seat and whacking William's knee with the book she was still holding.

He howled in pain, and Alexandra straightened Edith back onto the seat, though William refused any offer of assistance.

When everyone was settled down again—all

clutching the seat, Alexandra noticed—William picked up the topic again.

"I need not tell you what will happen if Mr. Osborne does not propose to Harriet," he said in a warning tone of voice.

"Perhaps you needn't tell Alex, but you can tell me," Edith said. She cocked her head at her brother. "What are you threatening her with?"

"This is none of your business," William said, sounding thunderous.

Alexandra put a warning hand on her step-daughter's arm. "I know the consequences, Your Grace," she said, meeting his gaze. "I know just what is at stake now."

My happiness, my daughter's happiness, and Edith's ability to keep her temper in check.

"Good," he said, giving his sister a sharp look.

And I'll be damned, she thought, *if I let you run roughshod over any of us.*

THEO AND FENTON arrived later in the day than Theo had planned. But Fenton needed to go make another few thousand pounds that morning or something, and Theo didn't want to keep his friend from genius-ing, especially since Fenton was doing him a favor.

Fenton's unique abilities had gotten him a sizeable fortune. Not as vast as Theo's, but healthy nonetheless. He'd taken a modest inheritance from his adoptive parents and invested it early on in domestic railway systems, then taken those profits and invested them into other budding enterprises, and now he was advising other wealthy gentlemen how to invest their monies.

It was teatime when Theo's carriage rolled up the drive to the duke's country house. Or, at least, one of them; Theo presumed any duke worth his salt had at least four or five of the things.

The house was enormous, as Theo had expected. It looked as though the original house had been added to by someone who didn't care for the original design; whereas the middle of the house, presumably the first iteration, was elegantly classical in design, the house got increasingly chaotic in style the further it spiraled out, so that either side of the house appeared to have been created by a fanciful pastry chef.

"Goodness," Fenton said as the carriage rolled to a stop.

"It's ridiculous, isn't it?" Theo replied.

"What is?" Fenton asked, sounding genuinely confused. The way most people sounded when speaking with Fenton, whose non sequiturs were legendary. "Certainly not Plato. I was trying to remember what he sees as the highest form of his ethical system. Goodness, that's what it is." He gave Theo a stern look. "Certainly not ridiculous. This is Plato we're discussing."

"You're discussing it, not—never mind, here we are."

A footman opened the door to the carriage, and

Theo and Fenton got out, looking up at the duke and his wife standing on the front steps. Deliberately, Theo thought, placing themselves above their guests in a literal representation of their status above everyone else.

Alexandra wasn't there. Was she here at all? She had to be. He knew her daughter was here, since that was the whole point of the visit.

And then he felt like an idiot for not asking her anything about this visit the night before. Instead he'd yammered on about lemon ices.

If she wasn't here—well, it would make everything far less pleasant, but he still had a job to do: figure out how best to solve his predicament.

"Welcome," the duke said, descending the stairs to greet them. "Lady Harriet and my stepmother are taking a walk in the gardens," he continued, his lips thinning.

Theo exhaled a breath he didn't realize he'd been holding.

"Thank you," Theo said. "May I present Mr. Ash?"

Fenton bowed as the duke gave him an appraising look. "You are welcome, Mr. Ash," he said. "We are about to take tea, if you'd like to wash up and join us?"

Theo would rather go find Alexandra in the garden, but he couldn't very well tell the duke that.

"Of course."

Thirty minutes later, he and Fenton were in a

vast salon, one stuffed with a hodgepodge of furniture styles, much like the building's exterior.

Gothic sideboards were set up against neoclassical chairs, while more modern pieces waged a valiantly fussy war against the stripped-down style of previous decades.

The duchess sat opposite them, wearing a gown that was almost fussier than the most ostentatious furniture items in the room. Made of watered silk, it was peach, and had flounces and ribbons and lace trimmings placed apparently at random, as though the dressmaker had been either drunk or suffering from vision loss.

Her hat was just as ridiculous, with several large feathers pointing straight up out of the crown. She wore gloves, and ruby bracelets on either wrist, with matching ruby earrings swinging from her ears.

"I can't imagine where Harriet and the dowager duchess are," she said, sounding disapproving.

Theo was just about to inform her that they were in the garden, or so her husband had said, when they heard movement at the door, and all turned to see the wayward ladies entering; Alexandra's face was flushed, and her eyes were bright.

Theo had never seen a more beautiful sight in his life.

Alexandra's daughter followed behind, her expression set, as though she wanted to make a face, but couldn't.

Theo and Fenton rose, and Theo stepped forward, swinging his hand out to indicate Fenton. "Good afternoon, my lady. Your Grace. May I present my friend, Mr. Ash?"

Fenton executed a faultless bow, making Theo wonder what corner of his odd brain that had been tucked away in. Surely Fenton hadn't had occasion to bow so deeply that often, and it wasn't as though his friend actually cared about societal norms.

"It is a pleasure to meet you, Mr. Ash," Alexandra said. She shot a quick glance toward Theo, then bit her lip, as though recalling the previous evening.

He couldn't stop thinking about it either, so he couldn't blame her.

"The tea is getting cold," the duchess said. "Do sit down, Harriet. Your Grace." She punctuated her command with pointing toward a chair as she spoke the two ladies' names.

They sat, Alexandra taking the seat next to Fenton, Harriet beside Theo.

"Harriet, do tell Mr. Osborne of your proficiency on the piano," the duchess said loudly, after the teacups were handed out and biscuits were offered.

Lady Harriet met Theo's gaze, a dryly sardonic look in her eye. "I am proficient on the piano, Mr. Osborne," she said, with all the enthusiasm of a piece of damp wood.

He smothered a chuckle, offering a solemn nod in reply. "I am pleased to hear it."

"Harriet will play after supper," the duchess continued.

Lady Harriet's eyes narrowed, and it looked as though she was going to contradict her sister-in-law, but Alexandra spoke instead.

"Mr. Ash, Mr. Osborne, do you enjoy music?"

Fenton, not at all perturbed by the sheer banality of the question, replied at length, talking about what effects varieties of music could have.

Apparently, some people—Fenton included—believed that music of the Baroque period encouraged diversity in thought, whereas earlier styles resulted in more regimented opinions.

"Mr. Osborne," Lady Harriet said in a low voice.

"Yes, my lady?" Theo said, turning to her.

He could see the resemblance to her mother; the large, wide-set eyes, the strong nose, and the shape of the mouth. But Alexandra had a presence, like a Greek goddess heading to war, whereas Lady Harriet looked as though she would inspire with lively conversation rather than action.

"I am sorry you had to come all this way," she said, speaking hurriedly while darting glances toward the duchess. "I want to make it clear that I have no intention of marrying you," she continued, color staining her cheeks.

"Oh," he said, too surprised by her forthrightness to say anything else.

Perhaps she was more like her mother than he'd thought.

"I've seen what marriage to someone you don't truly know can be like." She swallowed as she glanced toward Alexandra. "My mother is only starting to be who she should be. I want to be with her for as long as I can, and I do not want to live as she did." Her face was entirely pink now.

"Have you told your brother?" he asked, lowering his voice to a whisper. "He seems to think—"

"He thinks he can tell me what to do," she shot back. "I know he's told Mama she has to persuade me into it." She paused, then lifted her chin. "I also know Mama supports me absolutely."

"Oh, you two," the duchess said in a loud voice. Fenton and Alexandra both turned to look at them, Theo feeling his collar grow suddenly tight. "What are you whispering about? Something you cannot tell the rest of us, perhaps?" she continued in a sly tone.

What if Alexandra thought he had changed his—but no. She wouldn't.

"We're discussing a picnic, Your Grace," Lady Harriet said, so smoothly Theo wondered for a moment if that's what they had been speaking of. "If the weather is fine tomorrow, perhaps we could take our guests on a picnic on the grounds."

The duchess wrinkled her nose, and Theo wanted to clap Lady Harriet on the back for her quick thinking.

"Of course, if you think you would like that?" The way she spoke made it clear that a picnic was possibly the last thing she'd like.

Well, either that or a gown that wouldn't require a map to navigate around it.

"We would," Theo said. "Fenton and I both love picnics, don't we, Fenton?"

"Hmm?" Fenton said, apparently lost in his own Fenton world. "Yes. Whatever you say."

"Edith and I will go along as chaperones," Alexandra said, "so that William doesn't have to take time out of his schedule."

"Fine, of course," the duchess said, apparently bored of the topic.

AFTER SUPPER WAS finished, and Lady Harriet had been commanded to play, and dutifully complimented, and everyone had expressed how tired they were, Theo was finally able to escape to his bedroom. Which he promptly left, stepping into the hallway and walking quietly toward the opposite room.

He tapped on the door, and Fenton opened it within a minute, beckoning him inside.

Theo looked around the bedroom; like his own, this was done up in a far more restrained style than downstairs, leading him to believe the current duchess hadn't gotten her decorating hands on it yet.

The room was papered in a dark green, with green curtains on the two windows, while there were blessedly few pieces of furniture: only a bed, a wardrobe, a small side table, and two chairs arranged in front of the still glowing fire in the fireplace.

Theo sat in one of the two chairs, gesturing to Fenton to sit in the other.

"Lady Harriet doesn't want to marry me," he said, after Fenton had sat.

Fenton's expression was inquisitive, as though he was listening to a fascinating lecture.

"Did you want her to?"

"No, of course not. It's just that the whole point of this visit is so Lady Harriet and I can get to know one another, since her brother is so keen on us marrying. Only I have no interest in doing so, and it seems neither does she." Theo shook his head in a bemused wonder. "This would be a French farce if it wasn't my real life."

"I have no ide—" Fenton began.

"It's that I came here with the express purpose of figuring out how to get myself out of this situation, and it seems Lady Harriet has already solved the problem."

"But the duke doesn't agree, does he." It was not a question.

"No," Theo said, puzzling it out. "Lady Harriet might not have told him, since she intimated that the duke was threatening Alex—that is, the dowager duchess—with withholding her monies if her daughter didn't marry me." He dropped his head into his hands. "This is a mess."

"I think it's rather delightful," Fenton said, making Theo's head jerk back up in surprise. "Hear me out," Fenton continued. "All you have to do is delay long enough for Lady Harriet and her mother to come to their own resolution of their problem, and you needn't spend any brain thought on it."

"Brain thought?" Theo said, feeling his lips twitch into what might've been a smile.

"Exactly," Fenton said in an approving tone, as though Theo had solved a difficult sum.

And then what, Theo thought. *Then do I just return home to London and try to forget I ever met her?*

Even if I wanted to marry her, how could I ask her to marry a literal bastard? Giving up her freedom in the process?

But what will my life be like without her in it?

And why did that make him feel completely empty and lost?

Chapter Fourteen

$\mathcal{Y}$ou just . . . told him?" Edith said, sounding impressed.

Harriet nodded. "I thought he should know, so he doesn't get his hopes up. Though honestly," she said, frowning as she thought, "I think he was relieved." She turned to Alexandra. "Why would he be relieved? If he didn't wish to marry me, he could have just refused William's invitation."

Alexandra and Edith exchanged glances, and Alexandra put her hand on her daughter's arm.

They were in Harriet's bedroom—Alexandra had been given a guest bedroom a flight up, an indication of her lowered status in the house, and Edith was likewise on the same floor.

Harriet had been allowed to keep her former room after her father died, though she primarily lived with Alexandra in the dower house.

The room was spacious, three windows on each of the three walls, the fourth with a large door leading into the hallway.

William's and Florence's bedrooms—formerly Alexandra's and her husband's—were down the hall, but located far enough away that there was no chance they could hear anything.

Harriet sat on her bed, hugging a pillow to her chest, looking even younger than her years. "I just don't understand," she said. "How can William hold so much power?"

"Welcome to the patriarchy," Edith muttered.

Alexandra went to sit on her daughter's bed, wrapping her arm around her shoulder. "I know. I wish there was more that I could do—"

"Telling Mr. Osborne how you feel is an excellent beginning," Edith said. "Perhaps we can maneuver him into doing something William can't overlook?" she continued in a hopeful tone.

Alexandra glanced over at her stepdaughter. "Short of losing all of his money, I don't think there's anything Mr. Osborne *can* do."

"If he were to marry someone else . . . ?" Edith said, her tone deceptively innocent.

Alexandra narrowed her eyes. "That is not a possibility," she replied in a firm tone. Even the thought of it—of being tied to another gentleman, even one as charming and handsome as Theo— was enough to make her chest tighten. She felt as though she had emerged from a battle, and flinched from entering another one.

Marriage shouldn't be a battle, it shouldn't even

be any kind of conflict, and yet she felt terrified at the thought.

Yes, she could save her daughter, but at the cost of sacrificing herself. She would exhaust all other possibilities before entertaining that one. And besides, there was no guarantee Mr. Osborne would even want to marry her. He did desire her, she knew that, but she knew he valued his freedom as much as she did. They both liked lemon ices, and baths, and their time together.

Marriages were certainly built on less, but Alexandra didn't want any part of it. Especially since every marriage came with the knowledge that the female part of the union would be required to obey the male part.

She'd had enough of that for one lifetime, thank you very much. No matter how agreeable anyone might seem at first—there was always the danger of change. A woman such as herself could not take that risk.

"What if *I* marry someone else?" Harriet said, then immediately scowled. "I don't want that either. Having to agree with your husband all the time, the way Florence does? No thank you."

Alexandra suppressed a smile at hearing Harriet say—much more succinctly—what she'd just been thinking.

"Not every potential husband is as decided in opinion as William is," Edith pointed out. "Or as frequently wrong."

Harriet shook her head. "No. I cannot." She leaned her head against Alexandra. "I deserve more than being forced into a situation mere weeks after I am able to partake in life."

Alexandra squeezed Harriet's shoulder. "You do," she said. "You do." That wasn't enough, though. She had to make it clear to Harriet, as had never been made clear to her, that Harriet had a choice.

"More than that," she began, "I want you to do whatever you need to, as long as you are safe, to keep from being forced into anything you do not wish." She took a deep breath. "I will support you, no matter what you decide."

It was all that Harriet deserved. She was her own person, not a pawn in William's schemes. She deserved better.

And so did Alexandra.

THEO AROSE THE next morning feeling an unaccustomed ache in his chest. He'd spent the night in a restless sleep, his dreams punctuated by images of Alexandra, of imagining various scenarios he knew were untenable—never seeing her intimately again, conducting a public affair with her, persuading her to marry him.

Telling her how he felt about her.

Because whenever he thought about her, he got that very same ache in his chest—an ache of longing, and potential heartbreak. He'd never experienced that before in his long line of love affairs.

Why was she different?

Though that was a disingenuous question—there were myriad answers, from her curiosity, to her intelligence, her kindness, and her vulnerability. Her honest enjoyment of sex didn't hurt either, though he'd had that with other women.

But he wanted to be the only person she was ever intimate with again. Beyond their temporary arrangement. An irrationally possessive thought, given that he had no claim on her. He couldn't, and wouldn't, prescribe what she was to do with the rest of her life.

Could he convince her he was a choice to make for perpetuity?

Did he want that?

He did. He'd gone and fallen in love with her, and he knew how tightly she held her freedom. But he wanted them, wanted her, in a way he'd never wanted anything before.

Now he had to figure out how to get it.

And how to survive if he didn't.

Because he would not persuade her into something that wasn't her choice.

Goddamn it, he loved her.

He dressed quickly, not ringing for a valet; the duke had been surprised when Fenton and Theo had arrived without personal staff, but the two of them had done for themselves for long enough to find additional people around a hindrance rather than any kind of help. The duke had offered one of his footmen as a substitute, but Theo preferred to take care of himself.

In most situations, in fact.

Once downstairs, he was directed toward the morning room, where he found a long dining table and a sideboard filled with every sort of breakfast item imaginable: bacon, sausages, toast, porridge, rolls, and eggs, as well as a variety of preserves.

He filled a plate, then sat as one of the footmen prepared his tea.

The duke entered soon thereafter, his immediate reaction of displeasure displaced by a forced smile. "Good morning, Mr. Osborne. I trust you slept well?"

The duke jerked his chin toward the side table, and another of the footmen sprang into action, filling a plate with several items, then put it in front of the duke, who had seated himself at the head of the table.

"I did, thank you," Theo replied. "I believe the plan today is to go on a picnic?"

That distasteful expression again. "Yes, the duchess mentioned that."

That Theo was even considering allying himself with the duke's family was a testament to the strength of his feelings—he couldn't stand the man, he had no wish to ever spend time with him, and yet here he was hoping he could become a permanent addition to his life.

Ugh. Love did terrible things to a man.

"Good morning." Fenton strode into the room,

his appearance marking the distinct lack of a valet—his hair was a mess, his buttons were askew, and it looked as though he was wearing two different shoes, but to be fair, even a valet couldn't help if Fenton was determined enough.

"Morning," Theo replied, while the duke merely nodded.

Fenton was visibly enthusiastic about the breakfast offerings, piling his plate with more food than Theo could eat in a day.

"Picnic today, eh?" he said, before spearing a sausage.

"Yes, so it seems," the duke replied, already sounding weary of the topic. "I will order a basket for you."

"I've already taken care of that," Alexandra said, entering the room. "I know Florence is already taking care of so much, I thought I would go ahead and speak to the housekeeper."

"Thank you," the duke said, his mouth pressed into a thin line. "Though Florence has everything well in hand. There is no need to bother."

"It's not a bother," Alexandra replied, waving a hand. Apparently wanting to provoke the duke by continuing to assert herself.

Theo had to admire that, though he didn't think it would do anything but irritate the man.

Or perhaps that was the point?

She settled herself at the table, nodding with a thank-you when the footman inquired about tea.

"You will ensure Mr. Osborne and Mr. Ash get a tour of the grounds," the duke said. It wasn't precisely an order, but it certainly sounded like one.

"I will indeed," Alexandra replied, offering a smile to each of the two men.

The duke tossed his napkin onto his plate and rose. "If you will excuse me, I have some work I need to attend to."

He didn't wait for a reply before striding out of the room, his bearing rigid, his whole mien one of disapproving unpleasantness.

"He's kind of an ass, isn't he?" Fenton said in a casual tone.

One of the footmen suppressed a chortle, while Theo winced. "You can't be blunt like that, Fenton," he said.

Alexandra held up a hand. "I, for one, appreciate that kind of honest opinion." She turned her head to address the footmen. "We do appreciate your discretion."

They nodded, looking uncomfortable, and Theo took that as a reason to rise; he didn't want Fenton's unguarded tongue to say anything else that would reflect on their employer. He and Fenton were just visiting, but these people's livelihood depended on the duke's goodwill.

Which reminded him that other people's livelihoods also depended on the duke's goodwill—that goodwill depending on Theo following through on what he and the duke had discussed by marrying the duke's half sister.

What a complicated mess he'd gotten himself into.

Alexandra rose as well, followed quickly by Fenton, who could be polite when he wished to; he just didn't normally wish to. And he was wealthy enough that his idiosyncrasies were just that—idiosyncrasies—and not blatant rudeness.

Money compensated for a lot.

"Would you be able to meet in the foyer in an hour? For our picnic and vast tour of the grounds?" A wry smile curled her lips, and Theo couldn't help but smile in response.

"Yes, that sounds perfect," he replied. "Come on, you," he said, speaking to Fenton, "let's go share some unguarded opinions in private."

An hour and a half later, Alexandra, Harriet, Edith, Theo, Mr. Ash, and a small cadre of footmen set out, heading for the park at the northwest end of the estate. The day was mild; not hot, but not cold either. Just cool enough so it wasn't an unpleasant prospect to walk a mile or two.

Alexandra walked with Theo, while Harriet, Edith, and Mr. Ash followed behind. The three of them began a lively discussion about their respective love of books, with Mr. Ash holding the most diverse tastes, ranging from scientific treatises to Gothic fiction.

"That should keep them occupied for some time," Theo observed in a low, amused voice. "Fenton never tires of discussing books—we have a monthly book meeting, and usually he's read not only the book under discussion, but all the rest of the author's works."

"You meet monthly to discuss books?" Alexandra said in an incredulous tone.

"What, you think I spend my days making money and my nights—well, you know," he said. He sounded almost embarrassed at what he nearly said aloud, and Alexandra smothered a smile. "I do have interests other than that and lemon ices," he said, mock reproof lacing his voice.

She nudged his shoulder with hers. "I know that. I suppose I am just surprised to find one of your other interests is books." She shrugged. "That is my own prejudice, I suppose."

"And your prejudice is pricking my pride," he quipped, making her laugh in response.

"So I know you read novels, even romantic ones," she said. "That shouldn't surprise me, but it does."

"You like to read, then?" he asked, eager.

"Yes. I've read so much during the past two years," she replied, her tone softly reminiscing. "All the things that my husband deemed unsuitable, or were too much of a bother to get." She gave him a wry glance. "As if we couldn't just summon someone and ask." She had been rebellious in a tiny way back then, she realized. "But I've read Ann Radcliffe, and loads of poetry, and Dickens, of course, and some American authors like Cooper and Hawthorne."

"We have those tastes in common," he said, and that he shared this with her made her heart squeeze in her chest.

"Harriet says she spoke to you yesterday," Alexandra said after another moment. There would be time—at least she hoped there would be—to talk books, but she needed to seize this moment of privacy.

"Yes. Speaking of surprised—I was certainly startled to hear that your daughter has no interest in marrying me. If I weren't just as set on not marrying her, I might have been insulted," he continued, his tone of voice gentle. "But none of us have come up with a solution to the problem, have we?"

"No," Alexandra said, thinking of Edith's suggestion—*If he were to marry someone else . . . ?* But she couldn't mention that. He was a gentleman, and he might fall on the matrimonial sword, so to speak, by marrying someone else, if she were to bring it up as a solution.

And while she didn't want to marry him, she also didn't want anyone else to.

Very selfish, Alexandra, she thought.

"What are you thinking about?" he asked. "All of a sudden your body went rigid, and then you sighed, and not in a pleasant way."

He was far too perceptive. "I want my daughter to be able to make her own choices," she said.

"Unlike you?" he said.

More perception.

"Yes," she replied firmly. She glanced up as she considered it. "Unlike Harriet, I didn't even realize choice might be an option for me. My parents told me I was to marry, and told me who it would be, and I didn't question it." Until a few months into the marriage, when she realized she was likely to be unhappy until one or the other of them died.

"Which is why you are so adamant about choice now," he said. He gave her a long, assessing look. "I want you, Alexandra. I think I've been clear about that, but let me state it in no uncertain terms now. However, I will not do a thing to press the matter. Not unless you ask."

"Oh," she said, on an exhale. "Nobody's ever—"

"I know," he said, "nobody has ever given you that choice before. But I have. I will. I am. Which means," he continued, his voice tight, "if you wish me never to speak of anything of the sort again, you can choose that as well."

"No, I don't," she said, then rushed to continue speaking as he stiffened beside her. "I mean, I don't want you to stop speaking of it." She took a deep breath. "I want to continue, in fact. We can't take a bath here," she said, her tone amused, "but we could find other things to do. Thankfully, I am not as hampered by protocol now that I am a widow. And twelve years older than you—no one would ever expect the two of us to—"

He squeezed her hand. "Stop that. You are older, yes, but that just means you're more seasoned."

"Like I'm a fancy entrée?" she teased.

"If you mean that I'd have a taste for both, then precisely."

She felt herself color, and glanced away. "You're very . . . direct."

"I thought you appreciated a direct opinion. Isn't that what you said before?"

She tilted her head in an implicit affirmation. "When Mr. Ash said what he did about William. You're correct."

"So what do we do now?" he asked.

She jerked her chin toward the park, which was just a few yards away. "I believe we stop and have a picnic, Mr. Osborne."

"That isn't what I meant, and you know it, minx," he said in a low tone.

He turned to speak to the other three in their party. "It seems we're there, and I presume we're all hungry," he said before shooting a quick, meaningful glance toward Alexandra, who felt herself color even more. Hopefully the others would just blame it on the sun, if they noticed.

She followed him as he appraised the area, checking with her about the best place to set up their picnic. Once decided, they directed the footmen where to put the baskets and other supplies, then dismissed the staff—it would be terribly rude to keep them waiting, standing, while they lolled around on the grass, and besides, Alexandra didn't want to put them into the position of hearing too many of Mr. Ash's opinions.

And then they had the afternoon stretched ahead of them—Alexandra was supposed to be spending time with Mr. Osborne in order to convince him to marry Harriet, after all.

Meanwhile, Harriet didn't want that, Edith knew all the complications of the matter, Alexandra was keenly aware of every movement Theo made, and Mr. Ash was likely to notice and then announce it all for everyone's ears at any moment.

But at least she wasn't *bored*, Alexandra thought wryly.

Chapter Fifteen

*O*h, I never want to see another piece of food again," Harriet said, collapsing onto her back with a groan.

"Until dinnertime," Edith said, smirking at her niece.

They had eaten most of the food packed in the baskets, and drunk a fair amount of the wine. The sun had hidden behind some clouds, and so it was a bit chillier, but that was likely for the best, since the combination of full bellies and warm sun would mean several hours of falling asleep and likely getting burnt.

The five of them sat in a circle on one of the large spreads the staff had provided. They'd talked while they'd eaten, a comfortable conversation ranging on topics as wide as politics, the weather, gardening advice, favorite sandwiches, and the thing one would miss most if they moved out of England.

He now knew she liked to garden, aligned with

him on most topics of public policy, and would miss seeing the variety of English gardens if she ever moved.

Theo had wondered if it would be awkward being around Lady Harriet, what with her announcing she had no intention of marrying him—but it wasn't. Rather, she seemed to slip quickly into a younger sister role, albeit one who had absolutely the wrong opinion as to the best sandwich, which she insisted was watercress, and he knew absolutely was roast beef.

"Fenton," Harriet said, after five minutes of lying on her back and groaning while holding her stomach, "would you want to go for a walk? Edith too, I suppose, since I need a chaperone," she said, wrinkling her nose. Theo noticed with amusement that Fenton had become Fenton, and not Mr. Ash, to both the ladies after only an hour's worth of conversations.

"I could come if Edith doesn't wish to," Alexandra said. She still sat upright, a glass of wine in her hand, her mouth stained red from the beverage.

Lady Harriet nodded toward her mother's glass. "You're still eating. Edith doesn't mind, do you?"

In response, Lady Edith scrambled upright, brushing stray pieces of grass from her gown. "Not at all. Come along, you two."

Fenton and Harriet rose as well, Fenton giving Theo a sharp look. Theo didn't know what it meant, just that it was likely significant.

He'd just have to ask later; he didn't always speak nonverbal Fenton.

The three tromped off into the woods just beyond the park, Theo and Alexandra watching their departure.

"It's just us again," Theo observed with a smile. "Does your daughter suspect anything?" He gestured between the two of them. "Just because this keeps happening."

Alexandra's expression grew considerate. "I would have said no, but she's been surprising me lately. She is more observant than I realized," she added. "I haven't asked what she wants because she's told me what she wants." She gave him a sly glance. "And doesn't want."

"Your daughter is enough like you, it seems, that she doesn't have to be asked as to what she wants."

Alexandra snorted. "I wish I could claim that for myself, but I think it's only after being on this earth for forty years that I know enough to even ask in the first place."

He paused for a moment, then met her gaze. "What would you ask for, if you could?"

How would she respond? He hoped, of course, that she might be feeling more . . . feelings, as he was, and would express them, since she admired honest opinions. Though he didn't think so. Given how adamant she was that her daughter not be forced into anything, he didn't think she'd view a lifelong commitment as something to even consider.

And he'd promised not to try to persuade her into anything, hadn't he?

A small smile played about her lips. "I would ask for—for you, to do with what I would." She shot a quick glance at him from under her lashes. "Would that be too forward?"

"Never," he said, taking her hand in his. He stroked the skin of the back of her hand, then turned it around and drew it up to his mouth, placing a kiss on her palm.

"Oh," she said on a sigh.

He inclined his head to where the three others had left. "Do you suppose we have time to . . . ?"

"To . . . ?" she asked, arching a brow.

"Do you want me to say it?" he demanded.

"Yes, please," she replied, sounding demure, even though her expression was anything but.

"Well," he said, sliding his fingers up her arm, then to her neck, to where her pulse beat, "I have to say I've been craving your taste."

Her eyes widened. "I hadn't expected that," she said, her voice low and breathy.

"Did you think I would ask for just a kiss?" He leaned over, cupping her jaw in both his hands now, angling her face toward him. "I could do that," he said in a whisper, his mouth almost touching hers, "and then I could kiss you there, right where you're aching for me. You're aching, aren't you, Angel? Right here?" And he cupped her there, right on her mound, and she could feel the weight of his palm even through the fabric of her skirts.

"Mmm-hmm," she said, her eyes fluttering shut.

He captured her mouth then, sliding his tongue over her lips, urging them open as he stroked the soft skin of her jaw.

She put her hands on his arms, dragging him down on top of her as she leaned back onto the spread that lay on the grass.

He followed her lead, their tongues sliding over one another, their soft breaths joining the birds' songs and occasional insect buzz as the only noises they could hear.

God, she was so intoxicating—just the way she kissed him, as though she'd never kissed anyone before, but was also keenly interested in learning, because it felt so goddamned good.

She felt so goddamned good.

His cock throbbed in his trousers, pressed against one of her thighs, and he shifted, making the friction even more acute.

As though she knew what he was doing, she laughed, low in her throat, her hands now sliding around his shoulders, down his back, and onto his arse.

Which she palmed and squeezed, pushing him even closer to her. His erection was nearly painful, but he didn't want to stop kissing her—didn't ever want to stop kissing her—and he ignored it, instead sliding his fingers over her throat, her neck, to her neckline, where he slipped one finger underneath the fabric as she squirmed under him.

She gave a low, soft moan, arching her back so

her breasts pushed against him. He spread his fingers to create more space between her skin and the fabric, and was able to fit his palm underneath. It was awkward as hell, but he didn't care. His hand moved to cup her breast, and it felt so good he nearly lost his mind.

He'd like to fuck her breasts, slide his cock between those two gorgeous mounds as she held them together, watching him from her desire-lidded eyes, knowing he would be more than reciprocating eventually.

Thinking about that made him break the kiss, knowing they only had a certain amount of time together. He moved down her body, grabbing the hem of her gown and raising it, tucking his head underneath, immediately smelling her warm, musky fragrance, feeling the heat of her body surround him.

He put one hand on either leg, spreading them wide as he kissed, first her knee, then just above, then nuzzled her there, where he could already feel how wet she was.

"That's it, Angel," he said, more to himself than to her, his fingers grazing her inner thighs as they wound their way to her mound.

Her knees splayed open, and he slid his hands under her buttocks, raising her a little so he could better reach her with his mouth.

"Mmm," he said, just as he kissed her there, ran one long, slow lick up her pretty pussy. She jerked, and he chuckled against her skin, burying his face into her, inhaling all of her soft, sweet scent.

He licked her again, another long, slow lick that made her gasp and shift.

"Please," he heard her say, and he brushed her clit with his tongue, making her yelp, then took pity on her and placed his mouth over the tiny bud, kissing it with measured thoroughness, his fingers kneading the soft flesh of her arse.

Gorgeous. All of her was gorgeous, and he kept up his rhythmic kissing, licking, and sucking her until he felt her legs tense and start to shake, her hands gripping his head over the skirt of her gown, all of her trembling as he brought her to climax, a shuddering spasm that seemed to last for hours as he kept kissing her there, until she cried out and sobbed, and he nipped at her inner thigh, then eased his way back out from under her skirts.

She raised herself up on her elbows to look at him, a warm, sleepy smile seeming to fill her expression as he tasted her on his lips.

Better than anything he'd ever tasted. More addictive than the most delicious food he'd ever had—she was the most delicious thing he'd ever had, and he wanted nothing more than to go back under and do it again, bring her to another shuddering climax that would make her bones melt and her worries dissolve under the euphoria.

But the others might return at any minute, and he wouldn't risk that for her.

For him, maybe. But not for her.

So instead, he dragged himself back up to lie beside her, turning to look at her face, see the sparkle in her eyes. He brought his fingers to his mouth and drew them in, licking every bit of her off, watching as her eyes tracked the movement, wide with excitement and sated passion.

"Whatever you want to ask for, Angel, I will give it to you," he promised, his voice raw and husky.

She licked her lips, then bit them, and he couldn't resist leaning over to kiss her, just a soft, gentle kiss that he hoped might convey some of the emotion he felt, but didn't dare say—he wouldn't oblige her to anything, and he wouldn't ask her for anything. Ever.

Instead, he'd give whatever she wanted.

Until she didn't ask anything of him at all. When they had gone their separate ways, and all he had left were memories.

ALEXANDRA'S HEAD FELT as though it was made of cotton—well-pleasured cotton.

She lay on her back, staring up at the sky, but not seeing anything. Just feeling. How it felt when they'd kissed, how it felt as he kissed her there, and how it felt when it was all over.

She'd never realized, though of course she should have, that these kinds of activities could be done out of doors, during the daylight hours. Her previous experience had been contained strictly in the bedroom, her bedroom, and there had been only one candle lit, just to provide light so her husband could enter and exit without stumbling over anything.

That it was outside made it feel even more splendid—not because she wanted to be caught or anything, but because what they were doing felt so natural, so true, and here they were in nature, alongside other species that did the same thing.

Not that she'd compare her own experience with that of a fox, say, or a badger, but at least the context was similar.

She laughed to herself at how ridiculous her thoughts were. The result of that much bliss, she supposed.

He lay beside her, one arm flung over his eyes, the other holding her hand at their sides. He seemed perfectly content to just let her be, think her thoughts, while he presumably did the same.

This . . . was Heaven. This was lovely.

This was . . . not real life.

The thought snapped her out of her reverie, and she sat up, so suddenly she felt light-headed, and not in a good way. She released his hand as she did so as well, and she felt the lack of contact immediately.

Ridiculous, given what they'd just done.

"What is it?" he asked, his arm still over his eyes. "Something has upset you."

Perceptive. Was he like that with everyone, or just her?

Did it matter?

After a few moments' thought, she knew it did. "I'm thinking."

He tapped her hip with the hand that she'd been holding. "Stop it. It's not worth it."

She rolled her eyes. "Imagine if you stopped thinking about your business for more than a week or so. Or, I have no idea—how long could you go? Wouldn't things fall apart if you didn't think about them?"

He sat up also, turning his head to squint at her. "Is this about your stepson? I was hoping that this—" he said, gesturing between them, a smirk on his handsome face "—would have pushed all thoughts of that ass away."

She shook her head, though she was smiling also. "Yes, it did help, thank you," she replied in a prim tone. "But my mind keeps wrestling with it, and I can't seem to find a solution. At least not one that doesn't compromise someone's life."

"I could just give your stepson my money," he said, sounding entirely casual, as though he hadn't just offered to do something extraordinary.

"No, you can't," she replied in a flat tone. "He'll take it, and then spend it, and then try to sell Harriet off to the next bidder—perhaps someone who isn't as kind and thoughtful as you." Someone who was not having sexual relations with Harriet's mother.

"You think I'm kind and thoughtful?" he asked.

She rolled her eyes. "*That's* what you gleaned from what I just said?"

He reached over to take her hand again, clasping it in his. "No, of course not. I know you're thinking about it all the time, even when—" and he made that vague, yet immediately understandable gesture, again. Making her blush at what they'd done. "And I wish I could solve it—money does cure a host of problems, to be certain." He sounded absolutely frustrated that it wasn't as easy as throwing pound notes toward it. "Though not this one, I see that. William couldn't be persuaded to let Lady Harriet make up her own mind?"

She gave him a dry look. "Do you truly believe that is even a possibility?"

He snorted. "I suppose not."

"In my experience," she added, "men don't respond well when you try to persuade them into anything. Women are the ones who have to bend or we'll break."

He gave her an intense, searching look, and she felt as though he understood what she was saying. Understood her.

"I wonder where they are," she said after more time had passed. "Do you suppose we should go look for them?"

He frowned, pushing to his feet as he glanced at the sky. "It is past time for them to have returned, I'd say."

Alexandra felt a fierce panic well up inside of her. Theo grabbed her hand, threading it through his arm. "We'll walk back to the house and see if they returned there. They said they might, didn't they?"

She couldn't recall. She'd been thinking too much about everything to notice—just that she'd been pleased Harriet had been seeming to enjoy herself, despite the awkward situation.

They walked quickly back to the house, Alexandra feeling sweat slide down her back because of their rapid pace, and the sun, which had decided to make a late appearance.

She ran up the stairs, holding her breath as the doors opened, revealing one of the footmen, who picked up a silver salver from one of the side tables. "There is a letter for you, Your Grace," he said, holding it out to her.

She took it, seeing Harriet's familiar writing, tearing the letter open and reading it with trembling hands.

She turned to look at him. "They've gone," she said flatly, feeling as though the world had tilted sideways. "Your friend, Edith, and Harriet. They've gone."

The footman picked up another letter, placing it on the same silver salver and holding it toward Theo. "A letter for you as well."

Chapter Sixteen

"What do you mean, gone?" the duke thundered.

Theo resisted the urge to define the word for him. That would be something Fenton would do in the same situation, and while it had its appeal, it wouldn't be helpful.

He glanced to Alexandra, giving her a moment to reply, if that was what she wished. She met his gaze, giving her head a small shake.

"Gone, Your Grace. To Paris, it seems. All three of them."

He unfolded Fenton's letter, which was as direct as his friend ever got:

Theo:

We all talked about it while on our walk, and decided that things would be best if we just removed Lady Harriet from the premises. Lady Edith and I are taking her to Paris, since we were talking about croissants. I have enough money, and we'll ensure her safety, if the dowager duchess is concerned. We'll return, perhaps, when things have settled down.

F.

"Paris?" the duke repeated, as though Paris was akin to saying they'd gone to the moon.

The city in France? Theo considered offering, since it sounded as though the duke might not know where it was. But he knew that would not be helpful either.

The last sentence—*We'll return, perhaps, when things have settled down*—was so typically Fenton, he would have laughed if it would not have been completely inappropriate.

The duke turned to Alexandra, whose eyes were red from crying, her hands clutching a linen handkerchief. "This is your fault. If you hadn't allowed her to—"

"Allowed her to what?" Alexandra interrupted, stepping forward to gaze down into the duke's eyes. "Express her opinions? I know she spoke to you about this marriage," she said, waving toward Theo, "and that she wanted more time before making such a final decision."

The duke's expression shifted briefly to a nervous one. Then his natural bullying instinct seemed to reemerge. "What does a young woman need time for in deciding this type of thing? It is decided for her."

Alexandra pointed at the duke, her eyes narrowed. "And that is why she left. She might have stayed, we might have worked something out, if you hadn't been so implacable."

"So now it's my fault?" the duke said, his voice rising in anger.

Theo spread his hands out in what he hoped would be a calming manner. "We can point fingers—" literally in Alexandra's case "—all evening, but that will be an exercise in futility."

"You have to fix this," the duke said, glaring at his stepmother. "You filled her head with nonsense, so you have to fix this."

Alexandra flung her hands up. "How do you suggest I do that? Go to Paris and drag her back?"

The duke nodded. "Precisely. That."

She glanced over at Theo, as if in disbelief.

"I will go with you," he said, "if you wish." Something he could do, in all these times of feeling frustrated by his inability to just solve everything.

"And why would you go with her?" the duke demanded.

It was on the tip of his tongue to blurt out that it was because he loved her, and he wanted to persuade her to commit to him for the rest of their lives, but he knew this definitely wasn't the time, place, or ideal audience.

And he had the sinking suspicion, based on everything she'd told him, that she wouldn't be persuaded into anything. Despite how much he loved her.

"I suppose it makes as much as sense as anything else," the duke continued in a grudging tone of voice. "Nobody will think it untoward for the two of you to be traveling together, and that way we can keep the gossip from spreading." He gave Alexandra a look full of disdain. "It is not as though anyone will think you and him—" he said, rolling his eyes.

Alexandra's expression made it look as though she was going to blurt everything out, so Theo stepped forward and clapped the duke on the back, making him stagger a little. "Excellent idea, Your Grace. We'll be on our way in the morning then."

The duke looked nonplussed, as Theo had intended, while Alexandra still looked furious, but at least she wasn't revealing anything she would regret later.

Theo wouldn't regret it if she told the world what they'd been doing, but he didn't want her to take away whatever choices she'd been able to take for herself. Even though, selfishly, that would mean he could achieve his own ends.

"I'll pack this evening," Theo said. "Could you ask the staff to send a tray up for me? I don't think any of us will feel like socializing over dinner."

The duke gave a derisive snort, glaring at Alexandra, who glared right back.

While Theo appreciated that she was displaying her backbone, he didn't want her to say anything that would cause the duke to do anything rash, financially or otherwise.

"Your Grace," he said, taking her elbow, "could we discuss the best route? I believe your stepson has some maps in his library."

Her natural politeness took over, and she nodded, walking out of the room and toward the duke's study.

Theo followed, watching the rigid set of her back and how her hands were clenching and unclenching by her sides.

He wished there was something he could do to ease her mind, but he couldn't know what she was concerned about most: her daughter's safety, the harebrained nature of the whole dashing off to Paris thing, or that this action might force her stepson into enforcing even stricter controls.

ALEXANDRA WAS ABLE to sleep, remarkably, though her dreams were anxiety-filled, with her always being late to something or not being able to find something crucial.

It was impossible to miss the direct correlation to her life and her current worries.

She had packed quickly, not leaving it to the maid who'd been serving as her lady's maid while she was at the country house. She didn't need any fancy ball gowns or any of the new items she'd bought from Madame Lucille; instead, she chose her most serviceable gowns, though even they were relatively elegant.

It was nine o'clock in the morning when a drab coach pulled up in front of the country house. Alexandra had been expecting one of the ducal carriages, and she gave a puzzled look as Theo leapt down from the seat.

"What?" she began.

He took her elbow and spoke in a quiet tone in her ear. "It would be better if we travel anonymously, and that means no crests, and no servants. I will drive us back to London, and we can take a steam packet across. We'll have to pose as man and wife as well."

"Man and—" she began, but he continued laying out his plan.

"I thought it all out," he said, his grip tightening. "If we were to say we were siblings, then we would be given separate rooms. That would mean that I couldn't protect you, if one of the places we stay at has an unsavory clientele."

"Protect me?" she replied, feeling her chest get tight. "I am perfectly—"

"You're not, Alexandra," he said, cutting her off. Leaving her furious. But at least that emotion felt powerful, as though she might be able to do something about it rather than just worry.

And she knew, if she asked him to, that he would let her vent her fury on him. In any number of interesting ways.

"You're intelligent, and kind, and determined,

and an excellent mother, but none of that will disarm a large gentleman when he's had too much drink and not enough respect for other humans."

"I suppose," she admitted grudgingly. It did make sense, even though she wished it didn't. And then she thought about it—sharing a room with him. Behaving as though they were actually married.

If she weren't out of her mind with worry about Harriet, she might actually enjoy the subterfuge.

He hesitated, an odd expression on his face. "We could—we could tell your stepson. About us, I mean."

She gaped at him. "What?" she said.

"You could marry me," he continued. "It would solve most, if not all, of your problems." He drew a deep breath. "You would have your freedom. Harriet wouldn't have to marry me. I would make the same arrangement with your stepson he was willing to make for Harriet."

"Are you—are you serious?" she asked. Feeling both bewildered and angry.

And then the anger took over.

"Have you not been listening to me?" she began. "I cannot do that, ever again." Her voice was shaking. She was shaking. "I cannot."

He had his hands up in surrender before she finished speaking. "I know," he said, sounding as though he was reassuring a skittish horse. "I know you cannot. I just wanted to—"

"You wanted to solve everything with your

money and your penis," she snapped, then gasped, startled by her own words.

He gave a rueful nod. "I see that, yes. I am sorry I said anything—please forget it ever happened."

She gave him a narrow look. "Only if you promise it will not happen again. Only if you agree to continue as we have been, without any other complications."

He exhaled. "I promise, Angel."

THEY WERE ON their way within half an hour, Theo skillfully steering the team of horses down the long drive and onto the road leading, he said, to London, where they'd board a steam packet for Calais, and then travel to Paris from there.

"Would they have taken the same route?" Alexandra asked.

They'd been on the road for two hours already, and neither of them had spoken much—Alexandra was too caught up with worrying about Harriet to engage in conversation. She presumed Theo knew that, and was giving her the quiet and privacy she needed.

Or he was staying quiet because he knew he'd misstepped.

Theo snorted. "Probably not." He sounded relieved. That she'd spoken to him? "Likely Fenton figured out some sort of way to bypass whatever it is he wishes to bypass—usually people or inefficiency—and so there's no predicting how he'd take them, or when they'd arrive."

She frowned. "Is it possible we would get there ahead of them? And we haven't even talked about how to find them, once we're there."

Theo glanced over at her, a wry smile on his lips. "It's difficult for Fenton to stay hidden for long. He's altogether too . . ."

"Interesting?" she supplied.

He laughed. "Exactly. I would also add aggravating, idiosyncratic, and remarkably obstinate, but *interesting* is an excellent beginning."

"Your Mr. Ash doesn't seem to have to worry about how he's perceived," she observed. Trying not to sound piqued.

Theo shrugged. "I assume he notices that people find him odd. It definitely bothered him when we were young. But he had us to protect him, and he learned how to ignore what other people thought. Our friend Bram pointed out that Fenton didn't care about anybody but the four of us and his adoptive family. So why should he care what others thought about him?"

"I wish I'd had a Bram in my life," she said.

He turned, regarding her with an intense look. "You have me, Alexandra. No matter what, no matter what happens between us, you have me." His expression relaxed, but she felt the force of his emotion still. "And because of that, you are free to borrow any of the rest of the Bast— That is, my friends, that you wish. Especially Simeon."

"What were you going to say?" she asked, smiling.

"The Bastard Five. Not quite appropriate to speak so in mixed company, but—"

"But given what we've already done together, I don't think using a shocking word would even make the list of our inappropriate behavior."

He waggled his eyebrows toward her. "What would make the list?" His tone was inviting, with just a hint of innuendo.

Thank goodness. They were past that moment, the moment when she'd thought he was just like everyone else. Now they were back to what they'd been, and she could forget all about it.

Or try to, at least. Which meant she should answer his question.

For a moment, her old self tried to push forward and declare she would not indulge him, but she quashed that within seconds. Her old self didn't advocate for herself, accepted whatever she was told, and generally behaved like a damp cloth.

To be fair, her role as an ornamental duchess was supposed to be damp-cloth-like. But she was free of that life now, and she didn't have to do or say anything appropriate if she didn't wish to.

Not that she'd be immune from the consequences of those actions; perhaps she'd be ostracized, or gossiped about, or any number of dreadful things that would happen to a woman who spoke her mind.

But that would be her choice.

Armed with that determination, she began to

tick the items off on her fingers. "One, us going together to that first cottage."

"That hardly merits a pursed lip," he objected.

She rolled her eyes. "*You* are not a female who is constrained because of her sex."

He dipped his head. "Point taken."

"The kissing," she continued, feeling her cheeks start to heat.

"That was very pleasant," he said, his voice deepening,

"The—the touching," she said.

"Mmm-hmm." His tone was silky.

Had she only done three items? Dear Lord, how did bold people manage to say the things they did without expiring on the spot?

Probably because they are bold, a wry voice that sounded remarkably like Edith said in her head.

Be more like Edith, she reminded herself.

"The—" she said, and then she flicked her fingers out toward there, there where he'd kissed and licked and brought her to climax.

"The . . . ?" he prodded.

She gave him a mock glare. "You know what I mean."

"I do. I want you to say it, though," he urged. "Do you mean when I slid my tongue through your folds, sucked on your clitoris, and brought you over?"

"Since you just said it, I don't have to," she replied primly. Though she felt anything but prim; she felt wild, exhilarated, and eager for more of it. Now that she knew how it felt, and what they could do together—she wanted more. More with no promise of forever. Just with a promise of right now.

"But I want to hear you say it. Please, Alexandra?"

Are you going to give it to me? Or do I have to beg?

He'd said that the first night when he'd said the only thing he wanted was for her to experience pleasure.

Or do I have to beg?

She inhaled, then looked over at him, keeping her gaze fixed on his gorgeous eyes and that sensual mouth. "The way you put your mouth on me, kissed me there, there where I didn't know people kissed, and listened to my body and found the perfect rhythm for bringing me to climax. That is item number four."

"Dear Lord, Alexandra," he said, his voice strangled.

She glanced down to his there, and noticed his erection straining against his trousers. Not able—no, not willing—to smother her smile of satisfaction.

"You know just what you do to me, don't you," he said, seeing where she was looking.

"And I'm proud of it," she replied. She put her hand on his hard thigh and squeezed. "Meeting you that night is something I cannot regret, no matter what."

"Is that item number five?" he guessed.

She huffed a laugh. "Given the consequences, absolutely."

He nudged her shoulder. "If you ever want to add more items to your list," he said, his voice low and sincere, "I am here. But only if you choose to do so." His tone was serious, which caught her off guard.

"I hadn't even mentioned the bath," she teased, trying to make the atmosphere less weighty. "That has to be item six."

"We've got some catching up to do, then," he said, shooting her a wicked grin.

His comment made no sense, but it resonated deep within. There was more catching up for her to do, more of her life to live. Time she didn't want to waste any longer being the old demure self. Even though it meant consequences.

First, however, she had to make certain Harriet was safe and happy.

Though that didn't mean, she reasoned, she couldn't have fun at the same time.

"WE SHOULD STOP here," Theo said, slowing the horses.

They'd traveled for most of the day, and were very close to London, so close the air had changed—it smelled more smoky, and less like the fresh air they'd breathed while out in the country.

She'd been a remarkably cheery traveler. He would have expected that most people not accustomed to long trips atop carriages would have mentioned their discomfort at some point, no matter how well-bred they were.

But she hadn't. Instead, she'd pointed things out around them with an eager innocence he found entirely endearing. She seemed to be particularly fond of bodies of water, from small streams to ponds to the occasional river.

Though he'd likely find anything she did entirely endearing, so it wasn't exactly a startling revelation. At least he would have the memory of this trip to keep him company after they'd parted ways.

Since he wouldn't be able to persuade her to make their relationship a permanent thing. She was so adamant that she retain her choices after having been tamped down for so long.

He could promise he wouldn't do that to her, but the fact remained that if he was her husband, he would have the right to do nearly anything he wished. He knew he wouldn't. But that wasn't the point. The point was that he *could*, and her prior marital experience had apparently been so bad she was naturally skittish.

He wondered if she'd ever share more about it with him. Though to what end? So he could offer sympathy?

Better to help her shake it off, let her live the life she deserved to live from here on.

Which meant not pressing her to potentially make the same mistake. He'd made a terrible mistake suggesting it. But he'd wanted so much to help, and he hadn't thought about what that decision might mean. How she might view his wanting to take over and fix everything.

"You don't want to go further, go into London?" she asked.

He jerked his chin toward the city, which loomed in the distance. "We could make it there, but we'd have to be very careful about where we would stay. I thought it would be better to stay as anonymous as possible. We don't want anyone talking about us."

"Oh," she said in understanding. "I hadn't thought of that." She gave him an assessing look. "There's more to you than your handsome appearance, Mr. Osborne."

He arched a brow. "You mean to say you judged me on my looks when we first met?"

She smiled. "Well, your looks are very appealing." She reached up to flick her finger on his temple, just under the brim of his hat. "And your brain as well, I'm finding."

"I did offer to teach you chess when we first met, if you recall."

"That is true, you did."

"I could still teach you," he said. The hope that he could keep their connection—whatever it ended up being—vibrated in his chest.

Her eyes were warm as they regarded him. "You could. Along with other things," she said.

He felt his throat—and other things—tighten at the implication.

Another opportunity to show her how he felt without telling her—he was good at business negotiations, but that was entirely different from this.

There, he could wield his money and power like a sword, cleaving through any possible objections to achieve what he wanted. On the rare occasions his opponents weren't swayed by that, he was able to find something that would resonate with them as to the deal's positive outcome: a higher standing in the community, a chance to let someone else do the work, or merely branching out into another area of business.

But none of that would work with her. She wasn't a business to be merged with, though he longed for that; she was a person to be listened to, and treated with fairness.

As well as desire.

His only asset in this situation was his admittedly robust set of sexual skills. Alongside his ability to hear her, to understand what she meant when she said she wanted to choose.

He would give her the right to choose whatever it was she wanted. His tongue, his fingers, his cock. All three, if she was feeling adventurous.

And then he would just have to wait. Perhaps she would realize she wanted to choose him, all of him, both his body and his brain.

Or not.

And he'd have to be fine with her choice either way.

Chapter Seventeen

$\mathcal{A}$lexandra looked around the pub with interest. She realized shc'd never actually been inside a modest inn like the one Theo had found for them; in fact, she'd never slept anywhere that wasn't owned either by her father, her late husband, or her stepson.

The inn had a sign hanging next to its shabby door proclaiming it the Turnip and Stoat. It was two stories tall, made of wood, with an attached stable on its left. Inside, it was surprisingly bright and airy, not nearly as dim as she'd expected, judging by the outside.

A lesson to be learned there, if she was being particularly analytic. But for now, she was just enjoying the first time she'd been in a pub that anyone could go to.

The past few weeks had been filled with firsts: first time deliberately shredding clothing, first time enjoying kissing, not to mention some of the kissing was outside. First time achieving orgasm with another person.

First time seeing the possibilities ahead of her.

While also fighting frantically to retain those possibilities for her daughter.

She knew, instinctively, that Harriet was completely safe, and no doubt having a delightful time with Edith and Mr. Ash. Fenton, as he seemed to prefer being called. She wouldn't feel settled until she saw her daughter with her own eyes, but that didn't mean she couldn't enjoy the journey to find her. She might never have the opportunity to travel to Paris with such an attractive man alone. She might as well take advantage of it.

Besides, if she didn't, Edith would be sorely disappointed in her. And she wouldn't be setting a good example for Harriet, not that she could tell Harriet everything that might occur on this journey.

"Do you want to have them send supper up?" Theo asked.

Alexandra was shaking her head before she even realized it. "No, I want to eat down here. With everyone else."

Retreating to her room while there were so many people here, people she would never encounter in her usual life, would be a waste.

"Over there, perhaps?" Theo said, gesturing toward a small table at the back of the room.

"Yes, please," she replied.

He took her elbow and guided her through the tables to where he'd indicated. She noticed that

some of the patrons gawked as they passed—
her clothing, while modest for her, was likely
opulent for these people—but nobody seemed
to care after a few startled glances.

The table was made of wood, and well-worn,
with a few pits and gouges showing past use.

Theo made sure she was comfortably seated,
then went to place their orders at the bar. He'd
asked if she'd had a preference for anything, but
since she'd never been to this kind of establishment before, she told him she would leave it up
to him.

She trusted he would make the best choice for her.

How had that happened? And when? When
they'd first met, that very first night, she'd regarded him only as a way to explore her own
pleasure—after his encouragement, of course.
She'd never expected to be here in this situation,
depending on him to repair the terrible mess
they'd gotten into, confident that, somehow, they
would work out a solution.

She gazed at him, watching as he engaged the
woman taking their orders in conversation. She
could tell it was more than just *one meat pie, please*,
because the woman had an interested expression
on her face, and she smiled a few times as Alexandra was watching.

He had the ability, she realized, to find common-
ality with anyone he might meet—that was likely
due partly to being born illegitimate, and having to ensure he was able to overcome people's

prejudice. But it was also likely because he seemed genuinely interested in people. That first night, when he'd said he'd wanted her to feel pleasure, that was real. It wasn't just because he would also have the opportunity for pleasure. It seemed to her, on reflection, that he just wanted others to find happiness.

She also realized, as he was returning to the table, two glasses of something in his hands, that it hadn't occurred to her he might be flirting with the woman behind the bar. It would have been fine if he had, she told herself. Even though she knew she was lying. But she knew, without his saying it, that she had his full and complete attention, in that way, at least.

"Food will be out in about twenty minutes," he said, putting the glasses on the table. The liquid from one sloshed over the side onto the table, and he quickly withdrew a handkerchief from a pocket to wipe it up.

He sat, placing the crumpled handkerchief on the table.

"What do we have?" Alexandra asked, leaning forward to sniff the contents of the glass.

"Ale," he replied, picking up his glass and holding it up. Waiting for her to hoist hers. "I didn't think you'd probably ever had any, and since you are interested in trying new things," he said, giving her a sly wink, "I thought I'd introduce you to it."

"Thank you."

"To the successful resolution of our journey," he said, clinking his glass against hers.

She dipped her head in reply, then took a sip of the ale. It was bitter, and tasted unlike anything she'd ever had before—not surprising, given that she mostly drank tea, with the occasional glass of wine.

"I thought you didn't care for alcohol?" she said, putting the glass back down.

"Ale is ale, not in the same category as alcohol," he said with a shrug. "It is something I grew up with, so I am more accustomed to it, I suppose."

She considered that, and then something else struck her. "What do you mean, a 'successful resolution of our journey'? That sounds quite vague."

He took another drink before answering.

"There is a universal answer, that a 'successful resolution of our journey' means your daughter, your stepdaughter, and my friend are all safe. Though that is just an immediate concern, not one for longer. We still don't know how to fix this—any of this—and yet we know it has to be fixed." He shrugged. "And selfishly, I want to resolve this so that we can figure out what we're doing."

She started at that. "What we're doing?" she echoed.

He met her gaze. His voice was low and resonant, making it seem as though it was the only thing she could hear at the moment, even though the pub was bustling with patrons, with conversation and the clatter of dishes and whatever else made noise in a public establishment.

"You have to know, Angel, that I—that this is more than what we thought when we began."

His words settled into her bones, a welcome warmth to them, and then she felt as though she was choking on them, that the words were smothering her.

He kept his gaze on her, his eyes widening as he saw the shift in her expression. "What is it?" he said. "No, never mind," he continued. "I am sorry, I didn't—I shouldn't have said anything. Forget I—"

She reached out to take his hand, which lay on the table between them, and squeezed it. "It's fine. I'm not—I'm not accustomed," she began, but he wrapped his fingers around her wrist and held it tight.

"You're not accustomed to being seen, Alexandra. To being valued. To being lo—" and then he stopped, his expression tightening as he froze.

To being loved.

She knew that was what he had been about to say, and she didn't know if she could bear to hear it.

No, she *knew* she couldn't bear it.

This was all too new, and she felt like an idiot constantly exclaiming how it was all new, but that didn't mean that she wasn't marveling inside. While also filled with fear that it would all go away, that it wasn't what it seemed, that something would jeopardize the tenuous, fragile sense of self she'd developed over the past two years following her husband's death.

Being loved was very different from being married. Those were two separate things, as she knew from her own experience.

"Theo," she said, leaning forward as she spoke. "Theo, this is lovely right now. I don't want anything—" she started, but her throat felt thick, choked with emotion. She had that same stifling feeling she used to have with her late husband, only this was Theo. Theo, who would never make her do anything.

Until he did. Would he? How could she trust he wouldn't? If she put her life, her decisions, into his hands, what guarantee did she have that he would respect her always?

She had no guarantees. Which was why this was lovely right now—but not for forever. Being loved for now was wonderful. But it didn't mean anything, not when he could do whatever he liked if their bond was permanent.

He gave a quick nod. "I know."

The food arrived before she could say anything else, and she was grateful for the respite. He'd ordered some sort of rich beef stew. It was delicious, and unlike anything she'd ever had before—another new experience, she thought wryly.

He watched her take a few bites, making sure she was enjoying her food, before settling into his own meal.

Did he know just how protective he was? Was it something that came instinctively, or was it something he'd learned because of his friends? The Bastard Five, he'd called them.

They ate in silence for a few minutes, and then Alexandra sat back in her chair, picking up her ale and taking a sip.

"Can you—would you tell me about your past?" She gestured toward herself. "You know who I am, but I don't know who you are."

He shot her a wry glance. "I don't know who I am either."

She nodded for him to continue.

"I was brought to the Devenaugh Home for Destitute Boys when I was around one year old. I don't have any memories from that time; they told me that I was brought there by a woman who was visibly ill. Young, so likely she was my mother. I don't have any other information than that."

"That is so—" she began, then stopped speaking.

"Sad?" he finished. "I suppose, but the Home was good. They took care of us, and fed us well, and made sure we all were educated. The Home was started not long before I arrived. The rumor is that it was funded by an aristocrat who wanted a good place to put his illegitimate child, and so all five of us, I think, had daydreams where a wealthy duke would arrive to claim us, and change our lives forever."

"Did you ever find out the truth?"

He shook his head. "No, though we do know

Bram cannot be the offspring. He and his birth mother were reunited this year. Fenton—true to his analytical self—did the calculations, but even he couldn't figure it out." He shrugged. "It doesn't matter. Mr. Osborne is my father." He looked up, and she saw the obvious warmth and affection in his gaze. "It doesn't matter that he and I were not related by blood, nor that the rest of my friends are not my brothers. I feel as though they are, and they are mine to protect."

He didn't say it, but he didn't have to—now she was under his protection also, at least for a little while.

"You're a good friend," she said softly, picking up her spoon again. He did as well, keeping his eyes focused on his bowl. Because he was hungry? Or because he was embarrassed he'd opened up to her?

She waited until she saw he'd finished his food as well, then took a deep breath as she placed her utensil to the right of her bowl. She couldn't have him forever, but she could have him now. "Take me to bed, please."

THEO ROSE SO swiftly, his leg bumping the table leg, that the glasses clattered alarmingly, but didn't topple off.

He seldom talked about his past with anyone beyond the Bastard Five, and it unnerved him. But this—this invitation, that was something he was confident in.

He held his hand out for her, and she took it, giving him a secret smile as she slid her fingers through his.

"Mrs. Osborne, if you would come upstairs," he said, hearing the urgent growl in his voice. How many more nights did he have with her? How many more ways could he show her he loved her without telling her?

He knew, as clearly as if it had been written on his skin, that if he told her, she would run away. She was still so scarred by her marriage to the late duke, still so skittish about asking for what she wanted.

But he would give her whatever she wanted. Even what she hadn't asked for—in this case, not saying words that would make her feel obliged in any way.

He couldn't stand that, if she somehow felt as though she owed him anything. What they were doing here they were doing as two free consenting adults without any kind of exchange.

To Theo's relief, the room was clean and comfortable. Perhaps a quarter of the size of the duke's foyer, but it had a bed, a washbasin, a wardrobe, and a small table and chair.

Someone had left a light burning next to the bed, and it cast a flickering light that made everything in the room look cozier somehow.

"You'll need to undo me," she said, turning to present her back to him. Their bags had already been brought up, and were to the left of the door, tucked under the table.

He undid her buttons, but not as frantically as he had before; now it felt as though they were truly a comfortable married couple, even though it was all a mirage.

She slid the gown off her shoulders and shimmied it down to the floor, stepping out as delicately as if she was Venus disembarking from her clamshell.

Her chemise was thin enough to let the candlelight reveal her curves, and he felt that familiar unsatiable hunger as he regarded her.

But he wouldn't jump on her like an animal; he needed to make certain that this was what she wanted. Perhaps she did just want to go to sleep.

As he pondered, she turned around, placing a hand on his chest and flattening her palm. "I want to stop worrying about Harriet," she said, her voice deeper. Sultrier. She slid her hand up to cup his cheek. His cock stiffened as she licked her lips, then leaned forward to speak against his skin. "I want you to make me stop worrying."

He wrapped his arms around her, his hand palming the delicious round flesh of her arse. Tugging her up, he leaned back against the door, somehow holding her against him as she laughed, looking down at him with amazement.

"You're very strong," she said in an admiring tone.

"Am I?" he said, raising his brow. "What else am I?"

She gave a rueful shake of her head. "Vain, for one."

"It's not vanity if it's true," he shot back. "I'm strong, I'm handsome, I'm incredible in bed, and I—what have I forgotten?" he asked.

Her body shook with silent laughter. "You're ridiculous. Put me down."

He released her immediately, and her eyes widened as her feet made contact with the floor again. "I didn't think you'd—but of course you would," she said.

"What?" he asked, genuinely confused.

"I was going to say that I didn't think you'd actually listen to me, but there hasn't been a time when you haven't listened." Her tone was appreciative, with a hint of wistfulness to it.

He wished he could banish all of her regrets with a few vigorous fuckings, but even he wasn't that talented.

But he could make her forget now.

He knelt down in front of her, curling his palms around the backs of her thighs and leaning in to nuzzle her *there*. Where he most wanted to be.

She gave a startled shriek, then put her hand on the top of his head, holding him in place. "Oh goodness," she said. "I never knew that—"

"That I could lick and suck your delicious pussy until you screamed my name?" he said, his tone innocent.

"Oh, God, Theo, yes. Please."

"I like it when you beg," he said, then raised the

hem of her chemise and gazed for a moment at the thatch of curls covering her mound, smelling the fragrance of her as he stroked her gently with his index finger.

She was already wet.

"Tell me," he urged. "Tell me what you want. Demand what you want, Angel. I want to hear you say it."

"Please, Theo," she said.

"Not 'please.' Just tell me."

"Lick me, Theo. Lick me until I climax."

His mouth curled into a satisfied smile as he placed his mouth on her.

Chapter Eighteen

He'd put his finger inside her, and then he'd licked her—as she'd ordered him to—and she'd come, but she wanted more. She *needed* more.

"I want to lie down," she said, backing up toward the bed.

The backs of her knees hit the edge of it, and she let herself fall backward, her arms outstretched, her body already relaxing.

That was what he did to her. He let her feel, and be, as if there were no worries, no restrictions, no constraints.

He wouldn't let himself control her in any way—at least, not unless she asked.

Interesting thought.

Which was flung out of her head when he rose from his kneeling position, his hands going to his clothing to strip it off as he kept his gaze locked with hers.

"God, Alexandra," he said, his voice husky with want.

His shirt flew up in the air and landed somewhere behind him, and then she heard the soft thud of his boots on the floor, followed by more sounds of clothing falling.

And then he stood at the end of the bed, one hand wrapped around his cock, the other holding on to one of the bedposts. His stare was ravenous, and she shuddered at seeing the palpable desire in his eyes.

This was how it felt to be wanted. This was how it felt to be an equal partner with someone who respected you and also wanted to do all sorts of erotic, forbidden things with you.

Glorious.

"Show me," she said, jerking his chin toward where his hand held himself. "Show me how you stroke your cock." She gave him a wry glance. "Your big, beautiful cock."

He grinned in reply, and twisted his hand around the shaft, pulling and yanking, his eyes still locked with hers.

"I told you it's not vanity if it's true," he said, and she laughed.

"I want you to show me," he said, nodding toward her.

Her eyes widened. "You mean—"

"Yes. What do you do when you're alone? When you're thinking of me?" His smile was as cocky as his—well. She smothered a grin at her own wit.

She put her hand down there, and covered herself with her palm, digging the heel of her hand

into herself, right there, where he'd kissed her the
first night they met.

She'd touched herself many times since that
night, always thinking of him, and how he gazed
up at her as he was licking her there, bringing her
to a frenzy of completion.

"That's it, Angel," he said. His expression was
dazed, as though he was in a haze of lust.

Likely the same expression was on her face.

She bit her lip and began to touch herself more
intently, rubbing that little nub as she kept the
pressure of her hand on her mound.

It felt so good.

Though not as good as it would if he were inside her.

"Come here," she said, barely recognizing her
own voice. It was husky, and low, and if there had
been any other noise in the room, she would have
been inaudible.

"For what?" he challenged.

She spread her legs wide, revealing herself to
him. "For this. I want you to put your big, beautiful cock inside me, Theo. And I want it now."

Alexandra was frankly amazed at herself for
her boldness. But it seemed to awaken an even
fiercer hunger in him, and she was delighted to
see it. Mostly because she would be the fortunate
recipient of his desire.

He joined her on the bed, positioning himself
on his knees between her legs. He had an excel-

lent view of her pussy, and she wriggled a little to expose herself even more.

He grasped his shaft with one hand and planted his other hand next to her head, leaning forward.

"I'm going to fuck you now, Alexandra," he said, his voice a rasp. "I am going to make you come so hard you see stars. And then I am going to do it again, if you're willing."

"Please," she said, sounding desperate and needy. "Please, Theo, please fuck me."

His lips curled into a wicked smile, and she felt her heart flutter in anticipation.

And then he entered her, his length pushing in as he kept his gaze on her face, clearly wanting to make certain she was comfortable.

When he was all the way in—deliciously large, making her feel as though she was stretched—he began to move, sliding in and out, the bedsprings creaking in an inexorable rhythm, him grunting as he increased speed.

He put his hand between them, placing his thumb on her clitoris, and began to stroke it as well in time to his own movements.

The combination of hand and cock was almost too much to bear, and she flung her head back against the pillow and let her eyes shut, reveling in how alive and sensual she felt, how she didn't want to be anywhere but here, with him, at this very moment.

And then the tension increased, and she felt

herself tighten around him. He groaned as she shattered beneath him.

He rocked against her a few more times, then held himself still as he came. She felt him spill inside her before he collapsed down.

"That was incredible," she murmured.

"I know," he replied, his tone full of pride, and she had to laugh again.

"WE'LL ARRIVE IN London in about an hour, and we should be able to get on a packet later this afternoon," Theo said as he drove the carriage onto the road. The horses had rested, and been fed and watered, which is more than could be said for Theo—he'd spent almost the entire night pleasuring Alexandra, but he wouldn't trade a moment of it for more sleep.

And, admittedly, he'd eaten a lot. A lot of her, specifically, resulting in several climaxes that were satisfyingly loud and dramatic.

His Angel liked to shout, he'd discovered.

She sat beside him, looking coolly elegant in her gown, which he'd helped her get back into this morning. She'd coiled her hair into a simple knot at the back of her head, and she wore a relatively plain hat without so much as a peacock feather or ornamental pear in sight.

He didn't think he'd ever get tired of looking at her—her face was so expressive, and her beauty was interesting, meaning there were several elements adding to the overall effect. Her eyes, with their unusual green color, were the first thing most people likely noticed, but then there was her straight, aristocratic nose, high cheekbones, and full, luscious lips.

He ached to have those lips wrapped around his cock, but thus far they'd found other things to do, and he wouldn't suggest it without her thinking of it first. It was crucial he not make her more skittish—she was clearly recovering from the trauma of her first marriage, and he didn't know just what had transpired.

Had her late husband been sexually demanding and demeaning? Had he ignored her entirely? Or had he displayed her like a trophy without bothering to know the woman inside?

If she would let him in—but *she'd* have to be the one to initiate that, he knew. And it was one thing to share her bed, but it would take a lot more time for her to share her confidences.

Time they didn't have together.

It was so tempting to try to persuade her into more—to use his Theo charm, as Benedict had dubbed it, in a tone that was both judgmental and admiring.

But he couldn't. He shouldn't.

What's more, his mild suggestion that would solve some of her problems had been met with a fierce pushback. He wouldn't do that to her again.

"Do you know how long the steam packet takes?" she asked, as if she was thinking about time as well—though likely she was just wanting the time to be short, because it would mean she'd see her daughter all the sooner.

"The trip takes somewhere between twelve and eighteen hours," he said. "We'll book a cabin and sleep on the boat."

"Goodness, there won't be anybody we know on the packet, will there?" she said, her tone suddenly concerned. "If anybody recognizes us and talks—well, I might as well hand Harriet directly over to William, since he will assert his rights over her guardianship if he believes me to be a bad influence."

Theo glanced over at her. She was distinctive enough he would have recognized her no matter what, even if he wasn't in love with her.

"We'll take a detour and secure something to disguise ourselves with," he said. "Simeon—one of my friends—is an artist, and knows all sorts of artistic folk, including theater people. Or the Garden might have something we could wear, if you'd fancy being dressed like a schoolmistress. It comes with a crop," he added, mostly to see her cheeks turn red.

"Oh my," she said, after a moment of comprehension. "I never—"

"Not a lot of people do," he said, not wanting her to feel as though she was ignorant of something everyone else knew about. "Dressing in costume is for a small percentage of our visitors."

"The schoolmistress outfit sounds interesting, though," she mused, and he could hear her working out the possible scenarios as she spoke. "But never mind," she said. "We'll discuss that another time."

"I look forward to it," he said, imbuing his voice with a deliberate emphasis.

He drove to Simeon's lodgings, which occupied the second floor of Mr. Finneas's Fine Establishment, which was also where Simeon purchased all his clothing.

Mr. Finneas had known the Bastard Five since they'd required adult clothing. Simeon had become particularly close to the gentleman, and had offered to move in when Mr. Finneas was struggling to pay the rent.

Theo handed Alexandra down from the carriage, glancing up at the second story windows. Simeon was remarkably methodical for someone who imbued the soul of an artist as much as he did—he painted every day from ten to five o'clock, then got ready for the evening. As it was just past noon, Theo was fairly confident he'd be home.

He walked up the narrow flight of stairs to Simeon's workroom, shouting his friend's name as they went.

"What is it, pest?" Simeon replied.

They couldn't see him yet, but a few steps more and they had arrived in his studio. He had his back to the door and was working on a large canvas, a nearly naked female posing just beyond.

Alexandra gasped, and then quickly turned around so she didn't see.

"I've brought a guest, you lout," Theo said, walking toward Simeon.

His friend pivoted away from the canvas, his eyes widening when he saw Alexandra's back. "Isn't that . . . ?" he asked, before Theo clamped his palm over Simeon's mouth.

"It is, but we're trying to keep ourselves incognito."

Simeon's brow rose. "Well, I know you're serious if you're speaking Latin. You could just say you're trying to keep hidden."

Theo ignored his friend's jibe. "Do you have any clothing we could borrow?" Theo gestured to Alexandra. "We need to keep the—the lady from being recognized. Or if not, perhaps one of your actress friends has something?"

Simeon glanced over at Alexandra before returning his attention to Theo. "No need to bring any more people into this. I am certain I have something that will work."

Within half an hour, Alexandra was wearing a plain gray gown that her lady's maid likely would have turned her nose up at and a massive brown cloak that was far too large for her, so when she pulled the hood up her face was almost entirely obscured, as were her arms in the enormous sleeves.

Simeon's model had dismounted from her perch

and thrown a wrapper on, then did Alexandra's hair in a style that was far more functional than fashionable.

"I'm a genius," Simeon said in a smug tone.

Theo punched him on the arm. "You have clothing available to you because you live above a haberdashery and you often have models posing for you. That's not being a genius, that's circumstantial."

"Genius," Simeon repeated.

"Regardless," Alexandra said in a coolly amused voice, "I don't believe anyone will recognize me now."

Theo looked at her and smiled. "Agreed. And I will take pains to ensure I don't stand out quite as much as well."

One brow rose. "You mean you'll disguise yourself so instead of being spectacularly handsome you'll only be moderately so?" She laughed as she spoke.

"Or I could go with you and everyone would end up staring at me," Simeon said.

Theo shook his head as he met Alexandra's gaze. "You see? I am not even the vainest one of my friends."

"I see where you get it," she replied.

"Thank you," Theo said, nodding toward Simeon and his model. "We'll be on our way. We've got a steam packet to catch."

"You're welcome," Simeon said, his tone serious.

"You didn't tell me what this was about, and I haven't asked—but if you need help, you know where to go." He turned to look at Alexandra. "Both of you," he said.

Theo clapped his hand on his friend's shoulder. "I do."

"Thank you, Mr. Jones," Alexandra added.

Chapter Nineteen

They were on the steam packet, Theo having reserved a cabin for them while Alexandra waited
with the carriage. Theo then arranged for his
carriage to be taken back to his house, and they
boarded, along with what seemed like a hundred
other people. Alexandra didn't recognize anybody she knew, but she also made certain to keep
her face covered by the hood.

Theo had borrowed clothing from his friend,
and was wearing an ill-fitting jacket and a drab-
colored pair of pants. He had a scuffed hat on his
head, and had ruffled his hair so it was deliberately messy.

Alexandra could still see all of his beauty, despite his efforts, although she was admittedly
biased.

The boat pulled away from the dock, and Alexandra and Theo leaned on the railing, looking out
toward the water.

"I've never—" she started, and then she stopped,

nudging him in the shoulder. "I think you can guess what I'll say next."

He shifted so now he was leaning his back against the railing, turning his head to regard her.

"You've never been on a boat? You've never dressed up like a washerwoman? You've never visited a painter in his studio?"

"All of those," she said, putting her hand on his arm. "And I wouldn't have experienced any of them without you. Thank you."

"Don't thank me for introducing you to Simeon," he muttered. "Arrogant peacock." It was clear, from his tone, that he loved his friend.

She tilted her head to regard him. "I envy that, you know. That feeling of comradery."

"A matter of necessity, what with the being raised in an orphanage and all that," he said dryly. Her eyes widened, and she opened her mouth, but he held his hand up. "I am only teasing you. I am fortunate," he said, sounding sincere. "It could have been so much worse. I could have ended up in a different home, with different parents, or no parents at all. I still would have been handsome," he said, eliciting a chuckle, "but I wouldn't have been me. And I quite like being me."

I like you too, she thought. In fact—but no. She wouldn't, she couldn't even say that to herself. Instead, she changed the subject.

Did that make her a coward? Or was she just advocating for herself for the first time?

"Tell me about Mr. Osborne," she said. "Unless you don't wish to."

Theo's mouth split into a smile, and she was dazzled. He looked younger when he smiled so earnestly. Even younger than he was, which was, she'd nearly forgotten, twelve years younger than she.

"Stop thinking about whatever it is you're thinking about," he ordered. "Pay attention to me instead."

She crinkled her nose at him. "Fine. Mr. Osborne?" she prodded.

"He was so kind, at first I thought there was something evil lurking underneath. I was twelve years old, you understand, when he took me in. He never married. I think he had always wanted a family—he had just been too busy with work to take care of it. He spoke, years later, of his regret of not finding more time for himself." He lowered his voice into a conspiratorial whisper. "Which is why I make sure I play as hard as I work."

She colored, recalling their first meeting.

"You certainly do."

"Though not lately," he said, as though wanting to reassure her. "That is, except with you. Only with you."

She heard something in his tone that made her want to press further, but also made her want to retreat, as though she might hear something she wasn't ready for.

But he couldn't—he knew how she felt, didn't he?

Actually, come to think of it, how *did* she feel?

Different from before, that was for sure. As soon as he immediately offered to assist however he could to find Harriet, something changed.

Or perhaps nothing had changed except for her perception—after all, the first time they'd met, he'd devoted himself to her pleasure, and he hadn't stopped since.

Despite everything.

He could have made their interaction, their relationship, a one-time occurrence, especially after their entanglements were revealed. But he didn't. Instead, he promised to do whatever he could to change the outcome, and continued to ensure her pleasure—not just in bed, though that was substantial. But also in terms of her comfort. Ordering dinner for her the night before, realizing she should not be recognized, trying to avoid William and his goals earlier than that.

Every time asking if she was comfortable with what they were doing. Not pushing her, not forcing her into anything. Because he was that kind of person, or because he sensed she needed it in particular?

Or both?

Her mind still clung to that moment when he'd been about to say *love*. Though she didn't know what love meant, to either of them. For all she knew, he could say that to every one of his tryst partners. Perhaps it was just how he felt in the moment.

For her? Well, she didn't know how she felt. Or perhaps she did, but it was all too new, too terrifying.

"If you want to tell me anything about you, I mean from before," he said, sounding less assured than usual, "I will listen."

A FEW HOURS later, Mr. and Mrs. Osborne—according to the tickets they'd purchased for the steam packet—were in their first-class cabin. There was only so much Theo would do to maintain the ruse of their identity, after all.

They'd eaten dinner, which was passable enough, and it was too early to go to bed, though Theo would if she asked.

But then, of course he would. He'd do anything she asked. He knew that.

But only if she asked.

They had moved from the small dining area to the just-as-small lounging area. Alexandra sat on a low padded seat with a window above, presumably to look out and see the packet's progress. Theo sat to her left, in a small cushioned chair.

The cabin was efficiently designed, with discrete areas for dining, lounging, sleeping, and washing up. It was done up in navy and green, perhaps a nod to the color of the sea they traveled on.

It was already dark, and felt comfortably intimate; they'd lit a few candles, and moonlight streamed in through the two windows on one side of the room.

"You asked me earlier," she began, her gaze lowered to the ground, "what it was like. Before."

"Mmm-hmm," he said, reaching to take her hand. It was an intuitive gesture, one that now felt as natural to him as breathing.

What would it be like when she wasn't here any longer? In his life at all?

His chest tightened, and he pushed the thought away. He couldn't think about that now. Now he could only enjoy the time he had with her, before she realized she was in too deep, and ran away.

"It wasn't that he was cruel," she continued. "At least, not actively cruel. But he refused to admit I was a person in my own right. Everything I was, he wanted me to be. A wife, a mother, an object to be dressed up and brought out as tribute to his greatness." She took a breath. "He chose my clothes, my friends, my interaction with my daughter, and everything that could possibly be remarked upon by others. The only thing he didn't control was what I thought and felt. Of course I had to hide those things, because if he knew how I thought or felt, he would have an opinion about those as well." A rueful snort. "Not that he ever cared about either of those things. Likely it didn't enter his mind that I had my own thoughts and feelings."

Theo absorbed her words, hearing the deep hurt she still carried. "And then? When he died?" he asked gently.

"Well," she said, her voice shaky, "you know.

My going out to the Garden that night was my first—no, my second—independent act as my own person."

"What was your first?"

"I destroyed my mourning clothing," she said simply. Proudly. "I took a pair of scissors and I cut the gown off my body at Madame Lucille's shop."

"Excellent," he replied. "And then you ordered an entire new wardrobe?"

"I did." A pause. "For all the good it did. Look at me—still beholden to the Duke of Chelmswich, having to do what he says. The particular man may have changed, but the intent is still the same." Her tone was bitter.

"I could help, you know," he began. "Not with what the earlier solution I proposed," he added hastily, "but—"

"No," she cut him off. Her tone was sharp. "No, and while I know you have the best of intentions, the last thing I ever want is to be obligated to anyone. Even someone as kind and handsome as you."

He gave a rueful smile. "I can see why. And you forgot to mention quick-thinking and very inventive in bed."

He'd meant to lighten the atmosphere, and it succeeded—she laughed, and punched him on the arm. "I will have to report to your friend Simeon that I believe that you are the vainer of the two."

"Simeon is so vain he'll want to claim first place

in that contest as well," Theo predicted, and she laughed some more.

"But Angel," he said, moving to sit beside her on the seat, gathering her in his arms and holding her close against his chest, "you will come to me if you need to? I will do whatever you want, I will promise whatever you need, and will not oblige you to anything. You have my word, and because I know how valuable a gentleman's word can be, I will put it down in a legal document."

She smothered a half laugh, half sob, and looked up at him, her eyes dark with emotion. "Thank you."

"Well," Theo said, gazing into her eyes, wishing the trip to Calais took twelve years instead of twelve hours, "we should probably go to bed." He lowered his mouth to her ear. "So I can be absolutely certain you understand I am the best at what I do."

THE BOAT DOCKED at Calais only a little bit more than twelve hours after leaving London. The day was cloudy, but it didn't seem as though it would rain.

Alexandra dutifully pulled on her enormous cloak, drawing the hood over her face and clasping her hands together in front of her so her upper limbs were entirely covered.

Theo had mussed up his hair again, and smashed the hat down on his head on an odd angle. Their precautions were likely unnecessary, but it felt like more of an adventure and less like a desperate hunt if they were in costume. The result would be the same no matter how they approached it, so they might as well have fun with it.

And Alexandra had to admit she was having fun.

Theo was a delightful traveling companion, not just because he was a divine kisser and skillfully adept at giving her multiple orgasms, but because he was thoughtful and kind in so many other ways: fetching her tea when the air got a bit colder, asking what types of sandwiches she preferred, settling her under the covers so she would be warm and comfortable. After supplying her with multiple orgasms, of course.

"The train to Paris takes about three hours," Theo said as they disembarked from the boat. The other passengers streamed past them, none of them giving them a second glance. "And then we'll find your daughter."

"You make it sound so easy," Alexandra said. Admiringly, yes, but also skeptically.

"Things are easier if you have money," he replied simply. "All I have to do is wave around a stack of francs and people will tell me about the odd Englishman and his two female companions. Fenton sticks out wherever he goes, so I don't have much concern about that."

Alexandra considered his words for a moment, then nodded. "I can see that." She knew that, in fact. If she had money, her own money, she wouldn't currently be haring after her daughter.

She and Harriet would be living their lives, with Harriet free to choose whomever she wanted. If she wanted.

As would Alexandra. But then she wouldn't be here, with him. Would she have met him at all, if she was truly independent?

She liked to think she would have—that she would have found her own way to the Garden of Hedon. But none of this was getting her any closer to Paris.

"Shall we?" she said, gesturing toward the sign indicating the train.

He took her arm, tucking her against his body. She liked that. "Let us go, Mrs. Osborne," he said, and she startled, even though this wasn't the first time he'd called her that. She was not sure she liked it. Though she wasn't sure she didn't like it.

Or that she knew anything about her state of mind at all.

She just had to find Harriet, and then they would solve everything. Somehow.

"Let me guess," he said, holding up a hand, even though she had yet to say a word. "You've never been on a train."

He had booked another private cabin for them, and they sat on opposite sides, her facing forward, him facing back. The cabin's windows had shades for privacy, but he had drawn them open so she could see the country as they traveled. The clouds had eased somewhat, and there were dapples of sunlight as the train sped along the track. She caught sight of cows, sheep, and the occasional cart. It didn't look any different from the English countryside, but it certainly felt different.

She smiled in response. "Of course I haven't." She leaned forward. "I wonder if you've ever—" and she went over to him, straddling his lap and yanking his hat off, tossing it on the seat beside them "—kissed someone on a train."

His lips curled into a lazy smile. "I have not, Angel. Are you going to add to my education?"

"If you let me," she said.

At his eager nod, she lowered her mouth to his. His lips were warm, and she felt as though she was melting into him. The train jostled them, and he wrapped his arms around her to steady them both, clamping his hands on her arse, one cheek in each hand.

"Ingenious," she murmured, then slid her tongue out to enter his mouth.

His mouth tasted of the minty lemonade they'd shared earlier—tart, refreshing, delicious. She stroked her tongue with his, the feeling cascading through her body, all the way to her toes.

Lingering there where he so often kissed her. Where she pressed against him, her mound against his hard abdomen.

She kissed him deeply, leisurely, exploring his mouth with her tongue as he let her take the lead. No, as he wanted her to take the lead.

She knew he desired her—the proof was

hardening under her arse as she thought—but she also knew he respected her need for control. Even though she had so little experience, and he could guide her, if necessary. He wanted her to own what she was learning. To continue her education with someone else when this was all over?

She didn't know. She didn't want to know.

All she wanted to do was kiss him until the end of time, feel that same overwhelming spiral of passion and want and need wrapped up into one heady elixir.

His grip tightened, and he shifted under her so she felt his cock pressing up even more, no doubt giving him the friction he craved.

It wasn't enough, she knew that—she wanted more also. She rubbed her breasts against his chest, wishing there were fewer layers of fabric between them. Wishing he would draw her nipples into his mouth and lick and suck her there, too. Slide those clever fingers along her skin, tracing their way down to where she ached for him.

She was panting against him, and she couldn't stand it any longer—she rose, checking the cabin door was locked, then reached for the placket of his trousers and freed him, his cock waving proudly in the air, the veins throbbing.

"Mmm," she murmured, wrapping her hand around his hardness.

"What are you going to do, Angel?" he said, his voice hoarse.

She planted one hand—the one not on his cock—on the back of the seat near his head, leaning forward.

She kept her gaze on his mouth, then licked her lips. He groaned.

"What do you want me to do?"

He looked up into her eyes and drew a breath. "I want you to do what you want."

It was what she wanted to hear, even if it scared her—to be in control, to be in charge of what was happening between them.

To decide things that would affect both of them.

She trailed her fingers down his neck, then steadied herself as she lowered to her knees, keeping her other hand on him. Stroking it gently; not enough to bring him to climax, but enough to make him squirm. "Please, Angel," he said, begging.

She liked that.

She inched her knees closer to his seat so she was squarely between his legs. She put her hand on the inside of his right thigh and pushed it wider, then put her mouth just above his cock. It was so hard in her hand, and she saw a drop of moisture on the tip.

She glanced up to see his fierce, intense stare on her. "Do you want me to kiss it like you do me?" she asked. Her voice was throaty.

"God, please," he managed to rasp, and then she smiled, widening her lips to take him in her mouth.

He tasted musky and clean, and she worked her

mouth around him, keeping her fist wrapped at the bottom. Tentatively, she licked his shaft, and he jerked and groaned. She knew enough to figure out his reactions were entirely pleasurable, and she felt wicked and determined. Wanting to make him beg and plead as she had, wanting to know how it felt to control someone else's desire so thoroughly.

She sucked, and he grasped her head, threading his fingers through her hair. "Like that, please," he said, and she slid her mouth up and down, licking and sucking as she did.

He muttered a string of curses, and she felt positively gleeful at what she was able to provoke. Eventually, she figured out the rhythm he liked best, and she focused on doing that, until he was gasping and pleading in incoherent noises.

At last, he yanked her up and off his cock, pulling her to him and putting his mouth to hers, his hands frantically getting her into position until she was seated on him, his penis thrust up inside her, her hands on either side of his head.

He broke the kiss and looked at her, his eyes wild. "Ride me," he urged, and held her hips as she began to move. Up and down, feeling him slide in and out with every movement.

Meanwhile, he had buried his face in her chest and was nuzzling her breasts through the fabric of her gown, one hand working at her neckline to get access to her skin.

This contact was different from his hand or his

mouth, or even when he was atop her. It felt more intense, somehow, and she was able to adjust the rhythm so she could start to feel the urgency as well, the friction of their bodies, her clitoris rubbing against him in a brutally sexual way.

And then she felt it, caught the climax as it started to surge forward, moving up and down him even faster as his fingers tightened almost painfully on her hips. "God, yes, Angel," he gasped, and she felt him stiffen, felt him spurt into her as she summited her own hill, her head flung back, her lip caught between her teeth, crying out as she came.

"Dear Lord, that was good," she said, dropping her head onto his neck.

"It was, wasn't it?" he said, sounding smug.

She batted him lazily on the arm. "I did all the work," she replied.

"You have an excellently skilled teacher," he said, making her laugh.

And when the lessons were over? What then?

But she wouldn't think about that. All she would think about now was how they'd find Harriet, how they'd solve this problem, and if her clothing had survived this train interlude.

Nothing else was permitted, not until she had to face the rest of her life.

Chapter Twenty

It was impossible for Theo not to have fallen in love with her.

Not just because of her eagerness in sexual play—though obviously that was welcome—but because of her intelligence, her bravery, and her honor.

She had endured being ignored and belittled for years. She had had no recourse. And as soon as it was possible for her to live her own life, she had leapt on the opportunity—leapt on him.

She was level-headed, courageous, and curious. She knew her own worth, and she was insistent on valuing herself.

It was admirable. Theo couldn't imagine that her story was much different from that of other aristocratic young ladies—brought up to be reflections of their inevitable husbands, discouraged from doing anything that would express who they were separate from their spouses.

To escape from that would require strength of character which she obviously had.

But because he was in love with her, and respected her, he wouldn't tell her he loved her. He'd almost done it—at the beginning of their journey here. But he'd stopped himself, not wanting to put that on her. Because he loved her too much to tell her.

It was an idiotic conundrum that he didn't think even Fenton could solve.

"Where now?" she asked.

The train had arrived in Paris, and they stood where a row of hansom cabs—called fiacres here—waited for customers.

Theo shrugged. "We take one of those to the best hotel in Paris," he said. "With any luck, we'll find your daughter, Lady Edith, and Fenton somewhere nearby."

She gave him a skeptical glance. "That easy, hmm?"

He gave her a wicked smile. "Have I failed in anything I've said I was going to do?"

She blushed, and he laughed, taking her arm to escort her to the nearest fiacre.

They arrived at Le Meurice quickly thereafter, and it took only a moment for Theo to display enough cash to secure them a room. He registered them as "Mr. and Mrs. Osborne" again, and Alexandra kept her oversized cloak on, even though it was drab compared to what everyone else in the hotel was wearing.

A bellboy carried their bags to the room, then bowed deeply as Theo handed him a tip. The room was opulent, with an enormous bed at one end, windows from floor to ceiling, and delicately carved and clearly expensive furniture placed just so.

The room was done up in shades of gold and green, and the entire impact was one of luxury. If they were here purely for pleasure, they would have been entirely satisfied.

Alexandra glanced around the room, her gaze taking everything in with an expression of interest. The brown of her cloak was a discordant note in the overall sumptuousness of the room.

"Once we've found them, we can purchase you some stylish French clothing, if you like." Theo jerked his head toward her attire. "I know you brought clothes, but perhaps you want something a tad more elegant?"

She shook her head. "No, I just want to get home and tell William what he can do with his demands."

Theo's eyes widened. "So you're going to risk his cutting you off?"

She took a breath. "I have to. I cannot allow William to bully me or my daughter into anything anymore. If he retaliates, that is on him. I cannot force him to be a reasonable human being any more than I can force my daughter into a marriage she does not want. Regardless of anything else," she said, waving her hand in the air between the two of them.

"You know, if—" he began.

"Stop," she said. "You've offered. I've said I would ask if I needed. I don't wish to discuss it again."

Theo was nearly taken aback by the ferocity in her tone.

He nodded, then waited a moment. "Shall we go find them, then?" he asked.

"Please."

It wasn't the same *please* he had grown accustomed to hearing from her—the one she said when he was wreaking pleasurable havoc on her. It was a low, urgent word, one that told him she would be entirely focused on her goal until she achieved it. He would keep his flirtatious remarks and sly comments to himself, at least until she was reunited with her family. The ones she cared about, at least.

He held his hand out to her. "Let's go."

They'd already asked at the front desk if a Mr. Ash was staying there—Fenton might think he wouldn't have to use a false name. Unfortunately, Fenton wasn't registered, at least not as himself.

They'd decided their first course of action would be to go to the hotel's lobby bar, one with a good view of the hotel entrance. If the three they sought were here, it was likely they would be coming in or going out within the next few hours. It would be frustrating to just sit there, but they both knew chances were good that the three were there.

They took seats that allowed them to see both the side veranda and the front entrance. A server came and took their order, which Alexandra gave.

Theo cocked a brow at her. "I didn't know you could speak French, among your other talents." He'd never learned any other language because that kind of instruction wasn't offered at the Home. Another distinction between them, then.

She wrinkled her nose. "It's something a young lady is supposed to know how to do. I can also embroider, play a little piano, and manage a household. I do not know how to do anything for myself, nor do I understand the things you deal with every day."

"Business, you mean?" he asked.

"Mmm-hmm."

The server returned with their wine, and they each hoisted a glass. "To finding what we want," Theo said, even though he knew he already had.

"To what we want," she echoed, tapping her glass against his.

They each took a sip. The wine was light, almost sparkling, and was absolutely delicious, despite Theo's usual indifference to alcohol.

"My business isn't hard to understand, not if you understand people," he said.

She gave him an inquisitive look.

"By which I mean," he continued, "that yes, you do have to know how to balance ledgers, or at least tell if someone has balanced a ledger correctly, and it helps to understand the various terms, but that can be gleaned from context. The part that many businessmen lose focus on is that business only works when there are people involved."

"What does that mean?"

"My business ventures include shipping, wholesale buying, and investments. I have to understand the concerns of people in the various areas I ship to and from so I'll know if I should be sending my goods there or somewhere else."

"Oh, I see," she said, looking thoughtful.

Theo had never discussed business with someone he'd also fucked.

"That said," he continued—and then his tone changed. "Look, they're here."

They were both on their feet within seconds, and she ran toward where the three runaways—Fenton, Lady Harriet, and Lady Edith—were walking, clearly heading toward the front desk.

He stayed just long enough to throw some money on the table and then was after them, in time to see Alexandra fling her arms around her daughter and burst into sobs.

"You found us." Fenton frowned, as he did when thinking. "I wasn't expecting you until tomorrow. You must have moved quickly."

"We've had a wonderful time," Lady Edith said. Alexandra and her daughter were still hugging, and both were now crying. "Fenton took us to the Café de Paris for dinner, and we had absinthe during l'heure verte—that is the time one is supposed to drink absinthe, you see.

Though it seems odd that something renowned for sparking one's imagination would be so rigid in its timing. We all enjoyed it, I have to say." She spoke as if their visit had been planned, not a spontaneous reaction to a bad situation. Perhaps that was how she regularly confronted things, which would explain why she and her brother did not get along.

It appeared Alexandra and Harriet had ceased crying and hugging for a moment, and Lady Harriet turned to their group, a faintly defiant look on her face. "I told you when we met, I won't—"

Theo held his hand up. "That is the last thing any of us want," he said, meeting Alexandra's gaze for a moment. "We are merely here because your mother was very concerned, and we wanted to ensure you were safe."

"Of course she was. She is with me," Fenton said in a matter-of-fact tone. "Look, can we go have something to drink? We just walked all over, looking at things, and I need to sit."

The five of them returned to the bar, the server obviously recognizing the new arrivals, quickly bringing them a bottle of white wine and more glasses, along with a tray of breads, cheeses, and meats. Fenton began to load up a plate.

"Fenton, don't eat too much," Lady Harriet said in what could only be called a fondly indulgent voice. "You know how your stomach is."

Theo looked at his friend, wide-eyed, waiting

for Fenton to reply in a long monologue about the intestinal system and the workings therein.

Instead, however, his friend merely nodded, placing the plate in front of him and popping a bite of cheese in his mouth.

What was even happening?

"WE'RE NOT GOING back with you," Edith announced, just as Alexandra's breathing was returning to normal.

Alexandra sat bolt upright in her chair. "I'm sorry, what?"

Edith folded her arms over her chest. "Not going back. We want to stay and see Paris more. We've only been here a few days." She nodded toward Mr. Ash. "Fenton was sick as a dog on the crossing. I cannot stand having to see that again so soon."

"But—" Alexandra said, looking to Harriet.

"I want to stay here. If I'm here, William can't force me into anything." Harriet's expression darkened. "He only wants me to marry because he needs the money," she said. "That's obvious. And why should I sacrifice myself just so he and Florence can maintain their lifestyle? No offense, Mr. Osborne," she said in an aside to Theo.

"None taken," he replied, shooting Alexandra a quick, conspiratorial smile.

"What do you think we should say to William?" Alexandra held her hand up. "Never mind that, it is not your responsibility." She gave a brisk nod toward Harriet. "I am fine with you staying here, I will speak with him, and I will figure out what exactly to say."

Harriet gave Alexandra an admiring glance, and it seemed as though Theo was going to take Alexandra's hand, but then remembered who else was there, and just tapped his fingers on the table.

Edith made a noise that sounded a lot like a growl. "Just tell him he doesn't get his way for once. That he might have to solve his own problems."

"Solve his own problems," Alexandra repeated. Something she would have to do as well. Theo's presence in her life wasn't a problem, not now— but it was beginning to feel like it would be when he left.

But she wouldn't ask him to stay, because he'd only wanted her pleasure. Could she ask him to devote himself to that for the rest of his life? She would not. She was determined to make her own way, and her own way didn't include a much younger man who might change his mind ten years from now. Two years from now, even, when he turned thirty.

How could she possibly even entertain the thought?

And yet here she was. Entertaining it.

Even though it was a terrible idea.

"We'll leave in the morning, then," Alexandra

said briskly, picking up her glass of wine and draining it. "But tonight, I expect you three to show us the very best of Paris."

"Because she's never been here," Theo said, giving her a wink.

"Exactly," Alexandra replied.

Chapter Twenty-One

𝒯he return journey wasn't nearly as delightful as the travel from London to Paris, despite their having succeeded in their quest.

Alexandra was distant on the train ride back to the steam packet, and Theo wondered if she was already anticipating their inevitable break. When would she tell him he was no longer needed? Before speaking with William? After?

And what would become of him then?

His friends would support him, of course, but even their love and friendship couldn't mend the heart he knew would be broken.

And while she hadn't been sick on the boat ride over, she got ill nearly as soon as they boarded, with Theo holding a basin for her as vomited.

"I must have caught whatever your Mr. Ash has," she said, offering him a wan smile as he pushed her hair back from her face.

She lay in bed, pale and drawn, staring up at

the ceiling as though it owed her an answer about something.

"Would you like some tea? Some water? Something to eat?" That he wasn't able to solve the problem by sheer strength of will frustrated him to no end, though he wouldn't add to her problems by revealing his emotions.

"I am fine, truly," she said, curling around herself and holding her stomach. "I just need to rest a bit. Perhaps I had too much rich French food."

Theo didn't think that was it, but he accepted her explanation and went to sit in the window seat as she closed her eyes.

He had a book with him, the next book for his monthly book discussion with his friends, but he couldn't seem to concentrate on it. Nothing, not even Jane Collier's *An Essay on the Art of Ingeniously Tormenting*, could keep his interest, though he did make note of a few items that might irritate Simeon.

Instead, he kept looking at her, feeling the pang in his heart at knowing this would all be over soon. She would confront her stepson, suffer whatever retribution that loathsome individual would dole out, and then exercise her right to choose how to live her life. She might not have funds, thanks to her stepson, but Theo found it hard to imagine she'd want to do anything extravagant—likely just garden and read and spend time with her daughter, wherever Lady Harriet ended up.

He'd be a brief interlude, a pleasant memory

of her first forays into discovering who she was and what she wished for. He didn't want to think about it, but he hoped that she would continue her education.

Even though it hurt like he was stabbing himself in the heart to think about it.

"You don't have to worry about me," she said in a soft voice.

I do, he thought. *Because I love you. And that's what love means. Worrying about someone when they're not feeling well, thinking about them when they're not with you. Doing everything you can to ensure their happiness.*

Of course he didn't say any of that. "I do worry. I am hoping we could continue our discussion on books," he said, giving her a warm smile. "You haven't told me your favorites yet."

"That's like choosing a favorite type of flower," she murmured. "They're all beautiful."

"We'll debate that later," he replied, pulling her blanket up and smoothing it so it wasn't bunched. "I do think you should eat or drink something." He put his hand on her forehead. Thankfully, it still felt normal.

"I suppose," she said in a grumpy tone. "Tea would be fine, and maybe there's some bread? I don't think I can keep anything else down."

Theo sprang to his feet, relieved to have something to do that might possibly help her. "I'll fetch it right away."

"Wait," she said, putting her hand on his knee.

"I haven't said, but I have to thank you. For making this into an adventure, and for accompanying me. It would have been much more difficult without your help."

Theo felt something odd in his chest—was it discomfiture at being caught for his thoughtfulness?

Or the realization that he would do anything she needed?

"You're welcome," he said, his throat thick with emotion.

She squeezed his knee. "I'll be fine while you're out."

"I'll hurry," he promised.

ALEXANDRA SANK FURTHER into the bed when Theo had left their cabin. She felt as sick as she'd ever been, and she hated to inflict that on him, especially since he had just spent so much time and money assisting her.

He hadn't seemed to mind, though. She wanted to think it was because they'd forged a friendship beyond their sexual trysts. It could also have been because he was genuinely kind, or perhaps both. *Both* was preferable.

Her stomach roiled, and she let herself utter a moan, a noise she hadn't released when he was in the room. She wasn't going to be foolish and stoically push through whatever illness this was, but she also wasn't going to inflict her suffering on anyone else if she could help it.

At least the voyage would be over soon, perhaps

in as little as ten hours, and she could return to William's London town house to fully recover, since she knew she'd need her strength to confront him.

Harriet was entirely justified in insisting she stay in Paris, though it meant Alexandra would be the one to face William. But even if Harriet was present, Alexandra wouldn't want her daughter to have the face the brunt of her stepson's wrath. She should have told William when she'd first heard of the scheme that she didn't want her daughter to be any part of his plans. But she had accepted the premise, that gentlemen were always involved in arranging the marriages of their female relatives, even though Alexandra knew firsthand what a terrible idea that was.

It made her angry at herself, that she hadn't stood up for Harriet more thoroughly.

But what would have happened then? a reasonable voice asked in her head. *William would have done everything in his power to make you buckle, including cutting off your monies, pressuring Harriet, and perhaps even throwing you out of the dower house.*

At least this way she'd been able to buy some time, time for Harriet to know her own mind, to concoct the plot to go to Paris.

Though Alexandra strongly suspected Edith had a fair amount to do with that.

"My brave Harriet," she murmured with a smile. Alexandra hadn't been given any opportunity to decline her future, but her daughter had. Alexandra's parents had leapt at the Duke of Chelmswich's offer for their daughter's hand, even though the duke was at least twenty years older and had children older than Alexandra.

In hindsight, Alexandra could see that her husband had tried to control her from the moment they wed. From commenting on how much she ate during the wedding breakfast, to discouraging her from showing any affection toward him—she had, initially, because she thought that was what she was supposed to do—to being overly familiar with the servants.

And even though she wished he was less of an ass, she couldn't blame her stepson for behaving as he did.

Wait. No, she could. But she *could* understand why he behaved as he did—he'd watched his father constrict Alexandra's movements the entire time he'd seen them together, so it was obvious he would continue his father's manipulation.

The thing was, if he had been just a bit more flexible in his goals, she would have gone along happily. If he had urged Harriet to find a groom during her first Season, one with enough money to support her in comfort, one with sufficient standing in their world, Alexandra likely wouldn't have thought about it at all. She would have accepted what he'd wanted, and helped Harriet navigate the matrimonial field.

So in some odd way, perhaps she should be grateful to William for being such an overbearing ass; without his rigidity, she wouldn't have realized how ridiculous and unfair the whole situation was in the first place.

Not that she would express any gratitude at all. He was, after all, still an unmitigated ass.

The door swung open, and Theo appeared, holding a tray, his expression concerned. "How are you feeling?"

Alexandra pushed herself higher up in the bed so she wasn't entirely supine. "About the same," she replied. Her stomach fluttered again as she spoke, belying her words.

"I've brought you tea and some biscuits," he said, putting the tray down on the low table in front of the window seat.

"Tea, please," she said. The steam rose from the pot, and she smiled at thinking how quickly he must have come from wherever he got the tea to here, given how hot it was.

"Milk and sugar?" he asked as he poured.

"Yes please."

He prepared her cup quickly, then came and sat on the floor next to the bed, holding the cup out to her. "I can hold it for you," he offered.

"I can handle it," she said, taking the tea from his grasp. The cup was comfortingly warm, and she took a sip, feeling the liquid slide down her throat. "That is lovely," she said, taking a larger sip.

"Good." His tone was relieved. "I am so sorry you are not feeling well. We should be there in about nine hours or so. I want you to rest."

She handed the half-empty cup to him, offering him a wan smile. "I'm so tired I don't think I have a choice," she replied.

He gave her a wry smile. "You always have a choice, Alexandra."

ALEXANDRA WAS RELIEVED to be feeling better when the ship docked. Theo assisted her off, then swiftly found a hackney and loaded her and their belongings into it, giving the coachman the address for the Chelmswich town house.

"You'll send for me if you feel worse." It wasn't a request.

"Yes, sir," she said, trying to sound cheeky.

"I will worry about you," he continued. "I don't want to allow you to stay there alone—"

"There are servants, you know," she pointed out.

"I know. But I don't know them, and I assume they were hired by your stepson, so who knows if they will take care of you?"

"I doubt William gave orders for me to be mistreated, should I arrive," she said.

He gave her a skeptical look. She couldn't blame him. William and Florence were both petty enough to do something exactly like that, especially if it meant they would save money— giving Alexandra bread and water rather than full meals, for example, or neglecting to call for a doctor if she became ill. Doctors were expensive; dowager duchesses were also expensive.

"Anyway, I will expect you to send a note every

day until you feel well enough to travel back to the country."

She was touched by his consideration—he'd become so much more to her than a one- or two-night distraction. He'd become someone she trusted, someone she relied on, someone she enjoyed spending time with beyond the bedroom.

Someone she loved.

She gasped in shock, and he immediately wrapped his arm around her, drawing her close. "Are you all right?"

No, I am not. I am in love with you, and I am an idiot, she thought. Both things could be true.

"I'm fine. I just got something caught in my throat." *The realization that I love you, and I cannot do anything about it. Because I've told you not to say anything to me of it, and you will honor my wishes.*

How had she gotten herself into this situation? Oh, right, she'd destroyed her mourning clothing and gone to a pleasure garden.

He kept hold of her, rubbing her arm as he made some incoherent noises of comfort. She snuggled in next to him, despite knowing she should be working on getting accustomed to his absence from her life.

Why does this have to end? a voice said inside.

So many reasons, her rational self replied sternly. She was twelve years older than he, and if he was to think of marriage—which clearly he was, given that he'd spoken to William about it, and even spoken to her about it—he'd want someone younger, someone he could have children with.

He cared for her. Perhaps he even did love her. For now. But what about forever? She couldn't trust in that. Though she knew how she would feel to the end of her days.

And she couldn't continue to dally with him—if she did, discovery would be inevitable. Which would entrap him, since he was an honorable person and would insist on marriage, despite his not choosing it.

You always have a choice.

She smothered a rueful sob, wishing that choosing wasn't so difficult—choosing to keep her feelings quiet, choosing to let him go rather than risk his future as well as her own.

If he could just tell her. Admit how he felt, and they'd figure it out together.

He was certainly good at speaking his mind— *Kiss me. Touch me. Fuck me.* His silence on his feelings for her beyond concern when she was worried or ill had to mean that he thought of his feelings, even his love, as temporary—as they'd discussed at the beginning of their relationship. If they were permanent, he would have found the way to say something.

The hackney slowed, and she felt her chest tighten. Soon she would enter the town house, not knowing when or if she'd see him again.

She braced herself to speak when he spoke instead.

"You will let me know how you are doing—I expect I'll have pressing business concerns, so I might not be able to get back to you straight-away. But that does not mean I do not wish to hear from you."

She stiffened, wishing his words didn't feel like a death knell for any hope she had for them. *I'll have pressing business concerns.* Valid, of course, especially since he'd just devoted more time than he must have planned for in the Harriet rescue. Reminding her that his business was a part of his life, whereas she . . . was not.

"Of course. I do appreciate your assisting me. As I said before." She wished she didn't sound so cold. She didn't want to seem ungrateful in any way, but if she let her true feelings out, she'd end up sobbing all over his chest, declaring her love for him.

And, gentleman that he was, he'd likely offer to do something to resolve it. She couldn't have that, not when he'd already done so much.

"You are welcome." He withdrew his arm from around her as the carriage drew to a stop. He leaned across to open the door, then got out, holding his hand out for her.

She took it, stepping down onto the pavement.

"I'll see you in," he said, gesturing to the front door.

She nodded, and he held her hand still, assisting her up the steps.

He knocked on the door, and they could hear it

echo within. Then they heard footsteps walking swiftly through the foyer.

The door was flung open, and instead of the butler or housekeeper standing there, it was William.

William with a furious expression.

Chapter Twenty-Two

"I did not realize you were in town, William," Alexandra said in a cool tone. Theo had been begrudging that same tone just a few minutes earlier—when she'd thanked him for his efforts—but now he wanted to applaud it.

"That is all you have to say to me?" William spat.

She arched a disdainful brow. "If you would like to have this conversation on the steps, we can do that." She gestured toward the other houses on the street. "If we are fortunate, perhaps we can speak loudly enough that everyone can hear. Is that what you want?"

William's jaw clamped shut, and he turned on his heel, striding away from the door, clearly expecting them to follow.

He indicated the direction. "I'll be right behind you."

"You don't have to come with me, you know," she said in a low tone. So she hadn't expected

Theo to follow. It hurt, that she'd assume he would want to leave when she was in difficulty.

"I do," he said in a curt tone. "Some of this is due to me, to my saying things I should not have. I have learned my lesson."

Her expression shifted, and he wondered if he'd said something wrong. But he'd been clear that he had had the discussions with her stepson before. This wasn't new information.

But he didn't have time to ponder it, not when William was already well down the hall and Alexandra was following him.

Theo stepped into the room at the end of the hall, the other two already inside.

They stood at nearly opposite corners of the room, as though they were boxers in a ring preparing to spar.

Theo turned to shut the door, then leaned against it, folding his arms over his chest. He'd do his best not to interfere—Alexandra would not want that—but he would not allow her stepson to browbeat her.

Even if it meant she was angry at Theo.

"You went to find her, and yet here you are, without her." William approached her, and Theo saw her straighten to her full height—at least two inches taller than her stepson—and brace herself.

"I went to see that she was safe," Alexandra corrected him. "She is. She is fine, and she is staying in Paris for now with your sister and Mr. Ash."

By now, William was almost touching her, his

fury palpable. He flung his arm out in Theo's direction, pointing his finger toward him, without taking his gaze off of Alexandra. "And what about him? He is supposed to marry into this family, only now he cannot because of you."

Theo opened his mouth, but she shot him a glare that dared him to say a word, and he snapped his mouth shut again. He would do as she wished, even if he didn't like it.

Unless he saw no other recourse.

"Harriet does not wish to marry Mr. Osborne," she said, again in that cool tone. He admired her demeanor—she would be excellent in a business negotiation.

William gave a derisive snort, then pointed his finger toward Alexandra. "Then I do not wish to support you. Since we are all declaring what we want."

Her cheeks flared with color, and he heard her take a breath. "Your father married me, whether you like it or not. My daughter is your half sister. I am part of your family, and you are obligated to assist, no matter how much we loathe one another."

Now it was William's turn to breathe hard and turn red. "Loathe one another? How dare you dislike me, after all I've done for you?"

She looked taken aback, and Theo couldn't blame her—he hadn't known either of them long, but he doubted whether William had done anything other than treat his stepmother horribly.

"You have done nothing for me." Her tone was

cold and furious. "And I will do nothing for you. I am sorry my daughter knows she does not wish to marry Mr. Osborne. I am even sorrier that you have mismanaged your financials so badly that you even attempted this devil's bargain. And I am the sorriest that I have the bad fortune to be related to you, though I do not regret my marriage to your father. Because it gave me Harriet."

William's mouth gaped open, and for a moment, he looked as though he might strike her. Theo stepped forward, prepared to take the bastard down, when instead William took a deep breath and spoke, his voice as cold as hers. "You will have no place in our family. You will vacate the dower house, you will receive nothing from me any longer, starting now, and everything you own—everything—rightly belongs to the estate, so you will be obliged to return it." He advanced closer. "You will have nothing. Nothing, do you hear me?"

Theo couldn't take it any longer. He strode up to them, moving Alexandra aside to glare down at William. "She will have plenty. She will marry me, and she will have my money. All the money you can't get your hands on. She will be comfortable for the rest of her life, and you won't be able to touch her ever again."

Theo vibrated with rage—rage against yet another aristocrat who was using his power as a bludgeon when he could be doing something useful with his influence. Rage that he couldn't just knock the man down in righteous retribution because he'd be demonstrating the result of his unseemly birth if he did something so violent. Anger that she hadn't already asked him to help when he had made the offer so many times.

The duke snorted. "You, marry *her*? She's old enough to be your mother."

Then Theo couldn't help himself; he swung his hand back, delivering an open-palmed slap to the duke's face, making him stagger back.

"How. Dare. You," the duke said, holding his blazing-red cheek. He pointed a trembling finger toward him. "I will blacken your name. Yours and your harlot wife-to-be."

Theo's hands were balled into fists at his sides, and he heard his own seething breath coming from his lungs. "You will not," he said in a measured tone, "or I will buy up all your debts and require payment. It wouldn't take much to ruin you, Your Grace. And I will, if you harm so much as a hair on her body."

William's lips curled with derision. "You two are welcome to one another. I am done. Get out."

Theo took Alexandra's arm in an attempt to guide her safely out of the room, but she shook him off, striding ahead of him as he followed.

He didn't spare a look toward the duke, just kept his gaze on her back, proud of how she held herself straight and tall, not faltering at all in leaving.

And she would be his wife. He could rescue her from the situation and be with the woman he loved.

It was unfortunate it had happened like this—he wished he had figured out a way to propose when it wasn't a crisis—but it had. He was secretly relieved it had required this immediate decision. She must see that this was the right way forward, even though all of it came at such a fraught time.

"Alexandra," he called, as she flung the door open and walked out of the house.

She didn't stop.

ALEXANDRA SHOVED PAST Theo to the front door, opening it without waiting for the butler, then marched through, tears blurring her vision.

She felt him behind her and she increased her pace, not wanting to speak with him or even touch him. Not with how she felt at the moment.

How could she have been so wrong? He wasn't supposed to rescue her, like some sort of white knight. He was supposed to support her choices. She'd made that very clear, and she thought he'd understood.

She knew he'd understood. But he'd done just what she'd feared—he'd taken the decision out of her hands at a moment of crisis. There was no way to prevent that from happening in the future, if they went through with his terrible plan.

"Alexandra," he called, and she kept walking, taking deep gulps of air untinged by the duke's malice.

He reached her side, and she felt his gaze on her, but she couldn't look at him.

"Let me hail a hack—" he began.

"No." Her voice was shaky, and she concentrated on settling herself down so she wouldn't burst into tears out here. Definitely not in public, and most definitely not in front of him.

He must've figured out something was wrong, or at least more wrong than he already knew, because he put his hand on her arm and squeezed. "It will be fine, I promise." His tone was well-meaning. Conciliatory. Which only made her madder. "I meant what I said in there. I will marry you. We can make all of this go away."

She removed his hand from her arm. "How. Dare. You," she said, repeating William's words. "You—you just decided for me in there?" Her voice was strained. "You just said what you were going to do to save the day without asking me anything at all about it?" The tears came then, pouring down her face as she felt her breath catch. He reached out to touch her again, and she pushed his hand away.

"I don't want to be saved, Theo. I said just that before. Many times, in fact. What I wanted— never mind. It doesn't matter." Nothing mattered. He had the chance to understand her, she thought he did, and then he just—announced what they'd be doing. Just as her late husband had. Just as all the men in her life before had done.

No. She would not tolerate any more of that. It was clear he didn't have any feelings for her beyond his innate kindness. Otherwise he would have known how upset she'd be at his presumption. More than presumption—arrogance. Assumption. Audacity.

"I do not wish to continue this conversation. I do not wish to see you again."

She flung her hand up, hoping a passing hackney would see her. She had enough money in her reticule to get her—where? Where would she go?

Her brain seized on an idea, and she resolved to follow it, not thinking about it beyond its immediate solution.

A hackney saw her and slowed, and she leapt in, giving the driver the address, not bothering to lower her voice. He'd figure out where she was soon enough, but it wouldn't change anything.

"You're going to Simeon's?" he said, sounding both angry and hurt. "Come home with me. We can talk about this. You don't have anywhere else to go."

The reminder of which she did not need at the moment.

"Alexandra!" she heard him call as the driver urged the horses forward. She leaned back against the seat and let the tears flow. Knowing that after the crying, her resolve would harden.

THEO STARED AFTER the hackney, feeling as though he had been gut-punched.

Scratch that. He *had* been gut-punched—by her. *I do not wish to see you again.*

What had happened?

He replayed the past twenty minutes over in

his mind, from walking in and unexpectedly seeing the duke, to watching the argument until he couldn't take it anymore.

What had he done wrong? His vision was a blur. The only thing he could see was her face—hurt. Betrayed. Anguished.

What had he done wrong?

He just wanted to help, he couldn't stand seeing her browbeaten by the duke. Even though she was hardly browbeaten. She was giving as much as she got.

She had it handled, and then he—

Fuck.

It hit him, then, what he had done. *She had it handled.*

After so many times reassuring her that he'd let her have her own choice, that she was free to do what she wanted, he'd pushed past all of that to assert *he* would be the one to solve her problems.

Even though she had implicitly and explicitly told him she did not want that.

Even though he'd tried to do the same thing earlier, and she had shut him down.

He'd done just what she'd been most scared of. And then he had the temerity to think she would be grateful for it.

His stomach clenched, and it took all his strength not to fall onto his knees and howl in pain. Ruining everything with one misguided attempt to fix things—when that wouldn't be the way to fix anything, not at all.

The hackney was well out of sight, but he still stood there on the sidewalk, staring out into the pain of the rest of his life. She might never speak to him again. She might never acknowledge his existence again, now that she'd made her decision to protect her daughter in the way she wished to.

She would definitely never accept his help, no matter what type of help it was.

Not even if he was to find a way to get help to her without her knowing who'd provided it—that too would be a violation of what he'd already violated.

At last, he turned away, glancing to figure out where his house lay from here. A long way, since the duke lived in the most fashionable area of town, and Theo . . . did not.

Time to think everything through was both the last thing he wanted and the first thing he needed.

People walked past him as he began to make his way home. People living their lives as usual, chatting to each other, carrying baskets with food from the market or ribbons from the haberdasher.

Carriages went to and fro on the street beside him, the constant clopping of the horses' hooves and jingling harnesses an auditory backdrop to his churning thoughts.

The day was relatively pleasant, and if it had been any other time, Theo would have welcomed the infrequent freedom—time when it wasn't possible for him to be working, or playing, but just being. When was the last time he had just *been*?

He was usually pursuing whatever it was he was pursuing at the time with such alacrity he didn't have time for walks, no matter how quickly he traveled.

But now, no matter how much he increased his pace, he couldn't run away from the truth of it.

He had done what she did not want. The epitome of the thing she did not want, in fact. That he knew it, though it remained to be seen if it was too late, was a place to start.

He couldn't let her think he never realized what he'd done—she had to know, to understand, that he respected her and her autonomy far too much. That his response in the heat of the moment wasn't reasonable, or even remotely correct.

She might still never speak to him again, but at least she might understand that he believed in her ability to choose for herself, not to have to be beholden to any man ever again.

Though that seemed contradictory, didn't it? Insisting she understand that a man accepted her autonomy?

It was pure male arrogance to want to correct her belief. The same pure male arrogance that had compelled him to rush in in the first place.

But he *was* male, he *was* arrogant, and he had to

make certain she felt—if not better, at least more settled, knowing that he understood he'd made a terrible mistake.

Because he had.

He'd made a terrible mistake, and it might be one from which he would never recover.

Chapter Twenty-Three

Alexandra bit back another sob, then forced herself to take a deep breath. She didn't know how long it would take to get to Mr. Jones's house, but she didn't want to arrive a sopping mess.

She would definitely be a mess, but she'd prefer not to be sopping.

Her handkerchief was buried somewhere in her gown, and she poked around until she found it, then wiped her eyes with trembling hands, relieved that it felt as though her tears were starting to slow.

The encounter with William had left her shaking and furious, but it wasn't until Theo spoke that she felt devastated.

She already knew William was an empowered ass who believed he was superior because of something inherent to himself, not because he was born into his wealth and privilege. And had then frittered away his wealth, apparently, leaving him only his privilege to bludgeon others with.

Theo, on the other hand, had been born into nothing—no name, no wealth, no privilege. He'd found a loving home, first with his friends and then with his adoptive father, Mr. Osborne, at which point he'd also achieved wealth, and then kept on growing it.

He was a self-made man, someone to be admired for what he had done. But still a man, with all the assumed rights of power that men seemed to have, as natural to them as breathing.

He had listened when she'd spoken. He'd seemed to understand what she was saying. He'd heard her when he'd tried to rescue her the first time. Or so she thought.

And yet, when it came time to prove he'd truly understood, he stomped all over her rights in order to assert his own. Negating hers.

Even when it was clear how upset she was, he hadn't gotten it. Meaning that while yes, he'd listened, he hadn't *heard*. Theo was a kind, thoughtful man, but that didn't mean he wouldn't trample over her opinion, her self-sufficiency, if he thought he knew better.

"You're a fool," she said to herself, then gave her head a vehement shake. Immediately disagreeing with herself. "No. No, you are not. You are a person who deserves the best, despite what you've gotten in the past. You should not blame yourself for something that is not of your doing." She was the woman who'd destroyed her mourning clothing, after all. Who'd looked for—and found—her own pleasure. The woman she used to be would never have done that.

In the past, she'd always questioned if a slight change or adjustment would improve things. If she was just more compliant, if she was quieter, or spoke up more, or wore fancier gowns, or dressed her hair differently, perhaps her husband would appreciate her more.

She'd come to realize, of course, that it wasn't about what she did at all. His dislike of her had nothing to do with her and everything to do with how he perceived himself: a man who should be able to control and manipulate everyone around him to suit his needs, who grew petulant and frustrated when he couldn't.

His son was just the same.

But unlike before, Alexandra did not have to tolerate the current duke's behavior. Nor would she; Harriet should be free to make her own choices, not be subjected to some weak man's wishes.

The same went for Alexandra. Theo wasn't weak, but she couldn't see him in her life any longer, no matter that she loved him, and she was already aching from the loss of him.

The carriage slowed, and she glanced out the window to see the sign proclaiming the building to be Mr. Finneas's Fine Establishment. She had arrived. This was the next step in her adventure. Without him.

She withdrew the scant coins she had in her pocket, her breath catching as she realized she wouldn't have access to any more funds, at least not until she figured out some sort of plan. But she would figure it out; her late husband had given her jewels, for example, that did not belong to the duchy, and she could sell them, if she could find a reputable shop. She'd also need to retrieve them in the first place, but that was all part of the planning process.

"Miss?" the cabbie said, impatient.

Right. Nobody would be at the door waiting to escort her out. She would have to do it herself.

The enormity of striking out on her own hit her, but not necessarily in a terrifying way; there were so many possibilities that were, well, *possible* looming in front of her, and she knew now she had the ability to make her own choices.

Her first choice would be to march into Mr. Jones's home and ask for his help.

She took another deep breath—likely the first of many today—and strode toward the door leading to the upstairs apartments.

"Your Grace," Mr. Jones said, his usually smoothly charming face showing surprise and a bit of shock. "Is Theo all right?" he said, peering behind her.

"He is." Alexandra lifted her chin. "May I come in?"

"Of course," Mr. Jones said, sweeping his hand out to indicate the room. "Can I get you some tea? Water? Something stronger?"

Alexandra walked into the studio, the same painting Mr. Jones had been working on set on an easel, looking closer to finished, but still in progress.

It had only been a few days since she'd first come here, and yet it felt like a lifetime ago.

"I'd like something stronger, please," she said in what she hoped was a suitably assertive voice.

Mr. Jones gave her a quick look, then left the room, doubtless to fetch the stronger beverage.

"Please sit, Your Grace," he called, and she glanced around the room, her brows drawing together as she looked for somewhere to do just that.

The only seat was a cozy love seat at one end of the room, probably something he used in setting up a scene to paint. Her cheeks heated at the thought of what could happen there, and she marveled at her own salacity, acquired only since—since that night at the Garden of Hedon.

She settled herself on the cushion, leaning against the back in a way that no proper duchess or even dowager duchess should allow herself to do.

But she was no longer going to be proper. She hadn't been proper since entering the Garden. At some point, she would want to tell Edith just how important it had been for her to go there—to tell Edith how valuable her friendship and support were.

She did have resources after all, didn't she? Here she was, confident that Theo's friend would help her, even though he'd only met her once before. Knowing that Theo's bond with the Bastard Five was so strong that they would extend their support to someone he cared about.

And he *did* care about her. She knew that. It was impossible to miss, even though she had tried her best to ignore it. That he had been so concerned on the ship when she wasn't feeling well, that he had agreed to go with her in the first place.

That he hadn't reacted defensively when she'd made it clear he'd erred. He'd been confused, but he hadn't then blamed his confusion on her as some lesser man would have. As her late husband or her stepson would have.

And he'd nearly told her he loved her. But love was a different thing than respect. And she didn't believe he respected her, not if he was so able to stomp on her wish to decide for herself.

"Here you are," Mr. Jones said, handing her a glass filled with brown liquid.

She brought it to her nose, taking a deep inhale. It smelled smoky and strong, and she took a small sip, feeling it burn as it slid down her throat.

He sat next to her, arranging his elegant limbs just so, stretching his hand across the back of the sofa so it was only a few inches away from her shoulder. She knew he wasn't being deliberately inappropriate, that his charm and sensuality were as natural to him as breathing.

"How can I help, Your Grace?" he asked, his tone serious. Completely at odds with how he was seated.

"I need to retrieve my jewelry from the Chelmswich dower house in the country. It's on the current duke's estate."

"What else?" he asked, as though her request was easily taken care of.

"Oh," she replied, taking another sip. "I will want to sell the jewelry, and I will have to find a place to live. A place I can afford, given that what I get for the jewels might be the only money I ever have."

A terrifying thought, but at least she had those resources. Many other people were not nearly as fortunate—they'd have to endure whatever life forced on them without recourse simply because of the position they'd been born into.

She resolved to do whatever she could to help those people, once she'd solved her own mess.

But first she had to solve her own mess.

"Do you want to tell me what happened with Theo?" he asked, speaking in a gentle tone. "Why he isn't here with you now, solving things?"

She gave a strangled laugh, then glanced away from his penetrating gaze, looking instead toward the other wall, the one with the windows that looked out onto the street. The sun was shining, though there were a few clouds floating idly by. No matter how much she hurt, she had to remember that the sun would continue to shine, that she would be able to see the beauty of each day, no matter how she faced it.

"My first instinct is to say no, I don't want to

talk about him," she began, her speech slower than usual, "but I think my instinct is wrong." She turned to meet his eyes. "Just as his was."

Mr. Jones gave her an encouraging nod.

"And I don't know what to do about it all, just that it felt—it feels like a betrayal. Of me, and what and who I am."

He didn't speak for a moment, but she could tell he was thinking about what she'd said. Formulating a thoughtful reply rather than an instinctive defense of his best friend.

She might not have a future with Theo, at least not a permanent, romantic one—but she could count at least two of his friends as hers as well. She had no doubt that either Fenton or Simeon would assist her, no matter what eventually happened between her and Theo.

"Theo is one of the most loyal people I've ever known," Mr. Jones began. "Not that I acquainted with that many people."

"You know the Bastard Five," she ventured, feeling audacious at saying the forbidden word.

He snorted. "He told you that, hmm?" He shook his head in fond reminiscence. "But Theo, like all of us, has his faults. I assume one of them appeared at the worst possible moment."

"That is a good way to put it, yes," Alexandra replied. "I needed him to do something for me, and he did not. He did the opposite."

"And telling you his intentions were good is beside the point," Mr. Jones said insightfully.

"Also yes," she said, feeling her chest tighten again.

Mr. Jones nodded in understanding. "I can't do anything to solve Theo's stupidity, but I can help you. Since you're a friend of his, you're also a friend of mine." He clapped his hands on his knees and rose, clearly preparing to tackle the tasks she'd mentioned. "The first thing is that you need a place to stay, at least until we find you a home." He glanced around the studio. "I'll vacate, and you can stay here."

"I couldn't kick you out of your own home," she exclaimed.

He waggled his eyebrows at her. "You're assuming I don't have plenty of places willing to offer me a bed?"

Her eyes widened, and she felt her cheeks turning pink. He laughed in response.

"I'll have to let Theo know you're safe, you understand," he said, more seriously.

"He is aware that I came here."

Mr. Jones looked startled. "He is?"

"He heard me give the direction to the hackney driver," she confirmed.

"Then we should be hearing—" Mr. Jones began, only to be interrupted by a loud knocking at the door.

"There he is," he said. "Do you want me to let him in? Or I can just tell him you're fine."

That he was willing to stand up for her against his friend, willing to let her choose what would happen next, made her heart squeeze inside her chest. Theo was a good man, with good men as friends.

"No," she said at last. "He doesn't deserve to see me so soon after—after everything." She lifted her chin. "I shouldn't have to listen to whatever he has to say, not now, not when he could have said other things earlier."

Mr. Jones regarded her for a long moment. "I think I agree with you," he said finally. "He should stew in whatever he did so he understands it—healing a wound takes time, doesn't it?"

"Exactly." And her wound was still fresh. It would heal. She had come too far to allow it to fester. But she felt raw and hurt, and if she saw him—if she saw him and he was sorry—she might forgive him because it would make the ache go away.

But it wouldn't be right.

He needed to understand fully why she was upset, and she doubted he did, not just an hour after the encounter.

"I'll tell him," Mr. Jones said.

THEO HAD INTENDED to return home, was nearly there when he realized that he wouldn't be able to go on as though things were normal when it felt as though every breath was a struggle.

How could he run his business, read the next book for the monthly meeting, even talk to his friends when every one of his thoughts was about her? There was no point in the facade when it wouldn't even fool himself.

Instead, he changed direction, making his way to Simeon's. Because he wouldn't be able to live unless he knew she was, if not all right, at least protected.

He ran through all the things he could say to her, all the ways he could try to explain.

But there was no explanation. There were only excuses, ones with which he'd try to justify what he'd done when there was no justification. There was just—apologizing. Telling her how he truly felt? Begging for her forgiveness?

All of it?

By the time he reached Mr. Finneas's Fine Establishment, he'd come up with nearly fifty different ways to say he was sorry, to ask that she understand that he'd only meant to help her, even if the effect was exactly the opposite.

None of it made sense.

Simeon answered the door, looking like his normal devilish self.

"She's here?" Theo asked, hoping her stepson hadn't somehow located her and carted her away.

"She's here." Simeon held the door open, but not wide enough for Theo to step through, which made the hairs on the back of his neck prickle in worry. "And she doesn't want to see you." Simeon made as though to shut the door, but Theo wedged his foot in, blocking it.

"She has to. I need to tell her—"

"Whatever you need to tell her can wait until she is ready. You can't just barge in and make whatever explanation you want on your schedule. She has to be ready to hear what you're saying." Simeon's expression was set. "Yes, you can knock me over and rush up the stairs to her, but that negates what she wants."

Theo's blood ran cold at hearing the truth of it. Simeon was right; if he insisted on seeing her now, he'd be doubling down on his making unilateral decisions. Not taking her own wishes into consideration because he was so desperate to make things right.

"What do I do?" he said, his voice breaking.

Simeon's expression relaxed, and he put his hand on Theo's arm, gripping his bicep. "You figure out what she needs to hear—not what you need to say—and you beg her to listen."

It was good advice.

"But what if she never . . . ?" Theo asked, running his hand through his hair in desperation. "What if she never wishes to speak to me again? What then?"

"Then you live with that," Simeon said, his tone regretful. "You live knowing you've managed to ruin the best thing in your entire life."

It sounded as though Simeon was speaking from firsthand experience. Odd, though, that Theo didn't know about the relationship, if it was something Simeon had gone through.

"Please tell her—please tell her," he said, shaking his head in frustration. "I don't know what to say."

Simeon pushed him gently out of the doorway. "That's why you have to go think about it. So you find the words. You only have one chance. Don't mess it up."

Theo met his friend's gaze, seeing the sympathy in Simeon's eyes, the resolve with which he held the door.

Theo's chest felt as though it was being squeezed in a vise, but he would have to get accustomed to that—as Simeon said, he had one chance to make it better, and he couldn't risk saying the wrong thing. Again.

Chapter Twenty-Four

"What now?" Simeon asked.

Alexandra looked up from her book to regard him. She'd spent the past week living in Mr. Jones's, now Simeon's, rooms. It was entirely scandalous, but she couldn't care.

Simeon had adapted easily, leaving his rooms in the early afternoon and returning in the late morning, working in his studio until teatime. Alexandra was busy trying to navigate her life, which was hard because she'd never done anything of the sort before.

People had always done things for her.

And she had to say, she didn't like it. The most recent example of someone trying to do something for her was not the most egregious, to be honest, but it was the only one over which she had any agency.

She was still feeling ill, though not as poorly as she'd felt on the ship—she blamed it on her unease, and it was better at some parts of the day than others. She hadn't wanted to call the Chelmswich family doctor, however, since she hadn't gotten money yet, and she certainly couldn't ask William to pay for it.

"You want your house back," she said. "I don't blame you, it's—"

"It's not that," he interrupted, a smile on his handsome face. "But I know you are struggling with all of it, and I wonder if it's time to speak to him." Theo had sent notes several times a day, and had come by the rooms once a day as well. Every time she'd refused to see him—it hurt too much to think about, and she was hoping that if she went days without seeing him, maybe someday she'd be able to bear it.

Thus far, her plan was not working.

She stilled at his words. "I don't—"

"If it's not time," he said hastily, "then I am wrong."

She gave him a wry smile. "If only it was so easy to get a gentleman to admit he was wrong."

"Ah, but I am no gentleman, Alexandra," he replied, waggling his eyebrows. "I am a bastard and an artist, neither of which is seen as anything remotely polite."

His canvases were propped up around the room, and by now, Alexandra had gotten accustomed to seeing paintings of random unclothed men and women in nearly every corner.

"But to be serious for a moment—which, as anyone will tell you, is not my favorite way to be—I care for both of you, and I can see that both of you are suffering. If you are able to talk it out, perhaps you can reach some sort of understanding with one another."

"You want me to marry him." Her whole body felt cold. "To forgive him."

"No!" he shot back. "Not at all. Not if that is not what you want." He nodded to her abdomen. "But you're going to have to figure something out before . . ." His words trailed off, and she looked at him, puzzled.

He gave another significant look toward her midsection.

"What do you . . . ?" she began, and then she froze.

Oh no, oh no, oh no. It wasn't . . . was it?

"Oh no," she said, wrapping her arm over her belly. "Do you think?"

Simeon cocked his head and regarded her. "I thought you knew?"

"No. No, I didn't. But—" But now it all made sense. Her nausea, the discomfort, the fatigue. She'd thought it was because of the stress, and that might have been part of it, but this—this was something real. Something she'd have to deal with.

This was momentous, and she felt the wonder of it all. She knew, whatever happened next, that she would be able to handle it. The child would be born of passion, and discovery, and ultimately love. Because she still loved him.

She groaned. "This will give him even more reason to want to marry me."

"Besides the fact that he loves you?" Simeon said, one eyebrow raised.

She brushed that aside.

"What am I going to do?" she asked. She gestured to her stomach. "If he finds out about it, I'll never know the truth." She took a breath. "Know the truth of how he actually feels about me, I mean. He's so honorable—" she said, her words trailing off.

Simeon shrugged, as though it was of no importance. "So don't let him find out. Talk to him, and see what happens. If it's right to tell him, you will."

"How am I going—I mean, you figured it out."

"I am remarkable, remember?" he said. "Seriously, there are ways to hide it, but you shouldn't leave it for too long. And I promise you, no matter what you decide, I will support your decision."

"Why couldn't I have fallen in love with you?" she said in mock exasperation.

"You love him." It was a statement, not a question. He hadn't pried, even though she imagined he wanted to. But it seemed now they were to the point where she should be honest.

"I do," she said, shaking her head. "It would be far easier if I didn't." She tilted her head to consider it. "If I didn't love him, I wouldn't care that he might be sacrificing himself for my security. If I didn't love him, he wouldn't be able to hurt me with his ill-chosen words. If I didn't love him, I could just demand he do the responsible thing and marry me." She exhaled. "But I do. So I can't."

"And that's why you need to speak with him." He rose from his seat. "As you know, I have a plethora of clothing available, so we should be able to find something that will disguise your imminent arrival."

She got up as well, her hand already going instinctively to her stomach. "I'll speak to him." She walked toward Simeon, catching his fingers in hers. "Thank you, friend," she said.

He looked unaccustomedly abashed, then recovered, leaning forward to press a kiss on her cheek. "You are welcome."

THEO FROWNED DOWN at the paperwork on his desk. He'd been trying to work on it all morning, but all he could do—all he had done for the past week—was think about her. He understood why she might not want to see him, to hear him explain, but it didn't mean he would give up. He'd written letters and went to Simeon's rooms at least once a day, with the temptation to go more often always lurking, but thus far he hadn't seen her.

But he had to believe some day she would agree to hear him apologize.

That's all he wanted to do—he didn't have any plans to make any sort of grand gesture, like showing up with a deed to a country estate or fistfuls of diamonds. He could well afford any of it, but it wasn't what she would want. And he wanted to give her what she wanted.

A simple apology.

And then he could try to mend what he'd broken with his stubborn insistence that he could solve her problem when she'd been clear she wanted to solve it herself.

It was no use. He wasn't going to be able to work, not until he'd made his daily visit to Simeon's. He rose, feeling as though this was a habit he was going to continue for a long while—work until he couldn't stand it any longer, then get turned away, then come back home and draft yet another apology.

There were sheafs of paper stacked on one side of his desk, all of the apologies he'd written, all of them lacking in one way or another.

He was at Simeon's thirty minutes later, not having bothered with calling for his carriage, but taking a hackney cab instead.

He knocked and waited.

The door swung open, and Simeon stood there, a smirk on his face.

Theo didn't think his friend enjoyed seeing him suffer, but he did think Simeon was taking some artistic inspiration from it—perhaps he'd do a painting titled *Man in Pain*, or *My Idiotic Friend*, or something like that.

"I would like to see Alexandra," he said, as he'd said every other day.

Instead of refusing, however, Simeon opened

the door wide enough for Theo to step through. "Come up," he said. "She'll see you."

Theo felt himself freeze in panic, then took a deep breath and followed Simeon up the stairs.

She stood where the model had stood the last time they'd been there, when they'd gotten disguises for going to France. Was that only a month or so ago?

It felt like a lifetime.

She wore a voluminous cloak over her gown, and she was holding something in her arms as if it was precious. She looked pale.

"Alexandra is posing for me," Simeon explained. "I asked her to hold the pose for just a moment longer, if you don't mind. I need to capture that expression."

Theo swallowed against the lump in his throat. She looked so beautiful it made his heart hurt. Her expression—the one Simeon was painting—was determined. Strong. Proud.

Like she was now, Theo knew. When he'd first met her at the Garden, she wouldn't have known how to look like that. But now, after what she'd been through and what she'd decided for herself, it was as natural to her as her inherent grace.

"I'm painting something based on a Mary Shelley work," Simeon explained, even though Theo only half heard him.

"Shelley?" he said at last. "Like *Frankenstein*?"

"Not *Frankenstein*," Simeon replied in exasperation. "It's *Valperga*. It's the story of a woman who has to make a difficult decision about her life. I'm painting the crucial moment. She's standing on the beach about to embark on a boat that will take her away from the man she loves because it's the right thing to do."

Theo winced at how appropriate that description was for what was happening in real life. He met Alexandra's gaze for just a moment, and that awareness was there in her eyes, along with a bright pain that made him hurt all over again. As if he'd stopped hurting a week ago.

"There," Simeon said, laying his brush down. "I'll go out for a bit and leave you two." He nodded toward Alexandra. "I will see you later, Alex."

Theo had a moment of intense jealousy at hearing the nickname coming from Simeon, but he knew it was only his male pride rearing up inappropriately again.

There was silence as Simeon made his way to the stairwell. Then Theo nodded toward her.

"Good afternoon, Alexandra." *Angel. My Angel.*

She nodded in reply, then bent down to place the parcel she'd been holding on the ground. "I need to sit for a bit. I've been up there for some time," she said, making her way toward the love seat. She did not invite him to sit, and he did not ask.

She kept her cloak on, and he saw her shiver.

"Are you cold?" he asked, looking around the room to find the fireplace. There wasn't one. "We could move into the other room, and I could build up the fire," he said, wanting to make her as comfortable as possible.

"I am fine. I do not want you to do anything." Her tone was cold. Distant.

"I see," he replied. "Can I— How have you been?"

She inclined her head. "Fine, thank you. Simeon says you have been by every day. And I've gotten your notes. You didn't say what you wanted to see me about in the notes, however, so I presume that is why you are here."

"I needed to see you," he began, then shook his head, frustrated with himself. "That is, I thought that you deserve an explanation for my behavior that day. Not an excuse. I want to tell you I understand now why what I did was the most wrong thing ever. The wrongest. I was so wrong, and I only wanted to help, but—" He paused, shaking his head. "It's not about me, about what I thought I was doing. It's about you, and what you wanted at that time." He met her gaze. "I am so sorry, Alexandra."

Chapter Twenty-Five

I am so sorry, Alexandra.

Five words. Five words she'd never heard from anyone before.

She nearly told him it was all right, he was forgiven, because that was what she had always done in the past—accommodated someone who was discomfited by something she may or may not have done.

But no. She deserved more than that. Not that she wanted to see him grovel—no, scratch that, she *did* want to see him grovel—but she needed him to understand the entirety of his wrongness.

"Thank you," she said. She gestured toward him. "You can sit, if you like."

From his expression, one would have thought she had invited him to go to the moon. If the moon was a place he intensely wanted to visit, that is.

He sat gingerly beside her, taking care to sit at one corner so he wouldn't crowd her.

"I told you about my marriage," she began.

"And you know that when my mourning period was over, I vowed to do what I wanted." She paused, searching for the right words. "I want to make my own decisions. All of them." Her tone was emphatic. "I acknowledge that not all of my decisions will be the right ones—but they will be mine. Not anybody else's."

He met her gaze. His stare was intense, as though she was the only thing he could see.

"That doesn't mean that I am so arrogant that I won't accept opinions." She gave him a rueful smile. "I'm not a man, after all." At this, he smiled back, making her heart ease a bit. "And if it ends up that there is something that requires collaboration, I will gladly do that. But what happened earlier—" she hesitated, still not sure how to put it all into words "—that was you deciding for me what was right." She felt herself tear up. "You didn't ask me first. It would have been so simple—'Do you want to marry me, Alexandra?'—but you didn't."

His expression tightened, and she could see him processing her words. She hoped he understood her, because this was the best she was going to be able to explain it, even if it sounded like a big mess.

"Asking you what you want," he said, his words slow and deliberate. "I asked you what you wanted in bed, but that wasn't enough."

Her throat got thick. "No. No, it wasn't." The urge to tell him that it didn't matter, because this was just a momentary interlude, was strong, but she resisted. Because she knew—she absolutely knew—that he loved her.

He'd respected her desires, had vowed not to marry her daughter because it was important to her, even when they'd had just one night together, had gone to the country with her and then to Paris, and had taken care of her so tenderly when she was ill on the boat.

Did he love her enough to adjust his thinking? Because he might love her, care for her, and want to provide for her and their baby, but if he couldn't recognize she was his equal, that she had her own opinions and thoughts, then he didn't love her enough.

Their baby. Her thoughts caught there, and she felt her breath hitch. Then he was asking, "Are you all right? Do you need tea, or water, or something?"

She gave a small smile. "No, I am fine." *Just thinking about the life we created.*

He got off the love seat, going to kneel in front of her, gazing up at her with a mixture of love and pain in his eyes. "Alexandra. I didn't ask you before. I didn't even tell you before. But I am here now, and I am so sorry for hurting you. I—" and he took a deep breath "—I love you. I want to marry you. I want to spend the rest of my life listening to you, and working things out together, and giving you everything we decide, together, that you want."

He waited, not saying another word, where

someone else might have continued to press his case, kept talking to fill up the space between them.

But he didn't. He waited.

She kept her gaze locked on him, saw everything he'd just said in his eyes. He was absolutely still, waiting—waiting for her choice. Her decision.

And then she knew, absolutely, what she must do.

THEO DID NOT stop looking at her. Stop staring at her, if he was honest. The first time they'd met, he'd obviously noticed and appreciated her beauty; but now, her beauty was only one aspect of who she was. She was kind, thoughtful, and was beginning to know her own worth. She was a fiercely protective mother, a good friend, an empathetic listener, and an excellent traveling companion.

The thing he wanted most in the world was for her to agree to spend the rest of their lives together, but unless that was what she wanted too, he'd have to walk away. This was it. He wouldn't try to persuade her into anything; he'd said what he should have said before, and now it was up to her. He wouldn't pressure her, or entice her with anything more than what he had said. She needed to make her choice with her whole heart.

After a moment, a lifetime, she rose, still wearing her cloak, and leaned down to put her hand on his shoulder, squeezing it as she gestured for him to rise also.

They stood face-to-face, she only a few inches shorter than he, both of them staring into one another's eyes. It felt as though he could hear her heart beating, even though he knew that was impossible.

"Thank you," she began, and for a moment, it sounded as though she would follow that up with a *but* . . . and his heart sank.

"There are things I should have said to you before as well," she continued. "The first is that I love you, too." She gave a warm smile as she spoke, and he knew it would be all right. That his heart wouldn't break. "But," she said, and then his emotions took a plunge into icy despair, "there is something you should know, because it affects both of us." She put her hands to her cloak and pulled it off, sliding it off her shoulders and onto the love seat behind her.

For a moment, he had no idea what she was talking about. He should know she could remove her own cloak? That she was wearing a gown underneath? That the love seat was a good place to put a garment?

And then she slid her hand over her belly in an unmistakable maternal gesture. He gaped at her, frozen, until he grabbed her in his arms and pulled her tight, feeling tears spring to his eyes.

"You're—" he gasped, and she nodded. She was weeping now, too.

"And we're—" she said as she nodded again. Her hands had wrapped around him as well. She was holding him so tightly he almost couldn't breathe, and he didn't care.

"Will you—will you marry me?" he said, speaking softly into her ear.

She drew her head back and gave him a disbelieving look. "You have to ask?" She rolled her eyes. "I suppose you do. Yes. Yes. Yes."

He held her even tighter, and spoke into her hair. "I just needed to hear you say it. I love you, Angel."

"I love you."

Epilogue

*C*heckmate!" Alexandra exclaimed in triumph.

Theo gave a mock groan, then gestured for her to come to his side of the table.

She was about six months along, at least according to their best guess, and they'd been married for three months now.

"I'm not too heavy?" she asked, when he held his arms out to her in clear invitation to sit on his lap.

"Never," he said. She sat down, snuggling up against his chest. Like that time they'd taken a bath together, long before either one of them suspected their feelings were more than temporary passion.

"Harriet has sent another letter," she said, drawing a piece of paper from her pocket. She unfolded it as she leaned her head against his shoulder. "She thinks we should name the baby Hardith, a combination of her and Edith's names." She shot him an amused glance. "And she helpfully explains that the name would be suitable for either a girl or a boy."

"I still think Alexander or Alix would be best," Theo replied, squeezing his wife. "How is Harriet, anyway? Does she say anything about Fenton, that scamp?"

Alexandra was silent as she scanned the letter. "Just that they are touring Greece now, and that Edith is obsessed with ancient Greek poets, particularly the female ones, so she is insisting they recite poetry at every stop."

"When are they returning?"

The traveling trio had returned briefly for Alexandra and Theo's wedding, but had taken off directly after with no promises about when they would return.

Alexandra was grateful that Harriet was getting to live her life as she wished, and she was also glad Edith was there to act as a surrogate mother.

Albeit a lot more adventurous a mother than Harriet's actual one.

"She says they don't know—apparently your friend Fenton is determined they go to Morocco, but Harriet says he is planning a very roundabout route."

"Of course he is," Theo replied in a fond tone.

He and Alexandra had speculated as to what kind of relationship Harriet and Fenton had, but Harriet had not said, and Fenton hadn't written at all.

But Fenton had pledged to ensure Harriet and Edith were well provided for during the trip, and Theo planned to argue with his friend about paying him back when they finally returned.

He had not been thwarted in giving money to the duke, however; Theo had asked his half dozen or so lawyers to draw up contracts so he would provide the Chelmswich duchy with the funds it required for improvements, but without allowing the duke to manage any of the money. That way the duchy's various dependents could continue to survive, from the household staff to the many farmers who rented the ducal land.

The duke had been furious, but Theo had merely shrugged, saying the duke could take this offering or nothing at all.

Theo and Alexandra had settled in Theo's London town house, with him cutting back the hours he worked on his business, and her gardening in the morning, reading after that, and then, more likely than not, taking a nap, followed by teatime, when she always took three biscuits.

He had promised to take more time off when the baby arrived, and they were looking at houses in the country to purchase so they'd give their child the opportunity to live in both London and the country—giving their offspring choices nearly as soon as they were born.

"We're going to teach Hardith to play chess as soon as they are able," Alexandra said, nodding toward the board. "And I want them to spend time with their uncle Simeon and all their other uncles." She turned her head to meet his gaze. "I want them to know what true family is like."

He felt himself tear up, and then he buried his face in her shoulder, holding her tight.

"I love you," he murmured.

"Me too," she replied.

"SHE'S BEAUTIFUL." THEO's voice held a note of awe.

The three of them were in bed, Theodora (not Hardith, after all) tucked between the two of them. She was all of a month old, and Theo was already wrapped around her finger.

Alexandra glanced over at him, feeling herself smile at his besotted expression. This man was very different from the suave, charming man she'd met at the Garden; she'd gotten to know more of him, know his depths, in a way only the Bastard Five could see.

They'd asked Simeon to be the godfather, and he was nearly as taken by Theodora as Theo was, already doing sketches of her as she was sleeping, calling her sweet names when he didn't think anyone else was listening.

Theo and Alexandra had both been concerned about the birth itself, given Alexandra's age. But it had been relatively easy, though Theo still reminded Alexandra how she'd slapped him during a particularly difficult labor pain.

She couldn't believe she was here, with him, with their child, and she was madly and profoundly in love. How it felt as though she'd been given a second chance at life, all begun when she'd taken a pair of shears to her black gown.

How he'd learned, and changed, and loved her.

And how they continued to visit the Garden every so often since Theo wanted to keep bringing her pleasure. More and more pleasure until she thought she might burst from it.

Don't miss Megan Frampton's next tempting
romance in the School for Scoundrels series

HER OFFER OF
TEMPTATION

Coming 2024!

EXPLORE MEGAN FRAMPTON'S TITLES

SCHOOL FOR SOUNDRELS SERIES

HAZARDS OF DUKES SERIES

A DUKE'S DAUGHTERS SERIES